Second
Thoughts

Michael Hemenway

ISBN: 978-1502364050

This book is dedicated to Mary, Amy, Sarah, Tori and Emilie, the next generation.

Many thanks to Becky for her tireless assistance, and to Priya, Edith, John, and Posey for all their help and support.

On July 16, 1979, a holding pond in Church Rock, New Mexico, filled with radioactive mining and milling waste, breached its dam and unleashed ninety million gallons of toxic liquid and 1100 tons of mill waste eighty miles down the Rio Puerco, lifting manhole covers in Gallup as it passed. It was the worst such accident in U.S. history, releasing more than three times the radiation of the partial nuclear meltdown at Three Mile Island the same year. Almost all of its eventual victims were Native American.

CHAPTER 1

Sam Shelton had trouble opening his eyes on his first morning in Santa Fe. Then the smell of the dirty urinal next to his bunk in the holding cell jolted him awake with grim efficiency. He sat up and swung his feet to the floor, trying to reconcile the fluorescent glare and the bars with the freedom and sunlit vistas of the cross-country motorcycle trip that had brought him here. He didn't succeed.

"Santa Fe? I hope you know what you're doing," Sam had said aloud just yesterday as he rode. Then, he had sensed that a good part of the answer lay simply in his arriving in the West, getting away from the East Coast, and taking a break from the pressure of school—and from his father, who had started bugging him again about what he wanted to do after graduation next year. How was *he* supposed to know? His summer internship in a law firm in Santa Fe had pacified his father, and he would get to see a new part of the country and maybe find out if law had some nook or cranny where you weren't always on a short fuse the way his father was.

Instead, he had stumbled into some nightmare—he could hardly remember how—and he had no idea how to get himself out of it. Clearly, he thought, holding his head in his hands, the answer to that implied question he'd asked himself was "No." He took a deep breath to keep from choking or—worse yet—bursting into tears. Little by

7

little he got a handle on his panic. Then he got slowly to his feet and put his hands on the metal bars, looking over at the intake officer.

"Excuse me. When can...When can I talk to my lawyer?" he asked with as much authority as he could muster.

Nothing. The man didn't even look up from his computer screen. Sam took a deep breath and tried again, this time louder. "Hey! I need to speak with my lawyer!" This time the officer looked over.

"What's your name?"

"Sam, Sam Shelton. Yesterday I asked for a lawyer named Mike Stone." In her note, Secunda Dumay had told Sam to look him up. How ironic that it wouldn't be a social call.

The guard peered back at his screen and after a moment got up and walked over to the cell. He was a short Hispanic man with cropped black hair and an acne-covered face. His uniform gave him an air of authority, but Sam noticed that his arms were covered with tattoos. He looked at Sam and then down at his clipboard.

"The magistrate decided to hold you because you have no local address, and he OK'd Stone instead of giving you a court-appointed lawyer. Stone just called and is on his way down to talk to you."

"I just got here. That's why I don't have a local address. If you would just let me out, I can straighten all this out!"

But the guard had already turned around to return to his computer. Sam's stomach sank. He stepped back from the bars and sat down on the bunk, still in a state of

shock, his eyes ranging slowly over the cinderblock cell
with its cement floor. What a far cry from yesterday.

"Coming all the way from Rhode Island?" the gas station
attendant had asked him yesterday morning, reaching
into his gray overalls and pulling out a wad of bills to peel
off change.

"Yeah, Providence. It's been a long ride. I'm just
coming down from Denver today." Sam took the change.
"How long till I hit the New Mexico line?"

"You'll be there in about an hour. When you get to
Wagon Mound, you're about a hundred miles out of
Santa Fe."

"Wagon Mound? Is that a town or a mountain?" Sam
almost let slip what he was really thinking: "What on
earth is 'Wagon Mound' and what am I doing anywhere
near it?"

"Both. It's a town in Mora County, this side of Santa
Fe. Sits at the base of the mountain. You'll notice it on
the east side of the highway—it looks like a wagon," he
said, gesturing with his left arm. "Back in the 1800s it was
a landmark for covered wagon trains and traders going up
and down the Santa Fe Trail. It's just a village, really. I
grew up there but came up here to find work."

"Thanks for the info. I appreciate it." Sam stretched.
He had been on the road for four solid days and was
ready to get to his destination. His original romantic
vision of riding across the country on a motorcycle had
vanished after about on hour on Route 95, but he'd stuck
to his plan to travel by interstate to make the best time.

Once he hit the plains, it was all wide-open country, and although he had become accustomed to the wind and the monotony, he had made the most of the periodic food and gas breaks.

Sam could see that this fellow was none too busy at this particular gas station in the Rocky Mountain basin in the southern part of Colorado. "I decided to go highway to make the best time. I've hit some rain and lots of wind, but basically it's been good."

"That looks like an old bike. A BMW?"

"Yeah, it's a 1964. Still running strong."

"Really? Where'd you find such an old bike in such good shape?"

Grateful for an excuse not to get right back on the road, Sam stepped back and gave the bike a once-over. He remembered as if it were yesterday the day he had first seen it in his neighbor's garage. "Believe it or not, it was given to me."

"You're kidding me. I know a bit about older bikes, and this one's a gem." He ran his finger over the ceramic circle on the side of the gas tank, with its blue and white pie wedges encircled by a black band with the letters "BMW," in silver, at the top. "It's an R50, isn't it?"

"Yeah, a '64. It's got some mileage, but as far as I can tell, it has all its original parts."

"But *that*'s not standard," the mechanic said, pointing to a two-by-three-inch block of numbers neatly scratched onto the side of the engine housing.

"Oh yeah, those." Sam had no idea what the three rows of numbers meant, but he'd looked at them so often on his travels he almost had them committed to memory:

192015145
81512419
208511525

"They were there when I got the bike. I got to know the lady back in Providence." The attendant nodded his head to acknowledge Sam's good fortune. "It's a long story," Sam continued, "but basically she got it from her father and then learned to ride herself. She was unusual, but nice. She never did tell me about those damn numbers," he added, putting on his helmet.

The more Sam had ridden the old motorcycle, the more he found himself thinking of Secunda Dumay. He first met her while housesitting for a professor in Providence over spring break. His main duty was walking Annie, the little wire-haired fox terrier. Tua— that was Secunda's nickname—was out getting her garden ready for spring, and they began talking each afternoon as he passed her house.

The attendant rubbed his hands on a dirty cloth he pulled from his back pocket. "I wish I could meet a nice lady who would leave me a sweet bike like this," he chuckled.

When she had first showed him the old motorcycle sitting in the corner of the garage, it was covered with an old Navajo blanket. She said it had been her father's and that when he died she had learned to ride it, an amazing story for Sam, who had a hard time imagining this fragile lady with long gray hair atop any bike, let alone this big black one. She had lightheartedly scolded him for his skepticism, reminding him that women could do anything that men could do, only better. And now she was dead.

"Well, I'd better keep moving. You have a good day," Sam had said, mounting his faithful steed. Then he reached down below the tank to turn on the gas switch and pushed the key into the top of the bike's headlight, where the ignition switch was housed. Reaching over to turn the right-hand throttle slightly, he stepped down on the starter pedal. The motorcycle came to life, then settled into its Germanic hum. Tua had named it "Pegasus," for the winged horse of ancient times. Now, practically at his summer destination, Sam decided to keep the name.

"Boy, that motor is quiet. Sure is different from the Harleys and imports that come by," observed the attendant. He looked southward into the sun, took off his baseball cap, and pushed his greasy hair back before putting his cap on again. "Have a good trip."

"Thanks," Sam replied, zipping up his worn leather jacket and putting on his gloves. He pushed the lever down into first gear with the ball of his left foot and let out the clutch. "On the Road Again" popped into his mind like a soundtrack. True enough, though what *he* couldn't wait for was getting off it. Working through the gears, he pulled onto the big highway under the open sky and soon hit 70 mph. This had become his regular highway speed, and he slipped into his travel zone, where wind, pavement, and movement blended into a space where ideas played through his head while he subconsciously noted the miles clicking by. It had been a long journey.

Twenty minutes later, Sam glanced down at the top of the black headlight holding the speedometer. The needle sat peacefully on 70, so he had drifted back to the inner recesses of his mind and the place where this whole trip began. Tua. There had been a cryptic little note. Ride Pegasus to New Mexico and it would tell him a story, uncover a truth, or something like that. Sam reminded himself to look at that note again when he got to Santa Fe.

Twisting the throttle to keep his speed steady against another gust of wind, he was glad to be flying at last through this desert landscape, pushed wide open by some prehistoric glacier as it was grinding down the Rocky Mountains. As the motorcycle hurtled effortlessly through the endless miles, Sam had found himself forming a bond with the machine even though it was only a few hundred pounds of metal and rubber dreamed up by some engineers fifty years ago. It had become, dare he say it, a living creature and a good friend. He patted the gas tank with his left hand.

In the distance he saw a green highway sign proclaiming that he was about to enter New Mexico. Making a fist with his left hand, Sam lifted his arm and shouted as he and Pegasus flew by it. "Yahooo!" They were getting close, and Sam dared to think again about how glad he was that Pegasus had not stranded him in the middle of the Kansas prairie or balked at the heat of the high desert.

An hour and a half later he noticed a sign for Wagon Mound and looked to his left. There, right on cue, was the little village set up against a mountain, a hill really, sitting in the middle of the open landscape. "Hey, it does look like an old covered wagon," Sam said to himself.

Over the last few days he had transitioned from the green of the East to the overriding brown landscape of the Great Plains and the West. Here, the sky was wide open and very blue, but everything else was dry, rocky, and brown.

"Pecos." Another hour and another sign. And then he saw the sign for Santa Fe, thirty miles away. With his goal in sight, Sam's adrenaline kicked in, and he nudged the throttle again and watched the speedometer needle move up to 75. The old bike was really flying now, although at this speed the wind now roared in his ears and the wind resistance was almost overwhelming.

The "Old Pecos Trail" sign at exit 22 told Sam he had arrived in Santa Fe, so he slowed down and left the highway. The city was nowhere in sight. Confused, he pulled over to the side of the road to get his bearings and check his map.

"Ah." Old Pecos Trail went directly into the center of Santa Fe, so Sam pulled back onto the two-lane road and followed the signs directing him downtown. He had decided to go to the center of town, a place called the Plaza, and then call the number where he was supposed to pick up the key for the summer sublet he'd found on craigslist. He'd only seen the place in photographs, but it had looked bearable, and it was the only choice in his price range: cheap. Just as well; too many options usually gummed up his mind.

As he rode along, more slowly now, Sam glanced around and saw a shifting mosaic of small shrubs, dirt, and rocks. The scattered buildings were constructed of beige adobe and hidden among the piñon trees that covered the hills. Little by little, *everything* seemed made of adobe. His face breaking out in a grin, Sam opined, "This is a very cool, earthy place."

He followed the road as it narrowed and the sidewalk and buildings came right up to the road. After a mile, Sam came down a final hill and saw a sign that pointed to the Plaza. The motorcycle slowed down and seemed to purr as he downshifted, as if Pegasus recognized the place.

CHAPTER 2

Sam parked Pegasus and walked across the street to the Plaza, a small, shady park in the center of the town square. It had benches all around and a fountain in the middle. Cars were excluded, and pedestrians clearly ruled—locals, tourists, business types, and kids hanging out. The open space was surrounded by buildings on all four sides. The old Governor's Palace had a fringe of Native American vendors under the long portico in front. Another side had a bank, a bar, and a couple of gift and souvenir shops, and directly across from the Governor's Palace, along with a couple of art galleries and stores and an ice cream shop, Sam noticed a 5 & 10 store advertising "Frito Pies." The fourth side of the Plaza had two more galleries and a few gallery-type shops...and about a hundred people protesting something.

Sam couldn't resolve their chant into words he recognized. Most of them looked like Native Americans. Some held posters, and some were thrusting their fists in the air. He heard the crackle of a hand-held loudspeaker and moved closer to check it out. The posters said something about the 30-year anniversary of Church Rock. *That*'s what the chant was: "No more Church Rock."

In front of an array of dignified but unsmiling Native Americans on the speakers' platform, an attractive young woman was shouting into a bullhorn to pump up the crowd. She appeared to be in her twenties and wore a bright red shirt. A blue bandana held back her long black hair, and she wore dark-rimmed glasses.

"No more white racist capitalism on our land! Ruin our land no more! No more mining!" The crowd cheered as she repeated the mantra into the bullhorn: "No more Church Rock—keep the ban! No more Church Rock—keep the ban!"

With each refrain, the crowd got more agitated, until it began to spread out like water. All of a sudden Sam was surrounded. To his right, a large, angry man wearing a black Metallica tee shirt gave every indication that he was out for blood. Sam looked down to avoid eye contact. He was tired and hungry from his trip and was clearly in the wrong place at the wrong time. He turned and tried to move towards the street but found himself boxed in by the chanting crowd.

He took a deep breath and cursed, telling no one in particular that he needed to leave, that he had to pick up his key. As he started to press outward, he felt the crowd congeal. "Get out of here, white boy," someone snarled. He was shoved from behind. His anxiety morphed into fear, and he lowered his head and twisted his body in an attempt to escape. The noise grew louder and the shouting angrier. From beyond the crowd came cries of "Go home, you damn Indians," and "Call the law!"

Sam's adrenaline was pumping now, and he found himself making headway through the ocean of bodies. Just as he was about to break from its confines, the sound of police sirens wailed in the distance. But the crowd engulfed him again, and this time he was shoved, lost his footing, and fell to the ground, knocking his head on the hard dirt. The sound of the crowd and the sirens faded out just before everything went dark.

When he came to, a cop and a paramedic were hovering over him. What was it they wanted? His name? His head hurt as much from disbelief as from the bruise. Wait. Was he really being lifted to his feet stuffed into the back of a patrol car? Where were they taking him? What about Pegasus?

"No. You've got this all wrong," he stuttered.

"Save it," answered the cop at the wheel.

Still slumped on his hard bunk, Sam heard a metal door sliding open by remote control. He looked up to see an old guy in worn khaki pants and a faded plaid shirt step through the doorway and into the main room. His old Nike running shoes made no noise.

"Hey Juan, I just got a call. They asked me to come down right away—said some kid from out of state was asking for me." The man looked around and peered at Sam's cell. "Is that him?"

The guard nodded and looked in Sam's direction. "Yes, that's him, over there."

Sam stood up as the man walked to the bars. He appeared to be on the far side of sixty and had an unkempt look. "Are you Mr. Stone?" Sam asked.

"Yeah, I sure am. My name is Stone, Mike Stone."

"Sam Shelton." Sam leaned forward and extended his hand through the bars. An odor of stale beer emanated from Stone's clothing, and the man hadn't shaved. "Uh...do you work for a real law firm?" Sam was suddenly apprehensive at the idea of his freedom being in the hands of a has-been lawyer, maybe an old drunk at that, even if he was a friend of Tua's.

The man's voice was raspy. "Look, kid, I don't know what you did exactly, or how you got my name, but you're in no position to question who the hell I am." He looked over Sam's shoulder at the cell and the urinal against the wall as if he had seen them once too often. "But yeah, I'll defend you, and if you do what I tell you, I might have you out of here this morning."

Realizing that he had insulted him, Sam tried to recoup. "Look, I'm sorry. I apologize. I'm a college student who just got here for the summer, and this whole thing has really knocked me sideways. I'm from Providence, Rhode Island, and Tua Dumay told me to look you up."

Nothing prepared Sam for the look on Stone's face when he heard Tua's name. It took the lawyer a minute to collect himself.

"How do you know her?"

"I house-sat for a professor who lives in her neighborhood, and when she learned I had an internship in Santa Fe this summer, she gave me her motorcycle to ride out here."

"Tua...how is she?"

"I wish I could give you better news. She passed away between the time I got to know her and the time I left. She was so tall and straight and...what's the right word?....'together'—the last sort of person to have a heart attack, in my opinion."

"Sometimes sorrow can wear you down," Stone said

cryptically. And then, shaking off some private thought, he heaved a sigh and changed the subject.

"I have a small office in town. I'm semi-retired and just take on a few cases. Especially when the public defender's office is conflicted out."

"Is that what happened?"

"Yeah, a bunch of people were arrested when the fight broke out, and the public defender's office got assigned to represent the Indian who decked you."

Sam recalled the militant-looking guy he had noticed before he went down. "Oh, I bet it was that guy in the crowd. I mean, I was there minding my own business and this guy, this Indian guy was spoiling for a fight. Actually, he looked like he wanted to kill me. That's when I decided to get out of there and someone hit me from behind." Sam was suddenly back in the moment and felt his blood pressure rising.

"That's what the sheriff told me," Mike said, nodding. "But since they couldn't really figure out who started it and who did what, they just arrested everyone." He chuckled. "Well, not everyone. Just you and the five people on top of you."

"So, what happens next? Can you get the charge dismissed? This is so crazy. I mean, can I sue for wrongful prosecution?"

Stone pulled out the paperwork for the case from a worn leather briefcase. After glancing over it, he looked at Sam and frowned. "Hmm. Unfortunately for you, when you were knocked out, the paramedic and the police officer on the scene went through your wallet to see who you were."

"Yeah, so what about it?"

"Well, they found your license, but they also came across an ID that had a different name on it. They went ahead and charged you with tampering with a public record—which happens to be a felony in the state of New Mexico."

"A felony?" Sam was shocked. "A felony? I can't have a felony! I'll never get a job if I have a felony on my record. My parents will kill me."

"Yes, it's a felony. You said you were a college student. Was this for buying beer?"

Of course it was, and Sam's stomach dropped when he realized that it hadn't occurred to him to ditch the fake ID when he turned 21 in May. He looked at his lawyer. "Mr. Stone, will you be able to get that charge dropped?

"Did you tell the arresting officer that you made the fake ID?"

Sam thought back to last night. "Well, yes. I guess I did. He read the Miranda rights from a card and then told me to tell him the truth. He said telling the truth would help me."

Stone rolled his eyes. "As the song says, 'When will they ever learn?' " he remarked to no one in particular. Looking back at Sam, he continued, "The District Attorney has taken up prosecuting these cases because of some recent car accidents that resulted in college kids getting killed. The statement you made to the police can be used against you to prove their case. Anyway, I'll do what I can, but right now, this is not going away."

Sam, crushed, leaned against the concrete wall of the cell. "Oh man. This is bad."

"Calm down, son. I suspect I can get the disorderly conduct charge dismissed. But we'll have to take the other charge seriously. You really don't want to play around with the criminal justice system."

After a long hesitation, Sam decided to put a lid on his dismay. "Well, I'm glad to hear that you can handle my case." He'd been concerned about this old guy acting as his lawyer, but something in Stone's voice and manner gave him confidence.

Stone pulled out a notepad and a pencil from his back pocket. "So you're a college student." A slight grin played over his face. "That's interesting. What are you doing here?"

Sam's story spurted out. "Like I said, I'm a student. I just finished my third year at Brown, and I'm just here for the summer to work as a legal assistant at the Fisher law firm." He took a quick breath. "You know, to see if I might want to go to law school. I just got here and walked into the Plaza and was listening to some protest and got knocked out."

Stone looked over his glasses and stopped writing. "Really? You weren't kidding when you said you just got here."

Sam nodded. "Yeah, just a few minutes before I got arrested. I was looking at the protest, and then there was some pushing and shoving, and I guess they thought I was part of it. But I wasn't. I mean I had nothing to do with it. Man, this is so crazy! And I didn't even need the ID!"

"So, you're gonna work for Walter Fisher this summer?

"Yeah, it's a small law firm. Mr. Fisher is the main lawyer. I'm working with his associate Stephen Schiff for the summer and staying in a sublet on Garcia Street." Then Sam lost it again.

"Mr. Stone, I've never been arrested before. I'm innocent." Sam could feel panic rear-ending him and took a deep breath as he glanced furtively at the inmates in the other cells. "You've got to get me out of here!"

"OK, why don't you calm down," Stone said, looking him in the eye. "I'll take care of this." He put his notepad into his pocket. Almost as an afterthought, he added, "Don't worry. I'll get you out on a personal recognizance bond. Give me a call when you get settled in. You can tell me more about Tua when we meet." He handed Sam a business card and abruptly turned and walked past the guard towards the exit. He paused in front of the metal door for a moment as invisible officers behind bulletproof glass hit a switch and the door slid noisily open. Sam watched Stone step through and disappear.

CHAPTER 3

Two days later, at 9:00 a.m. sharp, Sam stopped in front of another metal gate and looked at the sign in the yard confirming he was at the right place. The Fisher Law Office. Out of jail on a personal recognizance bond, he had decided not to mention anything to his new employer quite yet. The two-story building was right on Paseo de Peralta, the main road circling the downtown area, and was unusual in that it was made of brick. Sam could see it used to be someone's house. Taking a deep breath, he pushed open the door and entered. A petite woman of a certain age, with dyed brown hair in a bun, was sitting at the front desk and peered over her glasses as she placed a file on the stack in front of her. Sam carefully shut the door behind him.

"Hello, I'm Samuel Shelton." Sam smiled at the lady. Just then a tall man easily in his seventies entered from a doorway to the left. He was wearing a wrinkled grey suit and smoking a cigarette. Exhaling a plume of smoke, he first coughed and then said, "You must be Sam Shelton. Good morning, son. I'm Walter Fisher." He stubbed the cigarette out in an ashtray balanced on the copy machine and offered his hand to his new summer employee. As they shook hands, he nodded towards the secretary. "This is Sylvia, Sylvia Hernandez."

Sam smiled at Sylvia. Fisher was older than he expected, with large bags under his eyes. The loose skin on his jowls hung over his collar. Friendly enough, but

Sam could see he was used to getting his way.

A heavyset man with thick brown hair and wire-rimmed glasses came down the stairs from the second floor clutching a brown expandable legal file. "Walter..." he started to say as he entered the main room and spotted the newcomer.

Fisher made the introduction. "Stephen, this is Sam Shelton, the legal assistant you wanted for the summer. Sam, this is Stephen Schiff. I gather you haven't met."

"No. You remember that I was in law school with his older brother. Hello, Sam. How was your trip out?"

"Uneventful, even though I was riding a motorcycle. It took me four days."

"A motorcycle, hunh..."

Although probably only in his mid-thirties, the younger lawyer's pale complexion and extra weight made him appear older. "Glad to have you on board. I hope you're a quick learner, because we have a lot going on," he said glancing down at the file in his hand.

"Stephen, why don't you show Sam around," Fisher said. "Sylvia, I'll be in my office. I'm scheduled for a conference call in a few minutes, so let me know as soon as it comes in."

Sylvia nodded. "Yes, Mr. Fisher."

Schiff turned to Sam. "Come on upstairs. I'll show you your office." He pivoted, and they went up the staircase he had just descended and made their way to an office with two large windows on the front side of the building, overlooking Paseo de Peralta.

"This will be your office for the summer, at least until we hire a new associate. It's all set up with a computer and journals." Schiff added, "You'll be more useful than I ever imagined when Mark called and asked if you could intern. The lawyer we had just left."

Sam was impressed. You could see mountains in the distance. "Wow. Compared to the tiny student cubicles I'm used to at the college library, this is great," he said with a grin. "And it comes with scenery."

Schiff gestured toward the large maple desk. "Her name was Kendra White. She was an associate helping me out with my case load, but then she got pregnant and decided she didn't want to work anymore."

Sam was surprised at the sexist comment, but Schiff sounded irritated, so he didn't pursue the matter. "Well, I'm looking forward to working with you, that's for sure. I'm excited to learn something about environmental law."

Schiff examined Sam with a slightly skeptical look— Was this kid a tree-hugger?—then sat down in the chair behind the desk, took off his thick glasses, and rubbed his eyes.

"So how's old Mark?"

"Raking in the money in Cleveland, I guess. He seems to like tax law for some reason. I only ever see him in the summer when he and Laura and the kids come to Watch Hill on vacation."

"I think I've only seen him once since we graduated, at our tenth reunion. I'm not sure I could handle the pace of a big law firm like his. There's enough to do in a small one like this," he added, handing Sam the brown file he had been carrying.

"A lot of what we do actually does involve business and environmental law and litigation," he continued.

"Mr. Fisher does all the bond work for the northern counties and handles his own cases, especially the big ones, and he does a lot of lobbying. I handle almost all of the other litigation matters. That's one of Kendra's files. It would be helpful if you could be responsible for organizing the cases I gave her. I realize you can't practice law, but you can go through them and give me a summary of what she's done on each case. And then later in the week I'll give you a short lesson on doing legal research." He pointed to a filing cabinet against the wall. "All her files are in there."

"Sounds like a plan."

Schiff didn't get up right away. Instead he sat back and looked out the window towards the mountains.

"You'll see that our expertise is in the areas of mining law, oil and gas law, and water law. We represent natural resource industries in transactional, regulatory, and litigated matters."

"That must be a big deal in New Mexico."

"Fisher used to represent almost all the clients that came before the Environmental Improvement Board, the Water Quality Control Commission, and the Oil Conservation Commission in environmental rule-making proceedings, but I've taken on a lot of that work in the last few years."

"What do you actually do?"

"For one, we get solid waste permits from the New Mexico Environment Department and approvals of oil and gas developments from the Oil Conservation Commission. And another big aspect is negotiating cleanups. You name it, we do it: refineries, power plants, mine sites, underground storage tanks, and oil and gas plants."

"Sounds like you kind of walk the line between business and environmental interests."

Schiff suppressed a smile. "Well, it's true that we defend clients in litigation asserting environmental claims. Mr. Fisher also represents municipalities on environmental matters, mostly appeals of state certification of EPA permit conditions. He also defends them against citizen suit law. Stuff like that."

"What do you think I'll mainly be working on this summer?"

"Right now we're representing some clients in acquiring rights-of-way and in opposing lease forfeitures and tax assessments in Indian Country."

"So the firm doesn't represent the Indians then?"

"No, not really. Unless, of course, it has to do with the casinos. We generally prefer the bigger corporate clients. There's more money to be made."

The intercom buzzed on the desk, and Sam pushed the blinking button. Sylvia's voice came through the base of the phone as if she were in the room.

"Is Mr. Schiff in your office?"

"Yes, he's right here."

"Just tell him that he has a call waiting in his office."

Schiff left the office abruptly, and Sam was left standing silently in front of the huge wooden desk, his head awash in unfamiliar legal jargon. It sounded as if the law firm was a player, though it wasn't clear on whose team. A feeling of power pervaded the room. Pushing thoughts of his recent bad luck and pending court case out of his mind, he sat down in the plush leather chair and surveyed his new domain.

"Nice," he said out loud. "Very nice."

CHAPTER 4

Sam was sitting at his desk a week later when the intercom crackled. "Samuel," Sylvia announced, "Mr. Dickerman from the county legal department is on the line."

"Mr. Dickerman. Do you know what case it is?" Sam looked at the blinking button on his phone.

"I believe it's the case about the bridge at Embudo Station."

It rang a bell; it was a lawsuit filed to force the county to build a bridge across the river so a client could access his land. He spoke into the speaker. "Oh, OK, put him through."

"Mike Dickerman here," the caller said. "I understand you're working with Fisher and are handling the Embudo bridge matter."

"Actually, I'm a legal assistant, Sam Shelton. Mr. Schiff will be handling the case."

"OK. Well, can you give him the message to call me? We need to set up some depositions."

With that, the conversation was over. Sam stood up from his desk and paced around his silent office. Schiff was out filing some papers in a separate case, and Sam had been left momentarily with nothing substantive to do, now that he had finished the case summaries Schiff had asked for, all nineteen of them. "What I really need is to get outside," he said to himself as he pushed up the knot in his tie and made his way downstairs past Sylvia's desk.

"I'm taking an early lunch break," he announced as he headed for the rear entrance. "Can you tell Mr. Schiff that I will meet with him at 1:00 to find out what I need to do on the Embudo case?"

She nodded and jotted it down as Sam went through the kitchen and out to the lot where Pegasus was parked—faithful Pegasus, that he had found intact, saddlebags and all, in the lot of a towing company after his unscheduled night in jail. The guy behind the counter had said something strange—that it looked just like the one Dr. Blair used to ride. As the man counted Sam's cash, he recalled getting a kick, as a kid, out of seeing the dignified St. John's professor tooling around town. "So sad when he was murdered," he added. Sam hadn't asked him to elaborate.

Sam rode up Garcia Street past the Indian Museum and then past St. John's College. Just moving, being on his motorcycle, made him feel better.

"Beautiful day," he murmured, taking a right onto Upper Canyon Road. The sun lit up the hills on either side of the small canyon, where the piñon trees relieved the dry, rocky landscape. A sculpture of a blue coyote stood in the front of a walled compound he often passed. It never failed to make him smile. A sign and a metal gate marked the lower boundary of the water district. He looked at his watch. "11:30. I really did take an early lunch."

In the first few days after his arrival, Sam had become acclimated to the thin air of Santa Fe, at 7,000 feet; it even seemed to make the colors brighter. He slowed down as the paved road turned to dirt. A painted white sign, "Randall Davey Audubon Center," announced what had been a large, private estate before the Davey family turned it over to the Audubon Society in 1963.

Sam parked and headed for the two main adobe buildings, but a swath of bright green deflected him. Between the buildings, a stone pathway headed off to the right to a huge, lush lawn enclosed by an old adobe wall, with green deciduous trees that shouldn't have been there. Maybe the Daveys had gotten homesick for the East.

In the yard, a girl appeared to be meditating, sitting back on her heels on a small red and black blanket. A thick braid of long, black hair falling from the back of a baseball cap stood out against her yellow t-shirt, their splashes of color leaping out from the green background. She had light freckles across her nose and cheekbones and a small scar on her left cheek. But it was her dark-rimmed glasses that arrested Sam's attention. Any discretion he had about not distracting her suddenly vanished. She had disturbed his peace; he could certainly disturb hers.

"I remember you!" he said, walking up to her. "You were whipping up the crowd on the Plaza during that demonstration! I hadn't been in town for ten minutes, and one of your goons knocked me out, and I ended up spending the night in jail."

Her eyes narrowed. "Is that so?"

"Yeah, I was in the crowd. In fact, I had just arrived here from the East Coast." He thought about the felony charge hanging over his head and warmed to the topic. "And that's when all hell broke loose, and next thing I knew I was at the bottom of a pile and then in jail. You should never have let those thugs get out of control."

"And who kept the Flagship Mining Corporation under control in 1979 when it allowed 1100 tons of radioactive mill waste and more than 90 million gallons of contaminated liquid to flood the Rio Puerco when the Church Rock dam broke?" she answered hotly.

Sam was taken aback. "Church Rock. You guys were yelling something about Church Rock."

She sighed and gave him an impatient look. "You don't have a clue, do you?"

"Listen. I wasn't born yet when it happened! What was it all about?"

"Do you really want to know?" she asked, standing up.

"Well, yes. Yes, I do," Sam stammered.

The girl looked Sam over and then spoke resignedly, crossing her arms over her chest. "For your information, in the late '70s Flagship Mining Corporation put up a big mining complex on a reservation at Church Rock, which is a little town on the Rio Puerco in the western part of the state near the Arizona border."

She began walking back and forth. Her eyes smoldered.

"In the milling process, acid was used to separate the uranium from the sandstone it was in. Needless to say, it ended up laced with radioactive isotopes. The company stored it, along with the solid waste and some water pumped from the mine, in a huge pond held back by an earthen dam 25 feet high and 30 feet wide. The idea was to let the liquid evaporate and deal with the solids when they were dry." She paused to let him picture it. "And early in the morning on July 16, the dam burst and sent the whole toxic mess eighty miles down the Rio Puerco. They say that the wall of liquid backed up sewers and lifted manhole covers in Gallup, twenty miles downstream." She paused again for effect.

"The Navajo all along the river didn't know where it came from, and no one even bothered to tell them for the first few days. It was the worst radioactive accident in the United States—three times worse than the disaster at Three Mile Island that had happened three and a half months earlier. Except for the first atomic test explosion at the Trinity site in 1945, it was the biggest single release of radioactive poisons in America. Hundreds of Navajo families got sick and many ultimately died from the poisoning of the water."

"My God. I've never heard about this. What did they do about it? Did they sue the company at least?"

"Nobody could win a lawsuit against the mine, at least that's what they were told. It was too hard to prove the actual link between the flood and the sickness." With a twinge of sarcasm she added, "And, of course, nobody really took notice or cared, since they were all just Indians."

The story felt both immediate and remote to Sam. "Well, I guess I understand why you and the rest of the Indians are protesting, though I don't think they needed to pull me into their problems."

The girl's retort was sharp. "You *are* the problem!"

"Wha…?"

She stopped and took a deep breath to calm herself

down. "Look, I'm not blaming you in particular. I'm talking about your people, 'Anglos,' white folk. You chose not to look into this disaster, not to take action against the mine, not to prosecute FMC for the death and destruction they caused. Your people chose not to care, and, as you just admitted, you're *still* ignorant."

Sam felt his own anger return. "Look, I'm sorry, but I'm not too happy about taking the blame for an accident that happened before I was born."

She looked up at a large oak tree against the adobe wall and then back at him. "Who said it was an accident, and who said you had to take the blame?" Her tone became more conciliatory. "I just get upset when I think of the abuse my people have taken from Anglos and corporate America over the years. It's all about exploiting the land," she said, "Navajo land. First oil and gas, then uranium. If we don't fight back, if we don't do something to protect the people and the earth, it will just happen again."

"I... I don't know. I guess I should take a little criticism for not being a bit better informed, especially since I care about the environment." In a way, he didn't mind backing down. He *was* ignorant, and he didn't like confrontations in general—sometimes he wondered why he was interested in law.

"So, you're not from around here?"

"I go to school in the East. I'm just here working for the summer. I guess you live here, though."

"I live in Gallup, which is west of Albuquerque. Santa Fe gets rain, not like Gallup. That's why I like it up here." Glancing at the large trees surrounding them, she added, "Juniper, aspen, there's even an oak tree."

"I'm from New England, so I can recognize an oak tree, at least. So you come to Santa Fe for your work."

"That's right. I'm working this summer for the Native American Action Committee, NAAC. There's litigation going on for Native American rights. How about you?"

"I'm working at the Fisher law firm for the summer as a legal assistant."

"Fisher...hmmm. Seems to me I've seen that name on some of our documents."

She looked at Sam with the hint of a smile. "Now that we've met, I'll try not to get you thrown in jail again."

"Yeah, keeping out of jail is one of my goals for the summer. So, what do you do for the Action Committee besides incite to riot?"

"Paperwork mostly, and legal research," she responded, ignoring the barb, "and attending different rallies and protests." Then in a serious tone of voice she added, "It's the only way to be heard."

"So, uh, my name is Sam, Sam Shelton. How about you?"

"My name is Nina."

After a moment of silence, Sam looked at his watch, "Well, I guess I'll move on. I took an early lunch break, and I have to get back. I'm sorry I interrupted your meditation...and thanks for the history lesson. Maybe I'll see you around town."

As Nina knelt down again, Sam noticed a spider tattooed on her left ankle.

36

"We'll see."

Sam turned and walked towards the gate. He rode down toward the town feeling drained and elated at the same time. It dawned on him that he had never actually met a Native American before, not to mention a good-looking Indian girl who's militant one day and meditative the next.

"Not to mention one whose tribe has just beaten me up and had me thrown in the slammer," he said over the rumble of the twin cylinders.

Sam picked up speed. He could smell the sweet aroma of the piñon as he hit the pavement of Canyon Road.

CHAPTER 5

At 4:00 p.m. that Friday, Sam rode out the Old Santa Fe Trail and pulled into the parking lot of a two-story office building. Stone's office was one of several grouped around a waiting room on the second floor. His door was ajar.

"Greetings. Come on in," Stone said as he came to the door. He looked somewhat less rumpled than before.

Sam looked around the small office. Two chairs stood in front of the cluttered wooden desk. He sat down in one of them as Stone returned to his chair behind the desk.

"So how are things going over at Fisher and Company?

"Pretty well, actually. I hardly ever see Mr. Fisher, though. Stephen Schiff keeps me pretty busy doing legal research at the Supreme Court library and staying on top of the cases left behind by an associate who left. I don't know whether this is going to inspire me to apply to law school next year, but at least I seem able to do the work."

"So no more Native American rallies?"

"Mr. Stone, I can't get the first one out of my head. I hope you can get the charges dismissed," Sam said earnestly. "My father will absolutely kill me if I get a conviction. He complains enough about college tuition as it is, and of course, having a felony on my record would kill any chance of decent employment. I mean, can you talk to the prosecutor or something?"

The old lawyer picked up a file and looked it over quickly. "You're charged with disorderly conduct and with making a fictitious license, as I think I told you before. The second one is a felony, and I'm afraid you're right about the effects of a criminal conviction. Not to mention that this is post 911, and you'd get flagged by every computer in every airport. To answer your question, though, I don't think talking to the prosecutor will do much good right now. Let's look at possible defenses, and then I'll contact him. I may be able to get the charge dropped from a felony to a misdemeanor, but in any event, it's always better to negotiate from a position of strength."

"I guess you're right. But how can the same charge be both?"

"It's a felony because you're charged with *making* the fake driver's license, whereas *possessing* a fake license is a misdemeanor. That's why your statement to the policeman works against you. In any event, we might be able to cut a deal. But as I told you before, the prosecutor is nervous about getting re-elected, so he is being tough on all charges related to underage drinking."

"So the best I can get is a misdemeanor. Any chance of expunging it?"

"Listen, young man," Stone answered with a tinge of impatience, "a misdemeanor is a crime just like a felony; it just has a lesser penalty. But it stays on your record— forever. There's no expunging a criminal conviction. The record of your *arrest* can be erased, but only if you're found not guilty."

"So what you're saying is that even if I get it reduced with a plea bargain, I would still have the criminal conviction on my record forever?"

"That's right. You either win the case or live with the conviction."

Sam felt as if he had been hit by a 2x4. He took a deep breath and exhaled it as a sigh. "So what happens next?"

"We go to a preliminary hearing for the felony, to see if there's sufficient evidence to take the case to the grand jury for the indictment. If I can get it knocked out at the prelim, then we're home free."

"How about the other charge, the disorderly conduct charge?"

"I feel confident that it will get tossed. I've reviewed the police report, and there's nothing to support a finding that you got into that mess willfully." Stone put the file back on the desk. "And the DA is much more interested in felonies than misdemeanors."

"So, what do I do? Do I need to testify or anything?"

"No, you won't be testifying, not at the preliminary hearing. You really don't need to do anything except keep out of trouble and let me handle this. I will look at 4th–amendment and other legal issues."

"You mean my right to remain silent?"

"No, right to remain silent is 5th amendment. 4th is the search of your wallet without a search warrant and without probable cause." Seeing his client's concern, he added, "Of course, I'll look at 5th-amendment issues as well."

"Sounds good."

"We'll see. According to the police report, it looks like it was actually the paramedic who searched your wallet in the course of treating your injuries, and the 4th amendment only applies to police action."

"You mean it's OK for non-police to search without a warrant?"

"That's right. Just like Federal Express and UPS get to search any package they want for any reason. The 4th amendment just applies to government intrusion."

Stone looked at the file again. "Just as you said, the police seem to have given you your Miranda warnings before your statement."

"Yeah. The cop seemed like a nice guy, and then he told me that it would be best if I just told him what happened. When I told him I wasn't really sure, he sort of refreshed my memory as to what he had heard."

"What did he tell you, exactly?"

"He agreed that I was probably there by accident, but that I should have left when the shouting started. I agreed with him there. Then he told me that they found the ID in my wallet and that all the college kids have fake IDs, so it wasn't really that big a deal. He made it seem like it would be best if I was open about it."

"Did he make any actual promises to you or force you in any way to talk to him?"

"No, not really. It was mostly his tone of voice. You know, kind of fatherly. I felt like I could trust him."

"Did he ask you if you made the ID?"

"Yeah, and I told him I did. Again, he made it seem like a minor thing."

"Yeah, well, unfortunately, that's an old trick the

police use. They urge you to talk and make it seem as if you'll get off. But of course, they never promise anything. That would be improper. But in the meantime, you admitted that you were there, that you knew you should have left when the shouting started, that the ID was yours, and that you made it. That's just about everything they need to convict you."

Sam sank back in his chair. "Shhh..oot....Please do everything you can to save me from this mess."

"I've been around a long time and know what I'm doing, so don't worry." He looked at the frown on Sam's face and added, "Actually, you can worry if you want to. Just don't do anything to violate your bond. It is much better to be out of jail than in."

"I'll be on my best behavior." Sam was feeling better about his court-appointed lawyer. "And I'll stay away from Indian protests."

"Normally they wouldn't be back until next year. It's been an annual thing for the Navajo tribe members for about ten years now. But because the ban on uranium mining is coming up for a vote in August, I think they're planning a number of rallies. The Diné got screwed. I don't blame them for making a stink. The government and the law sure didn't help them out, that's for sure."

"Dineh?" Sam asked. That's how Stone had pronounced it.

"That's another name for the Navajo. It means 'the People.' "

"Oh," Sam continued, "by the way, would you believe I learned about the uranium mine the other day from the girl who was leading the protest? I ran into her

42

up at the Audubon Center. She told me that nobody could get a lawsuit going, and no one would prosecute the corporation."

"Sounds like you got accurate information." He stood up, "Well, let's plan to meet in a couple of days. I need to take a look at the new police reports, and then we can talk some more. Looks like you'll be doing your formal training with Fisher and getting your practical exposure with me."

The two moved towards the door. "Here, I'll walk you out," Stone said. "I could use some fresh air." They walked down the stairs and out into the sunny lot.

Stone immediately spotted Pegasus. "Ah. There's your bike." Stone moved toward it and patted the rear seat.

"Can you believe that Tua gave it to me when she learned I was coming here?"

"How about these numbers on the side? Where did they come from?"

"I'm not really positive, but I'm pretty sure Tua did it. Some sort of ID or code or something. To be honest, I haven't really put my mind to it yet."

Sam stepped up to Pegasus, inserted the key into the headlight, and turned down the fuel lever in preparation for starting her. He had wanted to ask Stone about Tua while they were in the office, but it hadn't seemed right to pry, and he didn't want to risk rubbing his legal lifeline the wrong way.

Now that the question was on the tip of Sam's tongue, Stone said briskly, "Let's talk more in a couple of days. Call me." Then he turned and walked away.

CHAPTER 6

Not for the first time, Sam pushed open the heavy wooden door of the New Mexico Supreme Court library. He had some research to do for Schiff on the possible obligation of the state to pay for building a bridge across the Rio Grande at Embudo Station.

He looked around and entered a little study room to his left, setting his backpack on the wooden table. As he headed out toward the reference desk, he noticed the girl, Nina, across the hallway in a similar room, and by the time he returned, he had screwed up his courage to say hello, hoping she had no accusations for him today.

"Hey Nina, remember me? Sam Shelton. We met up at the Audubon."

She looked up. "Oh. Yeah."

He looked around at the legal books covering the walls of the room. "So, what are you working on?"

"Water," she said, somewhat impatiently. "I'm doing research for NAAC on Navajo Nation water rights. Probably not something you'd be interested in."

"Well, I wouldn't say that. In fact, I've read up on Church Rock since we last met, and my lawyer turns out to feel the same way you do. Actually, between you and me, I hope he's as good as he thinks he is. I got criminal charges from the Plaza incident."

"Really? Criminal charges?" She was interested now. "For what?"

"Disorderly conduct, for one."

"You said charges. Did you get more than one?"

"Yeah, stupid me. I had a fake ID in my wallet from school that I forgot to take out before I came west, and the DA has slapped me with a felony charge. I sure hope he gives me a break or that my lawyer can get that charge dismissed. I mean I'll never get a decent job if I have a criminal record."

"Yeah, I sure would hate for you to not get to Wall Street after spending all your time at some nice Ivy League college. Hey, maybe you could get a job in one of the casinos on the Rez."

Sam immediately realized he had made not one, but two mistakes, the first by talking about his case against the advice of his lawyer. And if he had thought he could gain Nina's sympathy by spilling his troubles, he had overlooked the fact that he was in New Mexico speaking to a Navajo girl who might enjoy seeing an Anglo on the receiving end of unfair treatment.

"Oh geez."

"That's OK. I was just kidding." She paused. "Sort of. So who's your lawyer, and what did you learn about Church Rock?"

"His name is Michael Stone. He felt that the uranium mine really screwed the Diné—he told me what that meant. And it was never held accountable."

"Well, I think your lawyer had it about right. You said his name was Michael Stone? I've heard that name. I think I read about him in one of the NAAC articles." Pausing for a second to think, she continued, "Yes, I think he may be the lawyer who tried to bring criminal charges against the mining company. As I recall, he either got fired or quit when the Attorney General refused to do it."

"Really? Mike Stone took on the mining company?" Sam was impressed. "I'll have to ask him about that." He gestured toward the reference area. "Better yet, maybe I'll just look it up right now. Want to join me?"

Nina looked at the pile of books on the table and hesitated, but she finally put her pen down. "Sure, why not? I could use a break from water law."

Sam sat in front of the computer next to the librarian's desk and punched in Stone's name, Church Rock, and various dates in 1979. A page full of entries came up on the screen.

"Hey, he was into a lot of stuff back then," Sam whispered to Nina.

"Yes, like I said, I remember reading his name."

Sam scrolled down. "Look at this. It's from the newspaper here in Santa Fe. 'Deputy Attorney General Resigns over Church Rock.' " Skimming the first paragraph, he looked over at Nina. "You're absolutely right. It says here that Mike Stone attempted to bring criminal charges against the Flagship Mining Corporation for fraud and public corruption, but that his boss, Henry Stratford, refused. Stone was furious and resigned under pressure. He agreed not to give a public statement, and after he left the Attorney General's office, he went into private practice."

He scrolled down some more. "Let's see what else is here." A few seconds later, Nina yelped, "Stop!" The headline on the screen read: "Former Deputy Attorney

General Represents Man Accused of Murdering Dr. Blair." "My mother used to talk about it. Dr. Blair was a friend of the Diné."

"What that's all about?" The name rang a bell with Sam too—the guy at the towing company had mentioned it, but Sam had dismissed the odd coincidence of their having the same motorcycle.

Sam pulled up articles in the *New Mexican* about Professor Blair's murder trial and started skimming the headlines. He read segments of one of the articles in a whisper as Nina looked over his shoulder: " 'The shooting took place in Dr. Blair's kitchen. The prosecutor laid out the scene....The star witness for the state was Trent Hurley, who admitted being present at the burglary gone wrong and gave an eye-witness account of the shooting....The autopsy showed that Blair was shot once in the chest and once in the head. The prosecutor pointed to the center of his chest and then to the right side of his forehead....The evidence showed that the shots were fired at close range.' "

Sam looked up for a second—Nina still appeared interested. He continued to whisper aloud, " 'A forensic firearms expert from the FBI analyzed the two bullets that were recovered from the body. She opined that they were 41 caliber and that, based on her analysis of the tool-marks and grooves on the bullets, they were almost certainly fired by a Remington derringer.' "

Sam paused, distracted in spite of himself by Nina's closeness, then scrolled through the article looking for Stone's name again. "Hey, here we go. Here are some details about the witnesses. " 'Trent Hurley, the codefendant, who had admitted participating in the burglary and killing, was represented by former prosecutor Michael Stone and testified under the terms of a plea bargain in which he pleaded guilty to a lesser charge in exchange for his testimony against Joshua Metcalf. Metcalf had insisted he was not at Dr. Blair's house that night and had nothing to do with the crime.' "

"It goes on, " 'Under rigorous cross examination by the District Attorney, Metcalf seemed stymied by the questions and unable to provide an alibi. Hurley's testimony was critical for the prosecution because the murder weapon had never been recovered, a potential fatal flaw in the government's case against Metcalf.' " Sam scrolled down some more. "Look at this. The jury found Metcalf guilty, and he got life in prison."

Nina's reaction was immediate and sharp. "I hate snitches. I wonder what Hurley got for testifying for the prosecutor?"

Sam looked at the next article, yet another by a reporter named Tom Smith. After a quick review, he answered, "Looks like he got seven years. A long time, but still a pretty good deal, considering the circumstances."

"I guess, if you compare it to spending your life in a cell. But it must have been hard to testify against his friend."

His own short time in jail gave Sam a very strong opinion. "To be honest, I think you do whatever you can to keep out of jail."

Nina stood up, breaking the spell. "Interesting. But I'd better get back to my research." She then added,

"Hope everything works out OK in court."

Encouraged by her almost friendly demeanor, Sam stood and smiled at her. "Nice to see you again. Say, how about if we meet for coffee or something? Or if you want, we could take a ride sometime. I need to do some exploring, and I bet you know lots of cool places."

"Ride what?" Nina asked.

"I have an old motorcycle. It's a great way to see the countryside."

"Hmm. I don't think so." But after what seemed to Sam like a very long pause, she added, "At least not this week. I have to go back to Gallup for a few days."

"Sounds good. I'll look for you here at the library."

Nina left, and Sam felt pleased with himself. But he was soon drawn back to the disturbing thirty-year-old case in which the victim had the same kind of bike he did and a defendant had the same lawyer. "I wonder what Hurley said."

He went to the librarian to see where to get information on the trial and in particular on the derringer. Roger Lane knew him by now. A pale, gray-haired fellow in his sixties in khaki pants and a sweater vest, he took off his horn-rimmed glasses and, to Sam's surprise, seemed personally interested.

"Yes, I remember the trial. It was a huge deal here in town because the professor was very well liked."

Sam pursued his inquiry. "It appears the police never found the gun that was used to kill the guy. Is that right?"

"Hmmm. Yes," Lane answered, cleaning his glasses with a small cloth he took from his pocket. "I remember that one of the boys involved testified against the other one. Now that you bring it up, I remember that something wasn't clear about the gun that was used, and one of the lawyers made a big deal out of the fact that it was never recovered. The jury had to rely on one boy's testimony to convict the other one."

Sam had a sudden brainstorm. "Say, do you know this Tom Smith who wrote about the trial? Does he still live around here?"

Roger nodded. "In fact, I do remember Tom Smith. It's a small town, and Smith was all over this story. I mean, it was big news. Smith retired back here a few years ago. I believe he lives south of town. He was a character even back then. I remember he liked old cars. He used to come in here to look up stuff. His place is outside of the city limits because he wanted room to work on all his cars."

Roger put his glasses back on. Sam thanked him and made a mental note to look up Smith sometime. Then he located the law volumes he needed and went back to his study across from Nina's. As intriguing as the old case was, he had come to learn about a bridge at Embudo Station, and he knew better than to return to the firm empty-handed.

CHAPTER 7

"Sometime" came sooner rather than later. Sam reached Tom Smith by phone the next day, and that Thursday after work, he found himself riding out to see him, taking Old Pecos Highway to the Old Las Vegas Highway and then heading southeast on Route 60. After two miles on it, he took a dirt road to the right and then, a quarter of a mile later, a rutted driveway to the left. Smith had given him good directions. As he managed Pegasus up the driveway, he could see that the house didn't fit the Santa Fe mold; it was made of wood and had a steep red roof. A trailer partially hidden by piñons was set perpendicular to the house.

Old cars were scattered around the property. Sam parked in the shadow of an old F-150 pickup as a large German shepherd pushed its way out of the house and came down the pathway to check him out.

"Easy Max," a booming voice told the dog, and it slowed to a walk. Sam stood still and waited for it to sniff him. "He's OK," the man said from the front door. He held the door open. "I'm Tom Smith. Come on in."

"Sam Shelton. Thanks for letting me come over," Sam said as the two shook hands. "I really appreciate your willingness to talk about Dr. Blair. I know it was a long time ago."

Smith stroked his bushy, gray beard, "Yeah, I'm happy to talk."

"This is some place," Sam observed as he walked into the front hallway. A metal spiral staircase on his left led to the second floor. To the right, a studio was taken up by a huge weaving loom; spools of brightly colored yarn were impaled on pegs on the wall. "What's this? Do you weave?"

"No, that belongs to my wife Kate. She weaves and has a little shop in town. She makes clothing and wall hangings. She's at a weaving conference in California this week."

The two made their way to the open kitchen area. The house had high ceilings, and Sam could see that the bedrooms ran along the balcony upstairs. "This seems different from most of the houses in Santa Fe."

"You're right. Most are single-story rectangular boxes, and just about all are adobe or adobe-looking, by city ordinance. That's fine, but I wanted something different. That's why this is outside the city limits. A friend of mine is a native and an architect, so I had him design and build the house about ten years ago. It's still got a ways to go." Tom pointed up to an interior wall that was still unfinished.

"I like it. How about the cars outside?" Sam asked.

"Well, I like to tinker, and I do some welding too. I like the old cars. Come on, have a beer, and I'll show you around." He opened the refrigerator and pulled out two bottles, handing one to Sam.

Sam pondered his bond conditions and decided to take the risk. "Thanks."

The kitchen opened onto a slate patio against the side of the hill, with a stone grill, and wicker chairs around a table. "I like the German cars," Smith said, gesturing toward an old BMW next to the trailer, a '68 VW bug up on blocks on the downside of the hill, and a Jetta parked in the front of the house next to the pickup truck. "Kate drives the Jetta. I mostly use the truck."

The German shepherd made its way over to the trailer and the two men followed. "Go ahead in, the door's unlocked." It was a combination workshop and garage. Tools and welding equipment took up a third of the space, and beside them were a windsurfer and two motorcycles.

"Where do you sail around here?" Sam wanted to know. "I thought we were in the desert."

"Lake Cochiti is southwest of town," Tom responded. "It's manmade, but the wind is good enough in the late afternoons for windsurfing. Can't say I've done too much lately, though."

"What kind of bikes are those?" Sam looked over to the larger bike, which looked sort of like a Harley Davidson.

"That's my pride and joy. It's a 1948 Indian Chief. They stopped making the real thing a half century ago, though the name has lingered on. I picked that up as a basket case about ten years ago and have been rebuilding it ever since."

"Cool, "Sam said. "Have you ridden it?"

"Sure. I've taken it on some trips. It's old, though, and likes to break down, so I always seem to be repairing and rebuilding it. A labor of love, I guess you could say."

Sam lifted the blanket covering the other motorcycle. "This looks like a racing bike. What kind is it?"

"It's a Triumph. I've taken that one apart every year. I used it for track racing up in Colorado." He paused, as if rueful about the past tense he had just used. "Actually, I crashed a few years back and broke my hip." He held up his cane. "That's why I have this old oak walking stick. Anyway, my racing days are over. It's a young man's sport."

The two moved toward the door, and Max led them back to the patio. Sam declined a second beer, and Tom went inside, returning with another for himself and a plate of quesadillas cut into wedges. The two sat down on the wicker chairs.

"Here, have one of these," Tom said. "They're a specialty of my wife's. She wouldn't be happy I'm serving them cold," he chuckled. Sam had no trouble complying. "These are seriously good," he said.

"So, like I mentioned on the phone," Sam continued, "I was in the library and saw that you wrote about the Blair murder case years ago."

"Yeah, I got pretty involved. So, tell me why you're so interested in that old story. It was thirty years ago."

"To be honest, I'm mostly interested in Mike Stone."

"Mike Stone? How do you know him?"

"Well, he's my lawyer. I got in a scuffle when I first got here, and a friend in Providence had given me his name before I left. He seemed pretty good, and then I started looking up stuff about him. That led me to the Blair trial. And his name also came up in my research on Church Rock."

"Church Rock? My, my. You're really getting into a lot of old cases. Now that's an issue you can sink your teeth into! That uranium mining is deadly stuff. I often wonder why your generation doesn't get more involved in these environmental causes. I mean, just look at the global warming fiasco."

His gaze was intense. "When I was your age we were protesting left and right against things we thought were wrong. I guess that's why I ended up becoming a reporter."

"What have you been doing since that murder trial?"

"I stayed here for a while, then moved down to Albuquerque. But I eventually got tired of city life and returned to Santa Fe when I retired. Now I'm focusing all my attention on the global warming problem. Those damn energy corporations are getting rich and pay nothing for burning up the atmosphere.

"That trial didn't do anybody any good," he went on. "Blair's wife got sick and died shortly afterwards, a stroke I think. His daughter…she had a teenage son. What was her name?" He looked up as if to pluck her name out of the sky and then smiled. "Yes, I remember now. Her name was Secunda. I remember that name because the professor enjoyed languages, and it's Latin for "second." Yes, Secunda Dumay. She had a nickname—Tua, kind of a pun on her real name, when you come to think about it."

Sam was incredulous. Tua's father had been murdered. "Did you say her name was Tua? Tua Dumay?" The past and the present were colliding in his mind.

"Yes. She was a real beauty. Tall, slender, dark hair, dark eyes. She was really upset, of course. She lived

55

nearby and was next on the scene after the professor's wife. Also, the kids that did the crime were neighborhood kids and actually knew her son. He was mentally handicapped, her son was." Smith coughed. "I guess I should say he had special needs, to be politically correct. Anyway, seems to me that I read that he was killed in a hit-and-run a couple of years back. Too bad. That woman had a lot of tragic things happen. First her father was murdered, then her mother died, and then she lost her son."

"This is so amazing. You're not going to believe this. She's the friend in Providence that I mentioned."

"No kidding."

"In fact, she's the one who gave me that old BMW R50 outside."

"Really? You have the old man's beemer? I'll have to look it over when you go."

"Yeah. She told me to ride it to Santa Fe." Sam decided not to mention Tua's cryptic note, but he had to mention her own death this spring.

"She died of a heart attack shortly before I left Providence."

"Oh, I'm sorry to hear that."

"Did she have any other family? I was hoping to get some information about her while I was here."

"Let's see now. She didn't have any brothers and sisters. She was married, of course, but they separated and got divorced. Maybe the stress of having a mentally handicapped son, maybe the murder of her father. Seems like everyone splits up these days. She had a weaving shop in La Posada, a hotel in town. I remember that because my wife works in one too. Tua gave me lots of background information on her father. After the convictions, she was crushed and went to stay for a while with a friend who had moved East. I heard she met someone there and remarried. In any case, she never came back to stay."

Tom was a gold mine of information, especially after a couple of beers.

"I deduced from one of your articles about the murder trial that you thought there was something more to it. What was that all about?"

"The case may be closed"—Tom's voice had an edge—"but in my mind it was never quite solved. It has always bugged me. Always. I remember at trial it all came down to the kids' testimony. I mean the testimony of the kid's partner, Hurley, his name was. A very unsatisfactory ending. But that's just the half of it. When I dug further, I learned that Dr. Blair had been spending a lot of time doing research about the uranium mine." He drained his beer. "Did I tell you about the uranium mine?"

"Well, you didn't, but I've learned about the uranium mine and what happened when the dam broke at Church Rock."

"That's it," Tom said. "He was a geologist, you know. Seems he was always out on the Navajo reservation taking samples. He was really concerned about the environmental risks of the uranium mine. I thought there might be some sort of connection between the research he was doing and the fact that he got murdered."

"Interesting. What did you find out?"

"Well, I didn't know him personally before the murder, but people at the New Mexico Environmental Law Center told me afterwards that he was worried about the dam. I never got any farther than that, and after the trial the whole question became moot. The police got a confession from Trent Hurley, and then he turned state's witness against the triggerman, with Mike Stone as his attorney. Sort of interesting under the circumstances."

"Why was that?"

"Stone was a Deputy Attorney General back then. He was a hotshot prosecutor and went after crime wherever he could find it. In New Mexico, that meant public corruption and fraud. Well, he took on some important people, and the politicians were getting upset with him. The last straw was after the Church Rock tsunami—he wanted to file criminal charges against the mine and its owners, and his boss, the Attorney General, told him to back off. Stone refused, and the next thing you know, he was out on the street."

Smith might have written that article in the *New Mexican* just yesterday, Sam thought to himself. "And it was related to his wanting to bring criminal charges against the mining company?"

"Well, that was never officially stated, and Stone is not one to go public with anything. But I'm as certain as I'm sitting here. After he left the AG's office, he went off on his own as a defense lawyer. It was sort of a shock for the law enforcement community to have him on the other side of the courtroom, but it was good for the state because Hurley provided the only real evidence against the other guy, Metcalf. They never found the gun that was used, so the DA had to rely on Hurley's testimony."

"But you had your doubts?"

"Yeah. The gun wasn't identified conclusively, either by the expert or by Hurley. The woman from the FBI lab talked about some derringers being so old you can't match up a gun and a bullet unless you have the gun, and the kid just said it was a little pistol. There was some interesting stuff about blood spatter that backed up the derringer idea. A lot of pistols eject shell cartridge casings, and to pick them up the killer would have had to smudge at least some of the blood spatter all over the floor. But he didn't—it was completely intact. Derringers don't eject the casings, and an over/under derringer would have accounted for the two shots."

"Over/under?"

"Well, you know that a derringer is a really small pistol," Tom answered. "People carried them in a coat pocket, a purse, or a boot. 'Over/under' means that there are two barrels, one on top of the other. The gun could fire two shots."

There was silence as Sam contemplated all this information. Smith, too, was silent, deep in thought.

Sam finally said, "So the gun used to kill Dr. Blair was almost certainly a derringer, and nobody ever found it."

"Right. "

"And the jury convicted Metcalf, so the case is over, right?"

"Correct. Metcalf went to prison for life, Hurley for seven years, and no one was really interested after that."

"Did you ever try and talk to Stone?" Sam asked.

"I did try after the trial, but I ran into a brick wall. Stone told me that Hurley was his client so he had a legal and ethical obligation to not say anything at all. Funny thing, now that I think of it, I sort of felt that Stone wanted me to keep working on the case—he just couldn't tell me anything."

"Because he represented Hurley."

"Right. I probed for a while after the trial, but nothing turned up. In fact, I tried to talk to your friend Tua, but she was too upset, and then she moved out of state. It's odd, you know—talking about this makes the whole thing feel recent."

"This has been great. You've given me a lot to think about," Sam replied, looking down at his watch. "But I think I'd better be heading back to town. Why don't you come and have a look at the bike?"

They stood up. "Come back anytime. Glad to have the company."

Sam picked up his jacket, and they walked down the path. "So you think if they found the derringer, they would know for sure who did it?"

"They could probably get some DNA off it. Trust me, everyone has looked for the gun. It just never showed up and could easily be in some dump somewhere or at the bottom of a lake.... Ah, the good doctor's beemer looks as good as it did 'in the day.' Tua took good care of it." He sized it up with an appreciative eye.

"And it's not just skin deep. It brought me across country without a hitch."

"I'll take it off your hands in a heartbeat if you ever

decide to put it out to pasture," Smith said with a chuckle.

"No time soon, I'm afraid. What you told me today really changes how I feel about it."

They shook hands, and Sam started the bike, maneuvered it around, and rode down the driveway. He made a mental note to pull out Tua's note when he got back to town.

CHAPTER 8

Sylvia had been Walter Fisher's secretary for over forty years, and Sam could tell she had an instinctive distrust of newcomers. He guessed she was at least in her mid-sixties.

"Hi Sylvia." Sam smiled his best smile as he moved across the lobby of the office towards the stairs. But something made him pause. "Say, Sylvia. I was wondering about something."

She looked over the glasses perched on her nose and put down the phone she had just picked up. "Yes, what might that be?"

"Well, I was at the library working on the Embudo bridge case, and I got talking to the librarian."

"That would be Mr. Lane." Sam felt she knew just about everyone in Santa Fe. "Roger Lane."

"That's him. Anyway, he was telling me some interesting stories about past goings-on in Santa Fe."

"I'm sure he was." Always looking as if she had something important to work on, she began opening some newly delivered mail. "He seems to spend most of his time looking up things that don't concern him."

Unsure where this response was coming from, Sam continued, "Yeah, he was telling me about an old murder case. Some kids killed a professor up on Old Santa Fe Trail."

A wave of anger crossed her face, "What the heck

was he bringing up that old case for? That was thirty years ago. They convicted the boy who killed him."

"That's what I understand. But there was another guy involved. Roger said he was represented by a lawyer named Michael Stone. He must have been pretty good—I mean one guy gets life in prison and the other gets a couple of years."

"Metcalf deserved what he got. And the other boy didn't get just a couple of years, he got seven," she replied.

Surprised she knew the kid's name, Sam nodded. "So, did you know this lawyer named Stone?"

"Michael Stone was well known in Santa Fe. And not in a good way, I might add. In fact, if you ask me or just about anyone else, he was an overzealous prosecutor and went after everyone. In fact, he even tried to charge some clients of Mr. Fisher's. And then he got fired."

Sam could see she had momentarily let her guard down. He decided to probe for more. "Yeah, the librarian said the trial was weird because the gun never turned up, and the kid who turned state's evidence was a little vague about what it was. Mr. Lane said it all sounded fishy to him."

"That's ridiculous!" The secretary, clearly flustered, put down the envelopes and took a drink of water from a plastic cup on her desk.

Deciding to take a different tack, Sam sat down in the chair next to her desk. "I'm sure you're right about that." He paused. "But then the librarian said there may have been some connection to the uranium mine and the dam that broke."

"Roger said that? How would he know?"

Remembering that he had actually gotten that story from Tom Smith, Sam backpedaled. "Or maybe I read that. I went and looked up some articles because I was kind of shocked that something as big as Church Rock had happened and I'd never heard of it. Anyway, is it true that Mr. Fisher represented the uranium mine?"

Pleased to change the subject, Sylvia stood up. "Yes, Mr. Fisher represented the mining company." She quickly added, "And a lot of other clients as well. I supposed Roger was talking about that, too?"

"Well, no, actually."

"Professor Blair was a kook, if you ask me," she said.

"Why do you say that? I heard people liked him," Sam countered.

"He was telling folks that the mine was hiding information about the dam. That all ended when he was shot by that boy Josh Metcalf, because there was nothing to what he was saying."

Sam decided to humor her. "Well, you must know, because Mr. Fisher was representing the mine." He stood up.

"And that frivolous lawsuit by the Navajo was just a way for the Indians to get some easy money," he heard Sylvia mutter to herself as he walked to the kitchen to grab a can of soda from the office refrigerator. When he turned around, he was surprised to find her standing in the doorway.

"Samuel," she said sternly, "I really think you should focus on the assignments that Mr. Schiff gives you. It is nothing but trouble when you start digging around in old cases. As you must know, all the material on clients is confidential for all lawyers. They can't and won't talk about them, past or present. The sooner you learn that, the better off you will be."

Just then, Walter Fisher walked into the building and shut the door behind him. At the sound of the door, Sylvia hurried back to the safety of her desk. Sam followed.

Holding a Lucky Strike in his left hand, Fisher took a long draw and then, with a sigh, exhaled a large cloud of smoke toward the ceiling. "Sylvia, how are we doing on the copies for the Rio Arriba bond closing this afternoon?"

"Just about all done, Mr. Fisher." She pointed to a stack of papers next to the Xerox machine.

"Good," he said. "Get Steven. I've got an announcement to make."

Sylvia pushed the intercom button and told Schiff to come down. With everyone present, Fisher walked to the middle of the room.

"Well, folks, I've heard that the boys down at the legislature will lift the ban on uranium mining." He paused to correct himself. "I guess I should say they're going to vote on it in August—though I'm confident the ban will be lifted. And you'll be happy to learn that after all our hard work these last few months, we are being hired by FMC to review all the procurement documents and contracts." He took a triumphant drag on his cigarette. "I can assure you this means lots of work for us. We'll be hiring two lawyers, not just replacing Kendra."

"Great news!" Sylvia proclaimed.

Fisher lit another cigarette, and the smoke rose slowly into his face. He smiled again, "Yes, it's a big break. Happy days are here again."

The meeting was over and Sam followed Schiff up the stairs. Before reaching his door, Sam pivoted and walked down the hallway to Schiff's office at the rear of the building, overlooking the gravel parking lot. Sam gave a quick knock on the door and opened it. Schiff was busy writing on a yellow legal pad.

"So this a big deal," Sam said, angling for some background on the announcement. He leaned against the doorjamb.

Schiff put down his pen. "The Flagship Mining Corporation handles a big chunk of the uranium mining in the Southwest. Mr. Fisher used to represent them back in the '80s, but then the New Mexico legislature enacted a uranium mining ban, and all our legal business with them dried up."

"So there was a ban. And it lasted all this time?"

Schiff gave him a puzzled look and then laughed. "I forgot you're not from around here. The ban continued for so long because there's been constant obstruction by a bunch of environmental groups." After a pause, he added somewhat spitefully, "Especially the Indians, the Navajo tribe."

Sam saw Nina in his mind, at the Plaza with her bullhorn. "So, what's different now?" he asked.

"It looks like the right people have finally gotten elected to the legislature. They see how important jobs are and are standing up to those damn protesters. Like Fisher just said, it's really good for us that they're going to lift the ban on uranium mining, because it's a huge industry, and where there's big business, there's always a lot of legal work to do."

Sam felt a knot form in his stomach. "Makes sense," he said noncommittally, though working for a firm on the side of the Church Rock perpetrator weighed on him almost as much as his felony charge and his recent discovery about Pegasus. Speaking of which, maybe he should park his bike behind the shed out back, so it wouldn't trigger a belated memory in Sylvia—or in old man Fisher himself—now that Sam had brought up the Blair case. What else would he have to hide this summer?

CHAPTER 9

Late Saturday morning Sam rode over to North Guadalupe, where he had noticed a store called Outdoorsman of Santa Fe. When he entered, a friendly-looking young man in a blue-collared shirt stood up from behind a glass case.

"Can I help you?"

"I hope so. I'm interested in a certain type of pistol, a derringer made by Remington."

"A Remington derringer," the salesman repeated. "Yeah, they made a double-barreled pocket pistol. It was a classic. We don't have anything like that in the store right now. I could look it up pretty quick and give you some information, though. Maybe you'd be interested in another brand, something more modern like a Cobra or a Bond." He moved down the counter toward the cash register and flipped open a thick, well-worn book with a plastic cover.

As Sam wandered over, an older, balding man with a white beard and gold-rimmed spectacles emerged from the back room.

"Hey, Fernando," the clerk said, motioning him over. "This will be even quicker," he told Sam. "Fernando here knows everything about guns, and I mean everything." Turning to the older man, he asked, "Fernando, can you give me some information on a Remington derringer?"

"Who wants to know?"

"Me," Sam offered. "I was doing some research and came across a reference to a derringer, a Remington. Seems like it was popular in the 1800s but is not that easy to find anymore."

"Derringers were first manufactured in the 1700s. A guy by the name of Deringer made the first one. His name was spelled with one 'r.' It was a small pocket pistol. In fact, as you probably know, it was a Deringer pocket pistol that Booth used to shoot President Lincoln. The small guns became very popular out here in the west, especially for personal protection when inside. Later, they were referred to generically as derringers, with two 'r's.'"

"How about the Remington over/under? When was that made?" Sam asked.

Fernando walked over to the catalog and flipped quickly to an entry. Pointing it out to Sam, he used the figures he found there to fill out his description. "In 1865, Remington made a very popular double-barreled derringer. It was a .41 caliber rimfire. Since a derringer isn't a revolver with a spinning barrel, the two barrels, one on top of the other, gave it two shots instead of one. It weighed about 11 ounces and was just under 5" long."

"What does the ".41 caliber rimfire" mean?" Sam wanted to know.

"It's basically describing the size of the bullet the gun used, like a .38 caliber or a .22. And 'rimfire' means that the firing pin strikes the rim of the base of the cartridge, not the center."

"That's a new term for me. And I've never heard of a .41 caliber bullet. Is it rare?"

"Yeah, they don't make them anymore. The .41 short rimfire was a fat, slow-moving bullet that could kill easily at short range."

"How did the two barrels work?" Sam asked.

Fernando reached under the cabinet and pulled out a small silver-colored gun with a white pearl handle. "Here's a Cobra derringer. I can show you some of the basics. In fact, this looks pretty much like the old Remington 95."

"Thanks. That would be great."

With a confidence born from decades of handling firearms, the older man easily held the weapon in his left hand and pointed to a small metal lever on the right side next to the trigger. He flipped the lever forward with his finger and turned the gun upside down as he cracked it in half like a piece of hinged metallic fruit, exposing its insides–the two empty cylinders of the short barrel on the one side and the handle on the other.

"Uh huh, I see," Sam said as he looked at the gun over the counter.

Snapping the gun back together, Fernando switched hands and cocked the hammer with his right thumb. "Notice that since there's no trigger guard, the pistol won't fire until the hammer is cocked back." He pulled the trigger and the hammer clicked back into place.

"So how does the second shot go off?"

"Look here," Fernando said as he pulled the hammer back again and turned the back of gun towards Sam so he could see the space down inside. He pointed to a small slot. "See that little pin in that slot? When you squeeze the trigger, the hammer comes down and hits the pin, which hits the rim of the cartridge. That sets off the sequence that sends the bullet out the barrel. After the first shot, that pin slides down the slot and lines up with the second barrel." He pointed again to the space between the cocked hammer and the back of the body of the gun.

"Yes, I see it. That's cool."

After placing the gun back into the case, the proprietor pointed to the picture in the catalogue. "The Remington was a finely crafted gun. It was small enough to hide easily. The barrel was only 3" long, so it was really hard to hit a target more than a few feet away. But it did give you two shots."

Another question occurred to Sam. "What happens to the casing?"

"The derringer is really a pistol, but as with a revolver the casing doesn't get ejected after a shot." He reached back into the case, retrieved the Cobra, and opened it up with a single smooth, practiced movement. Reaching into his pocket, he pulled out two bullets. "These are .38s," he said as he slipped one into each of the barrels and snapped the gun together. Then he opened it up and pushed a small, encased rod located between the barrels, which raised the cartridges about half an inch out of the barrels. "This is a retractor that pushes the cartridges out just enough so you can either pull them out or let them fall to the ground."

"Pretty amazing." Sam grinned. "I really hit the jackpot coming in here."

"So tell me, why are you interested in the old derringer? Did you want to buy one?"

After the display of classic American history, the

thought had crossed Sam's mind, but instead he dodged the question. "Not right this minute." He paused and then added, "A friend of mine back East is a gun collector and keeps raving about the old Remington derringer he used to have. I saw your store and thought I would go ahead and ask about it. How much would it set me back?"

"Upwards of $500, depending on the condition. Rare ones can bring as much as $5,000."

"Whoa!"

"Well, come on back if you're in the market for the derringer or anything else," Fernando said, gesturing toward the glass cases lining the walls.

"I sure will," Sam replied. "You've been a big help."

Sam's next destination, the Georgia O'Keeffe Museum, was within walking distance, but halfway there he spotted Nina about a block ahead. Dodging a car, he crossed the street and followed her into a small lunch place on the corner of Johnson and Chapelle. He ordered his sandwich at the counter and approached the table where Nina had just pulled a book out of her backpack.

"Do you mind if I join you?" he asked, projecting a confidence he didn't entirely feel.

She hesitated, putting down her book. Sam pulled out a chair and sat down.

Her smile, when it came, was wry. "Sure, why don't you join me?"

"Thanks. What are you reading?"

"*Long Walk to Freedom*, Mandela's autobiography. Just like the blurb says, 'Should be read by every person alive'—especially organizers for causes with long odds."

But Nina surprised him by changing the subject. "So, where did you get that old motorcycle I keep seeing you on?"

"Ha! She notices me!" Sam thought to himself, and a warm glow suffused him. He hoped his face hadn't flushed. More relaxed now, he sat back in the wooden chair. "Well, if you really want to know, I got it from an older lady back East."

"A woman? You got that motorcycle from an old lady? Are you kidding me?"

"No, I'm not kidding. I was house sitting for a professor and walking his dog when I first met her. She was always gardening and liked to stop and talk, as if she didn't have too many people to talk to." He paused. "It's quite a story, actually."

"Go ahead. We Navajos like a good story. It's part of our tradition. She must have been an interesting lady."

"Yeah, you could say that. Really unusual. She got interested when I told her I was going to be working in New Mexico this summer. That's when she told me that she used to live in Santa Fe."

"That's a coincidence. So what did she do when she lived here?

"I don't really know, beyond the fact that she loved weavings and used to make weavings herself. Come to think of it, when I first saw the old motorcycle it had a woven blanket covering it. I've seen some Navajo blankets here, and I'd say that's what it was."

"Really? Weaving is sacred for our tribe, and the blankets that we make are very important—they tell stories." Their sandwiches arrived.

"We were just talking a couple of days later," Sam continued, "and all of a sudden she wanted to show me her garage, and there was the motorcycle, surrounded with junk and covered with this dusty blanket.

"She said it had been her father's and that she used to ride with him, and then solo. When he died, the bike became hers. She really liked riding—said it was better than riding a horse and cheaper to keep. I guess she was pretty wild when she was young. Married early, I think, and had a child. I asked her how she learned to ride— wasn't it too big for her to handle and all that."

"I was wondering about that."

"She just scoffed at me. Asked me how I learned to ride a bike, swim, or drive a car. It was the old 'anything you can do' I can do at least as well. Of course, I had to agree with her. It was just funny coming from this older lady. When she told me she wanted me to have the bike, I about fell over."

Sam looked down. "After a few more days, I went back to my own apartment. She seemed to be fine; like I said, she was always puttering in her garden, and in a week or so, an envelope came in the mail with the key, the title, and a note. But at the end of the semester, when I called her house to arrange to pick up the motorcycle, no one answered. Finally, I stopped by. A neighbor saw me wandering around the house and told me that Tua had died in late April. It came as quite a shock. The neighbor knew about me, and I left her my name and number in case anyone had questions. The garage was open, so I called a motorcycle repair place I had found to tow the bike and look it over."

"I'm really sorry to hear about Tua. It sounds like you were fond of her. What did she look like?"

"She was tall and thin, with straight gray hair that she wore in a pony tail. She was still pretty, really, and she had a warm smile. And her eyes. They were dark, and they could light up. She really picked up my spirits."

"Did she give you the blanket as well?"

"Yes, but I couldn't bring it with me, of course. It's in my apartment in Providence. And then there was a strange note."

"What did it say?"

"It was cryptic, scribbled so you could hardly read it. It said, 'Dear Samuel, you remind me of someone I knew years ago. I am giving you my motorcycle. I could not bring myself to go back to Santa Fe. Please ride it there for me. Perhaps you can fix the mistakes I made. Thank you.' She signed it, 'Peace, Tua.' There was a P.S. about looking up Mike Stone, the lawyer we did the research on. And then at the bottom she wrote a string of words that made no sense. I can't even tell if they're in English."

"Mmm, a mystery. I love mysteries," Nina responded.

"They're no fun unless they're solved, though. Believe it or not, I think the note was some sort of code. I know she was telling me something, and I've been puzzling over it ever since I got it. And Tua's not able to help."

Impressed by his earnestness, Nina raised her eyebrows and pushed her glasses back up to the bridge of her nose. "I wonder what she was saying to you. I wonder what secret life she had here, what mistakes she's talking about."

"Well, I can't answer that, but here's the clincher: I found out last week that Tua was the daughter of Dr. Blair. That motorcycle I'm riding was his."

"Oh my God!" Nina, stunned, sat bolt upright. "Do you still have the note?"

"Of course. I carry it around with me. I can show it to you." He took out his wallet and smoothed out a small piece of yellow paper on the table, and they read and reread its inscrutable closing words:

Mae dzeh dibeh yazzi tkin al an as dzoh lin tkin be klizzie no da ih nesh chee.

"She left three rows of numbers on the side of the motorcycle too."

"And you have no idea what they mean? They must mean something. This is no ordinary woman. You told me she was a weaver, and she had a Navajo blanket covering this gift she gave you. Yes, this definitely means something."

CHAPTER 10

Judge Helvin was a heavyset man with thick, light brown hair, and his glasses tended to slide down his nose as he looked down at his files. He wore his tie loose under his black robe. His voice was raspy but not unfriendly, Sam thought.

"Shelton, Samuel Shelton," the judge called out from the imposing wooden bench dominating the crowded courtroom.

Sam stood up and tightened his tie. He had broken out in a sweat just walking into the building a half hour earlier, in his first—and, he hoped, last—tangle with the criminal justice system, and he had now sat through two bond hearings and three first appearances of other defendants. Where was Stone? He had told Sam he would be a few minutes late, and Sam had no idea what to say.

He did know he was supposed to walk up the aisle and stand in front of the judge. A youngish prosecutor in a dark suit stood to the right, and Sam watched another three or four lawyers come and go, announcing they were representing someone or setting a case for a hearing.

"Good morning, Judge Helvin." Sam heard Stone's voice behind him as he reached the bench.

"Good morning, Mr. Stone." The judge smiled as he looked over his glasses. "I haven't seen you for a while. How's it going?"

"Fine, really. I've been pretty busy down in federal

court, but I always enjoy coming over to general district."

Sam noticed that his lawyer had no briefcase, no notepad, and no books he might refer to in his defense. Their last conversation had been a brief one, on the phone. Sam had repeatedly told him how concerned he was and how he hadn't told Fisher or anyone else about the criminal charges. But Stone had downplayed the court appearance, assuring him all he had to do was show up on time.

"Judge, Mr. Hall and I have reached an agreement as to the disorderly conduct charge in this case," Stone said when he finally stood directly in front of the judge.

"Is that so? And what might that be?'

At that moment, the prosecutor spoke up, "Yes sir, Your Honor. Mr. Stone and I have talked about this case, and the state feels there is good cause to go ahead and dismiss the charge. It seems Mr. Shelton was in the wrong place at the wrong time."

The judge looked down at Sam for a moment before deciding to accept the proposal. "OK, I will go ahead and dismiss the charge of disorderly conduct against you, Mr. Shelton." He shuffled through the pages in the file in front of him and held up a second set of papers. "I see there is a felony charge as well. What is going to happen with that?"

The prosecutor, an assistant DA, spoke up again. "Judge, with agreement of all parties, I understand that the defendant will waive preliminary hearing, and the case will be certified to the circuit court for a trial."

The judge looked over to Stone. "Is that right, Mr. Stone? Waive preliminary hearing, and the case goes up to the circuit court?'

Stone nodded. "Yes, Judge. We are waiving prelim."

The judge signed the back of the paper with the felony charge and then looked over at the prosecutor. "Mr. Hall, maybe you should tell your boss that charging felonies for these types of offenses may be a bit much, don't you think?"

"Yes, Your Honor, I'll relay your thoughts," the young man answered nervously. "As you know, we usually plead these down to a misdemeanor, but Mr. Shelton wasn't interested in that route."

The judge registered his surprise. "Is that right? Your client is going to risk taking a felony conviction over this?"

Sam looked questioningly over at Stone. They had discussed the options, but the judge made it sound as if he should take the misdemeanor. Stone did not hesitate. "That's right, Your Honor. The state initiated this harassment—I mean, this charge—and we are going to fight it."

Looking to his left, the judge handed the pile of documents to the clerk sitting next to him. "Mr. Shelton," he intoned, "you are ordered to appear in the circuit court for trial on August 12 at 9:30 a.m. In the meantime, you must obey all conditions of your bond and keep in touch with your attorney. Next case, Madam Clerk."

Sam took a second to realize that the vise had just tightened.

The judge smiled for a second before picking up the set of papers for the next case. "Good to see you, Mike."

"Always good to see you too, Judge." Stone walked

over and shook the young prosecutor's hand and thanked him as well.

As he and Sam left the building, he elaborated. "Always be nice to people when you can. If you're ever thinking of going into law or anything else of consequence, you will make enough enemies as it is, so start building good relationships whenever it's possible."

"Yeah, I'll definitely do that," Sam replied, not without a hint of sarcasm in his voice. Nonetheless, he was glad to have one of his charges dropped without the stress of a trial. "So, next is the trial on the felony charge."

"That's it. We'll have a bench trial. That means a judge will hear the case, instead of a jury. That's a good thing because our case is going to rise or fall on technical issues."

"And if we lose, we can always appeal, right?"

"Trust me," Stone said. "It's much better to win a case at the trial court level than to count on winning on appeal. Appeals usually don't succeed, and even if they do, the case is usually sent back to the trial court for a re-trial."

"Really? I mean, what about a case where it's appealed, and there's new evidence to show someone is innocent?"

"Newly discovered evidence doesn't help a defendant if it's presented to the court more than twenty-one days after a conviction."

"You're kidding." Sam responded. "I mean how about if someone else comes in and confesses to the crime? Are you saying that the court wouldn't consider that and free the guy who was wrongfully convicted?"

"That's right. They won't consider evidence after the twenty-one days. Part of what the criminal justice system does is create finality. There are appeals, but they generally look for mistakes that the judge makes at trial. They really don't consider new evidence."

The lawyer paused for a second. "Actually, that is not entirely correct. The courts have recently changed the 'newly discovered evidence' rule and *will* consider new evidence if it's scientific evidence that will prove someone's innocence, and if the science was not available at the time of the trial."

Sam turned toward his lawyer. "Like DNA."

"Yes, that's the classic example. It's relatively new, so if you had a case twenty years ago, and if DNA evidence could prove someone didn't commit the crime, then the courts will consider that."

"That's what I thought. Like in a rape case where the DNA shows the guy didn't commit the crime," Sam replied, though his thoughts had strayed to the Blair case.

"For example."

"Well, that doesn't do me any good, does it?"

"Right again. Like I said, we need to win this at the trial court level."

"OK. You're the boss. But tell me," Sam went on, "do you think I should tell Mr. Fisher what's going on?"

"That's up to you. Personally, I like to keep things low key, and the fewer people know about your case, the better." Almost as an afterthought, he asked, "Oh yeah, how's work?"

"Fine. The first week I spent summarizing all sorts of

files left behind by a lawyer who quit, and now I'm working on whatever Stephen Schiff, the associate, gives me. There was a case involving a little bridge over the river at Embudo Station, and now I'm working on a wrongful termination case at the Los Alamos labs."

"Embudo's up in Rio Arriba County. That's where a lot of Fisher's clients are from."

"How did you know that? Do you know Walter Fisher well?"

"It's a small town, and I've been here for about thirty-five years. So, yes, I know Fisher and a lot of his clients."

Sam smiled. "Look, Mr. Stone, I told Mr. Fisher I had to take the morning off for personal reasons. Do you have time to have a cup of coffee? I'm really grateful for what you're doing, and I'd love to find out more about the legal landscape of Santa Fe, and the rest of New Mexico for that matter." He knew that Stone had been a very good lawyer, but his fate depended on him and it felt right to get to know him better, even without his intriguing connection to Tua and the Blair trial .

They had reached Palace Avenue and were walking towards the Plaza. Stone thought it over and then nodded. "Sure, let's get some coffee."

They found a spot in a newspaper and coffee shop on Otero Street. Sam led off with some questions he already knew the answers to. "So, is it true that you used to be a prosecutor? How long have you been a defense attorney?"

"Hmm, two questions in one," Stone said good-naturedly, taking a sip of steaming coffee. "I'll give the quick version of my career, if you're really that interested."

Sam nodded his head. "Yes, I'm interested. Like I told you at your office, I'm thinking of going to law school after college." How empty his stock phrase suddenly sounded to him! "That is, if I'm not a convicted felon."

Stone put his cup on the table. "Sam, you need to go ahead and live your life. Leave the details of this case to me. I've been around, and it will work out. That's the one really good thing about having a lawyer: you leave the case in his or her hands. In fact, I'm instructing you not to discuss the facts of this case with anyone. Just let me handle it."

Sam felt a wave of relief. "Thanks. I really appreciate your saying that. It's hard for me to shake off my anxiety."

As much to divert Sam's attention from his problems as to comply with his request, Stone continued, "I went to Stanford Law School and then moved to New Mexico in the seventies. I started out as public defender up in the Four Corners, but after about two years decided to try the other side of the fence."

"Oh, so you went into civil law?"

"No, not that. Funny, I never had any interest in the civil arena. Anyway, I became a prosecutor and did that for about twenty years. Worked with the DA in Farmington and then moved down here to Santa Fe and worked for the Attorney General."

"Really, the Attorney General? I didn't know he prosecuted criminal cases. What kind of cases did you do?"

"Mostly white collar cases. Fraud and corruption, things like that."

"That sounds pretty cool."

"Well, the AG at the time, David Benjamin, figured out that being tough on crime was good politics, especially taking on some of the corporations."

"So what were some of your cases? Gee, you weren't by any chance involved with the company responsible for Church Rock, were you?"

Stone looked away and didn't answer right away. Then he looked back at Sam. "Yes, I did weigh in on Church Rock. In fact, that's why I left being a prosecutor and took up defense work again."

"Oh, I'm sorry. You sound as if you'd rather not talk about it."

"No problem. It's ancient history." He paused nonetheless, as if gathering his forces. "The Flagship Mining Corporation had developed a big uranium mine up in Church Rock. It's a small town, a village really, out by Gallup, right near the Arizona border. I had reports about some stuff they were doing, tax manipulation and illegal loans to the locals. Mainly they were defrauding the Navajo tribe. But then Hank Stratford got elected AG and he wouldn't let me pursue anything. He was a solid Republican and was getting plenty of financial support from FMC, so prosecuting the mine or any other corporations in New Mexico became a no-no. Our office was told to go back to other, more politically safe, criminals."

"So you left and started defending criminals?"

Stone laughed out loud. "Pretty ballsy question from

someone who is charged with a crime and insists he isn't a criminal."

Sam saw his blunder and his cheeks turned red. "I guess I should say, defending people accused of a crime." He choked down the last bite of humble pie. "Like me."

"Actually, I usually tell people I'm defending the Constitution. Seems like most of my cases involve the 4th, 5th, and 6th Amendments."

Sam had looked them up after flunking Stone's test at the jail: search and seizure, right to remain silent, and right to a lawyer. "So, did you join a firm?"

"I went out on my own. In fact, my first big case had an oblique connection with Church Rock. I'm not going to bore you with the details right now, especially since I have to head back to my office to meet with a client." Stone finished his cup of coffee and signaled the waiter to bring the check. "Basically, there was a murder at about the same time as the Church Rock disaster."

"A murder related to Church Rock?"

"Well, no. Not officially." Stone looked at Sam as if trying to decide whether he should go on. "There was a professor who was murdered at about the same time. Two kids broke into his house, there was a scuffle, and one of the kids shot and killed the old man. I represented one of the kids charged with the crime. My client took a deal and agreed to testify against the other kid. That's how the DA won the case. My kid got seven years and the other kid, who took the case to trial, was found guilty and got sentenced to life in prison." He paused. "That's what I can tell you...because it's in the public record."

"You seem to be implying there's more to the story."

The check arrived and Stone stood up and put down a $10 bill. Sam stood up as well and pulled out his wallet, but Stone waved him off. "This one's on me."

Out on the sidewalk, the two shook hands and said good-bye, and Stone rounded the corner and was gone. There certainly *was* more to the story: Stone hadn't mentioned that Tua was Blair's daughter.

CHAPTER 11

Sam had promised Nina a ride before they parted company at the sandwich shop, so the Sunday after his court appearance he pulled up at 10:00 a.m. in front of the place where she was house-sitting, eager for relief from the Los Alamos case and his own legal troubles. Nina was waiting out front, wearing a deep orange t-shirt and faded blue jeans. Her long black braid fell straight between her shoulders.

"So, tell me again about this. You say it's a BMW motorcycle? Like the car maker?"

"That's right," Sam responded. "It's a model R50/2 made in 1964." He pointed to the metal cylinders that projected horizontally almost ten inches from each side of the engine like two stubby wings. "It has an air-cooled engine, and these are the cylinders. Each has a piston inside that connects to the crankshaft. The design was unusual for motorcycles, but it's very effective."

"A couple of kids on the reservation near Gallup used to have motorcycles. They looked different, though, mostly small dirt bikes. So you really rode this all the way across the country?"

"Yes, I did. It surprised me too," Sam added. "When I got it I didn't even know how to ride it. I had to take a sixteen-hour course on one of the training company's bikes and a shorter course on this one." He patted the oval tank and admired the bike's gleaming black paint and white pinstripe. "Ol' Pegasus got me all the way, my mother's misgivings notwithstanding."

"So, tell me about it. I mean how do you actually ride this thing?"

This "thing?" Sam thought. It suddenly struck him that the more he rode Pegasus—the more they trusted and depended on one another—the more he intuitively thought of it as alive. Or maybe it was simply the curves of the fenders, not unlike Nina's, he thought, as she moved around the motorcycle. Sam was learning to recognize beauty and dependability when he saw it.

"The ignition and speedometer are both in the headlight, right here on the top." He pulled out his key. "On these old BMWs, the key is just a piece of plastic over a short metal spike, like a small nail." To illustrate, he pushed the piece into the slot, which lit up the ignition indicator light. "The great thing is, you never get stuck if you lose your key, because you can use a nail or even the little metal piece from a belt buckle."

"Hmm...Interesting."

"The front brake lever is on the right-hand side of the handlebars with the throttle, and the clutch is on the left side." He pointed downward towards the right-hand cylinder. "The rear brake pedal is down there, under the cylinder."

Nina bent down a bit. "I see it. Looks like your foot tucks underneath."

"That's right. And on the other side is the gear lever."

Nina pointed to the oval-shaped piece of black rubber attached to the right side of the fuel tank. "What's that for?"

"That's padding for your knee when you ride." He pointed to the large dual seat. "See, when you're sitting on the saddle, your knees straddle the gas tank. There's one on the left side as well."

"I see." Nina put her hand on the saddle. It, too, was black and extended from the base of the tank to the chromed metal luggage rack secured to the back of the motorcycle. "The saddle looks comfortable."

"It should be. This is a fine German touring machine, and they're famous for their engineering. Everything's well done, including that saddle. Hard to believe it's over fifty years old."

"And those are the numbers you were talking about."

"Yes. Any ideas?"

Nina squatted down and read them. "A couple of them look like social security numbers. They're not the right length for phone numbers. Maybe an ID number? I really don't know."

"I thought the same thing, but nothing panned out. I don't know what kind of an ID it would be. Anyway, it continues to mystify me."

"And the lady etched those numbers?"

"Yes. Well, either she or her father, since they're the only two that ever owned the motorcycle. I keep thinking it must be her, because she obviously likes codes."

"You know, I've been thinking about her and that note. There was something familiar about it."

"Familiar? What do you mean?"

"I think I recognized one of the words. It's Navajo for 'goat.'"

"Goat! Oh gee, that really clarifies things. But yeah,

thanks for thinking about it. So, ready to go for a ride?"

She ran her hand along one of the fiberglass saddlebags attached to either side of the rear wheel and answered, with a sparkle in her eye, "Yes, on condition that you teach me how to ride it one of these days."

"Uh, sure," Sam nodded, not at all sure if he could convey how you ride a motorcycle without its falling over. "How about if we take a spin up to the ski basin? I haven't been there yet, and I hear the ride up is really nice."

"OK," Nina said. She had gotten a hold of a helmet, and Sam put on his as well and turned the ignition on and kicked down on the starter pedal. "Oh yeah," he said over the roar of the engine, "I forgot to mention that you have to kick start Pegasus."

They headed toward Fort Marcy on Bishop's Lodge Road, and after a block took a right on Ski Basin Road, heading to the mountains. The road went up past two adobe-colored condominium developments and numerous private homes spreading out into the piñon-covered desert. The blacktop followed a small river that originated as a spring higher up on the mountain. Soon Sam and Nina were leaning into endless curves as the road carved into the mountain pass up toward their destination fifteen miles away.

The views became more spectacular with every gain in altitude. Nina pointed out each new panorama, poking Sam on the shoulder and gesturing to the left or right. They climbed for eight miles until they arrived at a big switchback with a huge aspen grove to the right. Thousands of trees waved in the breeze, sending out shimmering waves of green. Nina patted Sam's shoulder, signaling him to pull over.

Sam pulled into the small parking area. Nina immediately dismounted and pulled off her helmet. "I just had to take a look. These aspens are so beautiful!"

An old dirt fire road led up into the woods. Sam and Nina followed it to a small stream cascading from a rocky ledge, where Nina knelt down and took a drink of the ice-cold water. "I must say, this is a great way to travel. You feel like you're sort of flying, flying up the mountain." Sam could not have agreed more.

Soon they were on the road again, and five minutes later they pulled into the large, almost empty parking lot of the ski area.

"Let's hike up a bit," Sam suggested.

Fifteen minutes later, they crested a hill and were able to look east over the pine trees. Nina also turned and looked back at where they had just come from, at the big metal towers strung with cables and lift chairs, and the huge pulley set next to the small shed at the top of the ski run. She shook her head. "It makes me so mad."

Drinking in the distant scene, Sam was caught short. "What?"

"It's so typical of you Anglos. I mean, here we are sitting on this beautiful mountain, and then I look around and see what's really important to you."

Her tone signaled to Sam where she was going, but he asked his question anyway. Although he was wary, he sort of enjoyed seeing Nina light up with indignation, as long as it was only generically at his expense. "What exactly do you mean?"

"I'm talking about exploiting the environment. Look at this," she said, pointing to the grassy, rock-strewn ski slopes carved out of the thick pine forest. "You cut down all the trees so that you can have your sport and so the corporations can make a ton of money. In the meantime carbon dioxide spews into the atmosphere with fewer trees to soak it up. And don't get me started on the possibility that the legislature will lift the ban on uranium mining during the special session. I have my work cut out for me in the next few weeks. The next rally is on July 16th, the Church Rock anniversary."

"You mean 'my' rally wasn't the big one?"

"No way! We were just warming up. The really big one is on August 16th, two days before the vote. A lot of organizations are involved."

Sam guided the conversation back to the present scene. He had no trouble sympathizing about the altered state of the land; his real discomfort lay in being a summer intern for the enemy. "You really do notice the bare slopes during the summer. All the same," he added, daring himself to push back, "Native Americans can't think that capitalism is all bad, can they? I mean, I see plenty of casinos around."

"I see your point." Sam was surprisingly relieved by her concession. Maybe they could actually have a discussion, instead of just thrust and parry.

"But," she continued, "they make money in a building in a commercial zone, rather than by cutting down the forest in order to have tourists loop endlessly up and down the mountain. And all just for money. I mean, these mountains, this forest, they belong to everyone, not just corporate white America."

Sam could add nothing, so he simply nodded. "Let's hike up some more."

A half hour later they reached the summit and were able to view the valleys in all directions. Sam sat down against a large boulder, winded from both the physical exertion and high altitude but glad for the bright sun and the light breeze moving across his face. "It really is amazing up here. Definitely worth the effort," he said slowly, waiting for more oxygen to reach his blood cells.

Nina sat down next to him and took a drink of water. "I feel like I'm on top of the world."

Sam raised his hand against his forehead for shade as he scanned the wide-open landscape. "Yeah, I don't get to see views like this very often on the East Coast. A lot of the mountains are lower and covered with trees. The West is all about open sky. I really like it."

Nina passed the water bottle to Sam and pointed to a large hawk circling in ever widening arcs. "When I was a little girl I really wanted to fly. We used to wander into the hills, and I would watch the hawks soaring. They seemed so free." They watched the bird in silence for a minute.

"Speaking of which," Sam said, "where did you grow up?"

"I was born and raised in Gallup. I'm the youngest of four. My brothers are pretty much on their own now. One's in college, one's a construction worker, and one's in law school in Boulder."

"I guess you learned to hold your own at an early age," Sam chuckled. "My brother is ten years older than I am, so he always seemed more like a young-ish uncle or something. My sister Sharon is two years younger than I am, and we get along pretty well. She just finished her freshman year at Brown."

"That's in Providence, right? So you go there too?"

"Yes. I've just finished my third year. I can't quite decide on a career, so I'm doing history as an all-purpose major."

"Well, I *can* decide," Nina replied with a laugh, "and I'm doing environmental science as an all-purpose major. I started out at NM Gallup, but now I'm in Albuquerque."

"But your activism is for Native American rights."

"They're inseparable from the land, Sam. Just look at Church Rock."

"I guess you're right."

"I may go to law school, but my best option would probably be a graduate program in environmental policy. I have my reasons. My father worked in a damned uranium mine and died of lung cancer in 1995, when I was seven."

"I'm so sorry."

"He was ten years older than my mother," Nina said with a sigh, "and he worked in the mines for eighteen years, beginning in 1965. That's more than twenty years after the uranium boom began. The mines were full of radon gas, and the mining companies were so negligent that they still hadn't installed ventilators. The first cancer cases showed up in the '60s, but federal safety standards didn't go into effect until 1971, and even then they weren't always enforced. After the fact, they've figured out that two-thirds of all lung cancer cases in Navajo men during the time my father worked can be traced to underground uranium mining....So you can see what fuels my need to protest." They sat for a while in silence.

"By comparison, my family will sound ridiculous to you," Sam said finally. "My dad's a lawyer, and my mom volunteers a lot at the local hospital in Bristol. She's a very good pianist. I've had it easy, maybe too easy."

"Like that hawk."

"Well, not quite—he's an expert flyer." Sam seized the chance to lighten up the conversation. "But lately I've come to think that when you're doing something you really enjoy or are really good at, like riding the bike or running, or maybe painting or making music—or weaving, I bet— it feels effortless, almost like you're flying. Effortless effort."

Nina, still watching the bird, saw it slowly circle toward an open space far down the mountain. She smiled and stood up, offering Sam a hand. He took it. "I used to dream I was a hawk. I flew over the mountains and the valleys, hunting, of course, in order to live, but also watching and protecting my mother."

"Your mother?"

"The Earth, Sam, the Earth," she explained as she let go of his hand and started to walk toward the path. "You know, the land, the sky, the flowers, the trees, the water, everything." She looked back and smiled. "C'mon, let's go."

She surprised him when they reached the motorcycle. "So, how about a 'flying lesson' right now? There's not a single car left in the parking lot."

Sam was perplexed. "You know, to be honest, I'm not really sure how to teach someone. I mean, it's like learning how to ride a bicycle, you just sort of have to do it. I can show you where the controls are, but at some point you have to use your balance and your instincts."

Nina got on the motorcycle and placed her hands on the handlebars. "Well, I know how to ride a bicycle, and, just to let you in on a little secret, I've ridden a motorcycle before."

"You have?" Sam was both surprised and relieved.

"Yeah, back when I was a kid. I rode one of those little dirt bikes. It's been a long time, but I remember the throttle, clutch, and gear thing."

"Well, that's the main thing. Actually, now that I think of it, there are two things. You need to be moving in order to keep your balance, and you need to use the back brake to stop, at least while you're learning. It's the foot lever on the right. The hand brake on the right operates the front brake, but if the wheel is turned at all, the bike tends to fall over." Sam conjured up the image of Pegasus falling over on top of Nina. "And we don't want that."

Nina practiced using the controls sitting on the stationary bike, pulling the clutch lever with her left hand, pushing down on the foot lever for the rear brake with her right foot, and changing gears with her left. Then she got off the bike and turned to Sam. "OK, I think I'm ready."

Sam took a deep breath and went over to start the bike. He put the key in and kicked down. Pegasus sparked to life. He rolled back the throttle, and the bike settled into her calm idle. "It's all yours," he said nervously. "Remember, it's like riding a big heavy bicycle."

Nina smiled confidently as she got back on. Sam could tell she had the most useful skill of all: she was not afraid. She flipped the side stand back with her left foot and revved up the engine using her right hand, squinting as she concentrated on Sam's instructions. Slowly she let out the clutch lever with her left hand, and as the engine engaged the transmission, the machine began to move. Nina lifted her right foot from the ground onto the riding peg, and the bike began to wobble.

"Give it some gas! You need some speed!" Sam shouted.

Nina hesitated for a second and then twisted the grip in her right hand. The engine roared to life and the motorcycle jumped forward. Soon girl and machine were moving smoothly across the parking lot.

"Bravo!" Sam shouted. "You've got it!"

Nina moved in a wide circle around the open space of the parking lot, and as she made her first turn to the left, Sam could see she had a big smile on her face. She shifted into the next gear and picked up speed.

After circling the lot three times, Nina rode back to where Sam was standing. She came to a smooth stop and put both feet to the ground, holding the clutch tightly. "Now what do I do?" she asked.

Sam had failed to tell her about how to find neutral and turn off the engine! He ran up with instructions. "You get to neutral by finding the space between first and second gear."

"With my left foot?"

"That's right. And keep the clutch in until you get neutral."

Nina jiggled the gear lever with her foot, and when she thought she had found neutral, she nodded. The green light on the speedometer lit up, and Sam gave her the thumbs up. "You've got it. You can let the clutch out now and then pull the key out."

Nina slowly released the clutch and pulled out the key from the top of the light. The engine fell silent. She pushed the kickstand down with her left foot and carefully leaned the bike over onto it, then dismounted and pulled off her helmet.

"Good job!" Sam said. "That was really great. You're a very fast learner."

Nina wore a big smile. "That was really cool."

Sam smiled back at her. It seemed to him that they had crossed a boundary, and he felt a pleasant chill down the back of his neck as he put on his helmet.

CHAPTER 12

Fisher came into Sam's office without knocking. "I want you to get on over to the statehouse and take notes on what the hell they're doing on the mining bill!"

Lighting a cigarette, Fisher took a drag. The edginess in his voice conveyed his irritation. "I just heard they moved up the Energy and Natural Resources committee meeting on the uranium mining bill. I guess they're anxious to get this thing in the bag. It's in room 315. I need you to find out who's attending and what they're talking about."

"Yes, sir, I'm on my way." Sam pushed his chair back and slid a pad of paper into his canvas briefcase. "Uh, anything in particular I should keep an eye out for?"

"Pay attention to Phil Deaton, Bobby Gonzales, and especially Jack Etsitty," Fisher said. "And take special note of any experts the Indians bring in. We know they oppose any bill that would even consider lifting the ban."

Sam grabbed his jacket and headed for the stairs but stopped and turned when he was halfway down the hall. "Is there a separate bill for the Indians?"

"Yeah, the Navajo passed a law a few years ago to prohibit uranium mining on Navajo land. That's probably never going to change, and they get a lot of sympathy from the liberals. The trouble is, they keep showing up for state bills and causing trouble. Focus on what's said about the bill to lift the ban on mining on state land, especially in Rio Arriba County. This is the last public discussion before the vote. It's going to be a close floor vote, and I don't want this bill killed by the damn liberals again."

Sam nodded and headed out the front door to the Capitol, right across the street. The American flag and the yellow New Mexico state flag, with its red Zia sign, flew overhead. "Symbol of the sun," he said out loud. The Capitol itself, with its round center and four radiating wings, was patterned on it.

He took the wide stone stairs two at a time to the third floor and opened the heavy wooden door as quietly as he could. The meeting had just begun, and he grabbed an agenda and slipped into a chair along the wall. Pulling out his notepad, he began to write. "Members: Rep. Phillip Deaton, Chair. Jeff Martinez, Vice Chair. Eleven members total, plus guest speakers."

The meeting was called to order by the chairman. Sam recognized the heavyset man with thinning gray hair, who wore a pinstriped suit. He had been meeting regularly with Fisher at the firm.

"I trust we will have an informative discussion on uranium mining," Phillip Deaton began. "I, for one, am looking forward to the economic benefits that a renewal of the uranium industry will bring to New Mexico."

A short man wearing a blue blazer stood up. "Mr. Chairman, I want to know why the time of this meeting was changed."

Deaton smiled. "Yes, thank you, Mr. Lujan. It was changed to accommodate our principal speaker. This will be the final public hearing before what I believe will be a close vote on August 1st, and his input is critical."

Representative Lujan retorted edgily, "I had a number of constituents who wanted to attend."

Deaton's tone was also sharp. "I need not tell you that we sometimes have to make last- minute changes." The two men clearly did not like each other. Thinking of Fisher's words, Sam felt sure that the chairman was trying to limit the discussion.

Deaton did not miss a beat. "The Chair recognizes Mr. William Rancard, the director of the Mining and Minerals Division of the Energy, Minerals, and Natural Resources Department."

A tall man stood up and moved quickly to the front of the room, where a laptop computer was already set up. "Good morning, ladies and gentlemen. Chairman Deaton has asked me to come today to give you all an update on the status of mines in the state."

The large screen on the wall lit up with a PowerPoint slide, a map of New Mexico with a spatter of red across part of the northwest. "These are the main uranium deposit locations in New Mexico." A more detailed map appeared, this one with hundreds of little red x's.

Sam was astounded. That many mines in New Mexico? He knew that the state was closely associated with the start of the atomic age—the first atomic bomb had been developed during the Second World War at Los Alamos, just northwest of Santa Fe, and the Trinity site where the first atomic bomb was detonated in 1945 was downstate, near Alamogordo. But Church Rock was the only mine he had ever heard of, and *it* had caused a disaster all by itself.

Rancard had anticipated his silent questions. He

reviewed the federal government's strong encouragement of uranium exploration and mining in the 1950s and early '60s and the gradual decline of the mining industry over the next twenty years. Then he got really historical. Putting up a succession of slides with red x's, one for each relevant county, he patiently detailed its geology and its current prospects, emphasizing the newer techniques like in-situ leaching available to industry players. His description of Cibola and McKinley counties prepared Sam for the Rio Arriba summary; always unsure of his geological eras, he had at least heard "Triassic" and "Cretaceous" often enough to be able to catch them when it was Rio Arriba's turn, and he had digested the fact that most deposits were found in sandstone. The "Morrison Formation" seemed particularly important. Interesting that there was also a significant limestone uranium lode with the odd name "Todilto." How did rocks get radioactive anyway? He would have to find out.

Sam was sure that Fisher already knew everything he wrote down about Rio Arriba; his crusty boss was more interested in the political vibes building in the room. When he looked down at his notes as Rancard was winding up his hour-long presentation with Valencia County, what was written in caps and circled concerned Church Rock, in McKinley County: a Texas company called Hydro Resources was going to open it back up!

"As you can see," Rancard concluded, "the Division has created an inventory of mines with verifiable production and reclamation status. We have identified hundreds of old mines with historic uranium, many of them 'uneconomic' until now, and another hundred sites that have uranium but no reclamation activities. A bright future for uranium mining in New Mexico lies ahead, and as a result the United States will no longer need to depend on countries like Kazakhstan for most of its uranium."

Deaton thanked Rancard, then looked over to a Hispanic man in his forties sitting across the table, who took the cue and spoke up. "Donald Chavez, from Cibola County. I'm confident that uranium mining can be conducted in a safe manner and that it will bring jobs to the area and enhance the quality of life in New Mexico."

Deaton nodded approvingly.

A short man with a walrus mustache raised his hand. "What about the Indian land?"

"Good question," Rancard replied in a patronizing voice. "As you know, the Navajo Nation has prohibited uranium mining on their land. This has created a problem with the checkerboard area around Indian land, and there are differing ideas about jurisdiction. However, there is a huge amount of uranium in Northern New Mexico that does not interfere with Indian land."

A sharp slam of a fist on the table jolted the whole room. "Lies!" A tall, thin, dark-skinned man in blue jeans and a plaid shirt stood up. "You are telling us the same old lies!" Sam noticed his long black hair pulled back tight in a ponytail.

"You must state your name for the record," Deaton interrupted.

Looking angrily around the room, the man took a deep breath and announced, "I'm Jack Etsitty, director of the Navajo Nation Environmental Protection Agency, and I am here to remind you again how uranium mining in New Mexico has adversely affected our air, land, and water resources." He stared at the director. "It's taken a devastating toll on Navajo human health and will affect the Navajo people for generations to come."

Deaton interrupted again. "Thank you, Mr. Etsitty." He looked around the table and added quickly, "Next speaker please."

Sam was on high alert.

Ignoring the ploy, Etsitty looked directly at Deaton. "The Navajo people do not have the option of relocating to unpolluted land and changing their life. I demand that, before any discussion of new mining proposals anywhere near the Navajo Nation, our polluted lands be restored, the uranium waste piles be removed, our sources of water be cleaned, and our air be restored to its original pristine state." He looked disgustedly around the room. "Why is it that you do not share the Navajo's concern about preserving New Mexico's environmental quality for your grandchildren?"

This was the confrontation Fisher had been concerned about. Sam felt his adrenaline pumping.

The menacing look Deaton gave Etsitty did not jibe with his overly calm answer. "We appreciate your concerns, which, I will point out, you bring to every committee meeting. However, as we all know, mining procedures have improved, and there will be complete oversight to make sure that any and all mining is clean and safe." He paused. "Not only that, the government, both state and federal, has cleaned up most all of those old mines. Also, as you know full well, any new mining will *not* take place on Navajo land."

"We've heard all this before," Etsitty retorted. "*You* know full well that the government has barely scratched the surface. The Church Rock disaster occurred in 1979, and the EPA didn't even sign on to a cleanup until 2007! And boundaries on maps are meaningless. I have personally visited the communities where pollutants have migrated from abandoned uranium mines, capped uranium tailings, and uranium waste piles. Some are located on adjoining state, federal, and private lands, and nothing prevents the migration of the hazardous pollutants from one piece of land to another."

Deaton attempted to cut him off, but Etsitty continued. "The discharge of billions of gallons of contaminated mine water from underground and open-pit mines would cause extensive ground water contamination. But your 'in-situ leaching,' your much-touted ISL, is just a variation on the theme of fracking and risks the contamination of entire *aquifers*, in an area of the country where water resources are already scarce!"

Sam stopped writing and looked up. *Billions* of gallons? Fracking?

"We will be sure to take all of this into consideration," Deaton answered and then looked around the room. "Remember, we are talking about lifting the *state* ban on uranium mining, not the Navajo ban."

But Etsitty wasn't finished. "And Mr. Rancard, you neglected to remind the committee that Kazakhstan is quite happy to sell uranium to the United States and that the number two and three producers, Canada and Australia, are close allies. The U.S. currently mines a mere 6% of its own uranium, and the devastation you are proposing would fuel only a handful of nuclear power plants in the course of a year. Thank you."

Etsitty sat down, amid electrified silence, and Deaton called a series of pro-mining speakers. Richard Horn, the executive vice president and chief operating officer of URI, was a fit-looking man in his forties wearing a tan suit, a starched pinstriped shirt, and red tie.

"Thank you, Mr. Chairman. Over the last three years, there has been an unprecedented increase in the price of uranium." He slowly panned around the table, looking at each member of the committee. "And I will tell you this: with the second-largest uranium reserves in the country, New Mexico can be at the forefront of the uranium mining resurgence."

Horn raised his voice for emphasis. "Uranium mining will provide 3,000 to 4,000 jobs in the uranium mining district. Northern New Mexico was a world leader during the first uranium mining boom, and current estimates are that 200 to 300 million pounds of uranium are waiting to be extracted."

Two other mining advocates followed, speaking about ISL, the new safety regulations and the huge economic benefits of uranium mining, but by this time Sam had tuned out. As he looked at the committee members, he could feel the momentum for the lifting of the mining ban.

After the last speaker finished, Deaton looked at his watch and reached for his gavel. "Remember folks, it's clear that the bill to lift the ban on uranium mining will bring huge economic benefits to the state and to each of your districts. I think your constituents will agree. As you have heard, this is now a highly regulated and safe industry. Personally, I see absolutely no downside. We're talking about bringing thousands of jobs to our state and being at the forefront of a booming, worldwide industry."

Just then the large wooden door was flung open. All eyes turned to watch a small, dark-skinned woman with black braided hair walked briskly over to the group of legislators, her arm raised over her head.

"Wait, Mr. Chairman, wait!" she said in a high-pitched voice. "I just found out about the change of time of this meeting."

Deaton looked at her and grimaced. "Please state your name and whom you represent, for the record."

She stood at the head of the table, caught her breath, and spoke. "My name is Abigail Watchempino. I'm a water quality specialist for the Acoma Water Commission. I want to tell the members of this committee that one of the areas being considered for mining is sacred to the Acoma people. I don't see how the government can allow another generation of contamination when our Navajo sisters and brothers are still suffering. It seems even now that uranium mining poses a threat to the aquifer that the Navajo people rely on for drinking water. We must address these issues before allowing this mining industry on our land!"

Sam looked around the conference table and noticed a couple of the members looking at each other, clearly startled by this small woman and her simple message. Remembering Fisher's words about this being the last public meeting before a close vote, Sam wondered how Deaton would respond.

"Duly noted," Deaton replied, and quickly pounded his gavel.

CHAPTER 13

At 4:45 p.m. on Friday afternoon, the phone rang as Sam was looking out the office window at the sun hitting the mountains. He hesitated to answer it, wondering if it was some official from Rio Arriba County demanding more research. He didn't need a new assignment just as he was ready to leave for the day. But he did pick it up, and a female voice said, "Sam, I'm in sort of a jam and wondered if I could ask a favor of you?"

It took him a second to realize it was Nina; she had never called him at work. "Oh, hi, Nina. Sure, you name it," he answered this no-brainer of a question.

"I have to go to the Navajo Council Chambers in Window Rock tomorrow for an assignment for NAAC, and my car died just outside of Albuquerque."

"What happened?"

"Something about the fuel pump. I had to have the car towed, and the garage said they can't get the part until Monday." She paused slightly. "Anyway, you mentioned taking me for a longer ride, so I thought this would be a good opportunity."

Quickly calculating that it was at least 150 miles due west to Window Rock, just over the Arizona line, Sam wondered aloud, "Well, yes. We could take Pegasus, but it's a pretty long ride. Are you sure you want to sit on the back of a motorcycle all day long?"

"I'm staying with my friend Rachel tonight, and it's

only about two and a half hours from here. I know this is asking a lot, and if you can't do it, I understand."

"Of course I can do it," he responded. "It'll be a good adventure, and I wanted to ride out that way anyway. Yes, I'll definitely do it. When did you say you needed to go?"

"I guess we would have to leave Albuquerque by 9:30 or so. I can meet you at the law school. It's right off the highway."

"That sounds about right," Sam responded. He figured he could easily look at a map. "So I'll meet you at the law school at 9:30. It'll be a long day, but we should be back before dark."

"That would be great. If we have time, I'd like to stop by and see my mother in Gallup. You'll be able to see where I grew up."

Amazing! Nina was not keeping him at arm's length. "Remember to wear something to protect yourself from the sun on the way there and the cold on the way back, in case we come back after sundown. And what about a helmet?"

"The one I wore to the ski basin belongs to the younger brother of my friend Grace. I'll call her and have her get in touch with you about picking it up."

"Sounds good. I'll wait here until I hear from her. If you can't reach her now, I'll be home after 6:00. Oh, and while I have you on the phone, you probably already know something I just learned just yesterday. Fisher had me sit in on a meeting of the Energy and Natural Resources Committee. Some big company is trying to reopen the Church Rock mine."

"Yeah, I know. That's why the demonstration you got mixed up in got so agitated."

"The industry guys sounded pretty sure of themselves."

"Don't tell me about it. I'll see you tomorrow," she said and hung up.

Excited about being on the road again, Sam cleared his desk and headed out of the office. At 7:00 a.m. the next morning, his saddlebags filled with provisions and gear, he settled in for the ride, elated by the sunshine, the wide-open space, and the prospect of a day with Nina. He passed over La Bajada, with the Sangre de Cristo Mountains behind his left shoulder, and plunged into the vast valley stretching to Albuquerque fifty miles away, flying along at 75 mph under the cloudless blue sky.

An hour later, Sam spotted Nina in the parking lot in front of the main building. "So, tell me again, what's in Window Rock?" he asked as they got ready to go, knowing the sound of the wind made conversations almost impossible at highway speed.

Strapping on her helmet, Nina said, "The Navajo Council Chambers. I need to get some information on Peter Benallie."

"Who's he?"

"He was the four-time chairman of the Council. He got lots done but was a bit controversial later on."

Sam started the engine and gestured for her to get on behind him.

Nina threw her leg over the saddle and put her arms around his waist. "I met him years ago when I was working on some research for school. He's must be ninety years old by now."

The two were soon on Interstate 40 heading west toward Gallup. Nina pulled down the helmet visor against the sun reflecting off the barren dirt landscape on both sides of the highway, and she and Sam each settled into their own thoughts as they hurtled through the hot sun and clear air, with the wind rushing past.

An hour and a half later, Nina pointed to the northeast, across a valley of wild grass and sage, at a rocky ridge to the right and a highway sign announcing that they were about thirty miles from Gallup. Sam nodded.

Thirty minutes later, Sam pulled into a gas station just outside of Gallup to fill up. He and Nina both got off and stretched as the noonday sun beat down. Nina pulled her map out of the saddlebag. "Window Rock is another twenty-five miles. And then, if you're up to it, we can see my mother on the way back."

Sam looked at the map. "Sounds like a plan," he replied.

"She lives in a little house she was able to buy with her RECA settlement."

"RECA"?

"The Radiation Exposure Compensation Act. It was passed in 1990 to help uranium widows. People who couldn't produce a traditional marriage certificate couldn't apply, though. My mom didn't qualify until the act was amended in 2000 to include couples married in Navajo ceremonies. Before then, we lived on the rez and she worked in a school cafeteria. She was able to buy her house in Gallup with part of her RECA settlement, and now she works in a cafeteria five minutes from home."

The 4.5 gallon tank took no time to fill. A half hour later, as they rode into Window Rock, Nina's hand signals directed Sam to the Navajo Nation Council House.

"Why is the town called Window Rock?" he asked Nina as they dismounted.

"There's a two-hundred-foot sandstone hill with a big hole in it located here. The town is the government center for the Navajo and also has the Navajo Nation Museum and the Window Rock Fairgrounds, where they hold the Navajo Nation Fair each year."

The heat reflected off the road, and beads of sweat formed quickly on Sam's brow. He and Nina both pulled out their water bottles and took a long drink. She put her hand up to shade her eyes and pointed across the street to the north. "Window Rock is over there. Its Navajo name is Tségháhoodzání, which means 'The Perforated Rock.' It's important in the Water Way Ceremony, called 'Tóhe.'"

"Tohe?" Sam asked, slurring the word.

"Tóhe," she repeated, gently correcting him. "Yes, it's a ceremony that's held for abundant rain. The rock is one of the four places where Navajo medicine men go to get the special water for the ceremony."

Sam enjoyed watching her lips as the words rolled off her tongue. As she pulled her backpack on, he asked, "Any other places for me to check out while you're doing your research?"

She turned and pointed past his shoulder. "About a mile south, there are the Tséta'cheéch'ih, which means

'Wind Going Through the Rocks'."

"Wow. I won't try repeating that one," Sam joked.

"They're huge sandstone rocks that look like haystacks. In fact, that's what they're called in English, the Haystacks," she explained. "If you have time, you could also see Tséyaató, which means 'Spring Under the Rock.' It's in a rock formation just south of the Haystacks beside the highway—a spring that seeps from under the rock. It was the first stopping place out of Fort Defiance when thousands of Navajo started their 'Long Walk' to Fort Sumner in 1864."

"The 'Long Walk.' I've heard of that."

"But let me guess—you weren't born then either." Nina rolled her eyes in what Sam hoped was mock frustration.

"Nina, help me out," he said with feeling. "It was just an inert paragraph in a history book."

"OK, the short version," she said, relaxing a little. "You'll recognize a couple of names. It started in 1864, during your Civil War. A general who was feeling left out of the carnage in the East decided to make a name for himself by wiping out the Navajo. He ordered Kit Carson to attack and kill us, burning our villages and destroying our crops and livestock. Finally, most Navajos surrendered at Fort Defiance, not far from here. They were marched in maybe fifty groups about four hundred miles to Bosque Redondo, near Fort Sumner, in eastern New Mexico. Many died along the way, and stragglers were abandoned or shot. The conditions in Bosque Redondo were atrocious too, and more and more died.

"In the meantime, William Tecumseh Sherman had

taken over the command, and in 1868 he realized the resettlement was a complete failure. He was no lover of Native Americans despite his middle name, but he made a treaty with the Navajo and allowed them to return to their traditional homeland. They say the return procession was more than ten miles long. The irony is that in the attempt to wipe us out, the 'Long Walk' sealed our identity forever."

"Oh geez" was all Sam could say.

"Well, I don't hold it against you," Nina replied with the first flicker of a smile. "In fact, you're not such a bad gringo, and you did give me a ride all the way here from Albuquerque."

Sam grinned. "Good point."

They walked towards the red sandstone building, and when they got close, Nina explained, "Like I said before, the Navajo Nation Council Chambers is the center of government for the Navajo Nation." She pointed to the desert landscape all around. "The building was designed to harmonize with its natural surroundings."

Sam was impressed. "It's nice looking. It's not new, though, is it?"

"It dates from 1934 or 1935, I think. The octagon shape is meant to represent a hogan, which is the traditional building form of the Navajo."

"So is this where the Navajo government keeps all its important documents?"

"That's right."

Sam looked down at his watch. "It's 11:00. I'll look around and let you do your research. What time do you want to meet?"

"I'll be a couple of hours. How about if we meet at about 1:30? We can have lunch and then head back. If we leave here by 2:00, we should have enough time to stop in Gallup." She touched his arm and smiled. "I really appreciate your bringing me here."

Sam smiled back. "It's been a smooth ride, and I'm more than happy to learn about your heritage, even if it hurts. So, tell me again how you say Window Rock."

"It's called tségháhoodzání."

Entranced by the strange language, Sam asked, "Have you always spoken Navajo?"

"Actually, not at all," she replied. "I learned a few words when I was a little girl and a few more when I got older and was more interested in our history."

"It's really like nothing I've ever heard."

Nina nodded. "Yes, it's a unique language, but mostly forgotten. I wish I knew more."

Sam smiled and turned toward Pegasus. "See you in a couple of hours."

CHAPTER 14

Under a blue sky with a wall of white clouds against the horizon, Sam and Nina rode down the wide main street of Gallup. It was honky-tonk, with signs for Arrowhead Lodge on the right, Uptown Plaza on the left, and gas stations and fast food everywhere. Sam felt the tug of history when he spotted an old sign for Route 66—its path crisscrossed the interstate they had just left, but here the famous old road and the upstart highway came together. He had felt the same tug earlier in the day as well, most strongly at "Spring Under the Rock."

He turned his head and raised his voice. "I read that Gallup is sometimes called the 'Indian Capital of the World' because it's smack in the middle of Native American lands."

They were moving slowly enough that Nina could hear. "That's right," she shouted back. "There are Navajo, Zuni, Hopi, and other tribes here. About a third of the residents have Native American roots."

It was exactly 3:00 p.m. when the two rode down West Aztec Street, on the south side of Route 40, turned down Stagecoach Road, and pulled over in front of an adobe-colored house on Calle Piñon, a typical one-story cinder block bungalow attached to a single car garage. Low green bushes separated the cement driveway from the pebble-covered front yard and a cement walkway leading to a solid-looking front door.   A spindly tree sat by the entrance. Nina pulled off her helmet and dismounted as she waited for Sam to turn off the bike.

Henrietta Lapahe was a heavyset woman with long black hair parted in the middle and pulled back. She wore a long T-shirt over blue jeans. Peering out of the window, she saw Nina and hurried to the front door. "Nina!" she exclaimed. "I'm so glad to see you."

Nina hurried up the driveway and the two embraced. "Ma, this is Samuel. He's the boy I told you about." Turning to Sam, she said, "This is my mother."

Henrietta ushered them inside. She had them sit on the worn couch in the middle of the open living/dining room and brought them cold drinks.

"Did you ride all the way on that motorcycle?" she asked.

"Yes," Nina responded. "I needed to get some research done at the Tribal Council, and my car broke. A busted water pump. I was lucky to get a lift from Sam."

"That's good. What are you working on now?" she asked.

"My group wants more information on Peter Benallie. They think he had good ideas and really want to know how he got so much accomplished."

Henrietta shook her head. "He was a powerful man, but he got in too much trouble."

Eager to join the conversation, Sam stepped up. "Nina didn't tell me you were involved in politics."

"Hardly," she said. "Back then, women were not allowed to govern." Then she added laughingly, "But I won the Miss Navajo competition in 1974."

"Really?" Sam wondered. "What did that involve?"

"Well, it was quite different from what you might think," she said with a sparkle in her eye. "You had to be unmarried, over eighteen years old, and a high school graduate, and you had to be able to speak the Navajo language and show proficiency in Navajo skills."

"Like...?"

"Fry-bread making, rug weaving, demonstrating a Navajo cultural talent..."—she winked at Nina—"and sheep butchering."

"Sheep butchering?" Sam's jaw dropped.

"Yes, sheep butchering," Henrietta said, as she and Nina both laughed at his surprised expression.

Sam had no doubt he'd just been played and enjoyed her sense of humor.

"You're not kidding!" he said when they had stopped giggling.

"No, I am not kidding. I was just thinking of it because the competition is fifty-seven years old this week."

"Where did you go to school?"

"I went to the Navajo Methodist School in Farmington, New Mexico, and then graduated from Shiprock High School."

"So did you know Benallie personally? What kind of trouble did he get into?"

Henrietta looked over at Sam. He smiled in as non-threatening a way as he knew. After sizing him up, she looked over at Nina, who gave her a reassuring nod.

"Yes, I knew him. Things were difficult back then. Peter tried to make things better, but he ended up making some deals with the mining company and was heavily into tribal politics. Later on, the federal government sent him to jail." After a moment she added, "He was prosecuted for things he did and things he didn't do."

"He was the only four-term chairman of the Navajo Tribe," Nina told Sam. "He was first elected in 1970. In 1989, he was removed from office by the Navajo Tribal Council, pending the results of federal criminal investigations headed by the Bureau of Indian Affairs. He was sent to prison in 1990."

Nina glanced at her mother and then looked at Sam somewhat defiantly. "He was accused of fraud and corruption. That's what I was looking into today. I'm planning to see him later in the summer."

"Really?" Sam was surprised that she wanted to interview this possibly corrupt old man.

"Not everyone charged with a crime is a criminal," she said, staring at him. Startled, Sam realized that she was referring to his own legal problems. "Many considered him a hero," she continued. "He was raised among sheepherders and then taught to be a medicine man, but when World War II started, he entered the Marine Corps. He may have been a code talker during World War II, though perhaps he just wanted people to think that."

"I've heard about them."

"Our history is full of stories about our warriors and their bravery," Henrietta interjected. "Back during World War II, many of the Navajo men joined the army or the Marines. It was so long ago, back in the 1940s, way before computers and cell phones. During the war, the army had a big problem with the Japanese intercepting radio messages and learning about its plans. They tried different codes to disguise the messages, but the enemy was always able to crack them. Then they discovered that Navajos had a unique language. Nobody anywhere in the world knew our language, even in America. So they used some of our men to make messages using a code made from Navajo words."

Sam leaned forward. "And Navajo men were willing to step up despite all that the Navajo have endured from the U.S. government." He turned towards Nina. "Nina spoke some words to me in Navajo. They were different from anything I've ever heard."

Henrietta continued, "Many credit the code talkers for helping to win the war. It was that important."

"So Benallie may have been a code talker," Sam said reflectively.

"Even if he wasn't, he knew the ones that were. I think only a couple of them are still alive."

Henrietta moved to the kitchen area and soon returned with a plate of sopaipillas and honey.

Sam took an appreciative bite and pointed to a weaving hanging on the living room wall. "Did you make that?" he asked her.

She nodded. "Many years ago."

"Nina was telling me how important weaving is for the Navajo."

"Yes, we have legends of holy people like Spider Woman. She was the first in the universe to weave, and she taught the Diné, the Navajo, to create beauty in their own lives and spread the 'Beauty Way' teaching of balance in mind, body, and spirit. Perhaps you would like me to tell you the legend."

Nina looked at her mother. "Ma, please, don't bore Sam with your old stories."

Henrietta hesitated, and Sam quickly added, "No, please, I'd really like to hear you tell the story of the Spider Woman." He looked over at Nina. "Really."

Nina sat back on the couch and grudgingly nodded her approval.

Henrietta sat up a little straighter. "The story of Spider Woman is part of the rich and complex Navajo creation story. It actually varies a little from place to place and even from person to person because our tradition is an oral tradition. We believe that the Black World, the Blue World, and the Yellow World existed before the White or Glittering World of earth and human beings where we live now.

"Spider Woman was created by the spirit holy ones in an earlier world. They told her that she had the ability to weave the map of the universe and the patterns of the spirit beings, but she didn't know what they meant. Then one day, as she was gathering food for herself and Spider Man, she came upon a small tree and reached out her right hand to touch one of its branches. When she pulled her hand back, a filament stretched from the branch to the middle of her palm. She could not shake it loose, so she wrapped it around the branch—so many times that she thought the branch would break. But still the thread came from her palm.

"She decided to move it to a new branch. She did this again and again and soon saw that she had created a pattern. For the rest of the day she perfected her new skill, breaking the thread from time to time with her left hand. Then she returned home to show Spider Man what she had learned.

"The spirit holy people then told Spider Man to construct a weaving loom and make weaving tools, each one associated with a special song and prayer. They gave Spider Woman an empowering weaving song as well. To this day, the two upright juniper beams on each side of the loom represent the pillars that hold up the sky and protect mother earth." Henrietta began to outline a loom with her gestures. "The beam at the bottom represents the earth, and the one across the top represents the sky, the universe, and the sunbeams and rainbows that also keep the earth safe. The weaving fork is used to push the weft down and bring the textile to life. The sound, when this happens, we call the heartbeat of the weaving.

"Spider Woman taught humans to weave, and Spider Man told the people, 'When a baby girl is born to your tribe, find a spider web and rub it on her hand and arm. When she grows up she will weave, and her fingers and arms will not tire.' "

Henrietta continued in a less chant-like voice.

"Today, weavings are bought and sold, but you must remember that weaving is a sacred ceremony expressing the Navajo's harmony with nature and the universe. It is the same harmony expressed in the best known of our chants. Perhaps Nina has told it to you:

> *In beauty may I walk*
> *All day long may I walk*
> *Through the returning seasons may I walk."*

Nina chimed in, "My favorite lines are:

On the trail marked with pollen may I walk
With grasshoppers about my feet may I walk
With dew about my feet may I walk."

The two women began to recite together, smiling
warmly at one another:

"With beauty may I walk
With beauty before me may I walk
With beauty behind me may I walk
With beauty above me may I walk
With beauty all around me may I walk."

Sam was moved, unwilling to disturb the silence that
followed. It was Henrietta who finally broke the spell. "I
have a weaving fork right here." She opened a small
drawer in the table next to the couch and pulled out a
piece of dark wood resembling a salad bowl fork, handing
it to Sam. It was about eight inches long, with many long,
thin fingers extending from the flat handle. He felt the
smooth wood.

"It's beautiful," he said as he turned it over in his
hands. Looking up, he added, "I feel honored to have
heard the Spider Woman story from you."

Nina stood up from the couch. "As you can imagine,
I've heard that legend many times. My mother really
wanted me to take up weaving and the other arts,
especially after having three sons."

"Nina adored her brothers, though, and wanted to
do everything they did—hiking, biking, exploring, playing
sports—but she finally came around."

"I was lucky that you persisted," she said to her

mother. "It taught me calmness and concentration. I love the rhythm of it, and the colors and patterns. I'll get back to it one of these days, but right now I don't seem to have the patience. I see things happening all around me that I have to do something about."

Sam was thinking about Henrietta's husband as he handed back the fork. "I must say, I've come to admire Nina's steadfast focus on protecting the environment. And you're so close to Church Rock here."

Henrietta frowned when he mentioned Church Rock. "That's right," she said. "And I think Benallie's troubles may have involved some big land purchase up there."

Nina turned the talk away from her environmental preoccupations. "Ma, why don't you and I go sit under the umbrella out back? Sam, my mom and I have to catch up on a few things. I'll get you another drink, and you can look at some of these books on weavings." She removed three large, illustrated volumes from a nearby bookshelf and put them on the coffee table.

"Take your time."

Twenty minutes later, mother and daughter returned. Nina gathered up her helmet, her jacket, and Sam. Henrietta walked with them to the curb.

"My neighbors will be asking me about my dashing visitor on a motorcycle," she chuckled. "Have a safe trip." She shook Sam's hand and gave Nina a hug. Sam put the bike in gear. They waved at Henrietta, and as they pick up speed and settled in for the long ride back, Nina leaned over Sam's shoulder and shouted, "My mother and I still think of Peter Benallie as a great leader."

CHAPTER 15

11:50. Sam unwrapped the sandwich he had brought from home and ate it quickly, looking out the window at the distant mountains. He would be booted from the office as soon as Fisher hired one of the steady flow of job candidates he'd been interviewing, probably to the little storeroom next to Stephen's office. He could live with that; he spent a lot of his time at the law library anyway. What really bugged him was the wasp's nest of problems he had stumbled on in Santa Fe, when he had expected to put in his forty hours, then fill his leisure time soaking up local color, culture, and cuisine and throwing back an occasional *cerveza*—using his genuine ID. "Right," he muttered sarcastically to himself. The trip to Window Rock and Gallup had stretched his boundaries at least.

He felt a stabbing pain every time he thought of his felony charge. The Blair murder case was another unknown, a labyrinth of dead ends. The possible lifting of the uranium mining ban added another layer of discomfort and uncertainty. To compound Sam's perplexity, the common thread in all his aggravations was Mike Stone. He hadn't seen his attorney since his appearance in General District Court, and he was due in Mike's office in twenty minutes.

Stone, wearing blue jeans, a T-shirt, and Nikes and sucking a Tootsie pop, was leaning back in his swivel chair with his feet up on the large pine desk when Sam showed up. The shades were half drawn.

"Not much to report, Sam. Pull up a chair," he said, swinging his feet off the desk.

"So what do we do next? Did you get a chance to talk to the prosecutor?"

"He said he was busy, and I figured I wouldn't push him right yet. Don't worry though. Your court date isn't for another six weeks."

Sam felt a familiar stab of panic. Was this guy really the right attorney to get him out of his predicament?

"So have you looked into a way to dismiss the charge?"

"I'm still digging for the facts. That's where most cases are won or lost. I don't know much about the arresting officer, so that's where I'm looking right now."

"Looking for what? I mean, he seemed like a pretty decent guy to me."

"Yeah, there are two kinds of police officers, the good guys and the bad guys. Seems to me that the nice guys get the most confessions—by making the accused person feel comfortable and trusting."

"Oh, God. I was so dumb. I thought he was going to give me a break. He seemed like a nice enough guy. Said all the college kids had fake IDs and it was no big deal, and that I may as well tell him the truth." Sam had played this scene over in head many times. "But what else could I do?"

"Well, for one, you could have said nothing. That's what the police expect. They have just two decisions to make. The first is whether to charge you and, if they do, the second is how to convict you." After a moment of silence, Stone spoke more reassuringly. "And that's why I'm looking at the facts. I've read his police report, but there's something I don't like about it."

"Really?" What had the lawyer seen that he had not?

"It's hard to put into words. It's just a feeling. I guess I'll have to go interview the officer, as well as the rescue squad team."

That sounded like progress. Sam decided not to push any further. His visit to Gallup and Window Rock had made him want to find out more about Stone's early career, and maybe that would segue into talk about Tua.

"Can I change the subject? I'm doing some research and have come across Peter Benallie. Seems he was prosecuted, convicted, and then pardoned for corruption and fraud."

Mike Stone sat up. "Peter Benallie?"

"Yeah, the old Navajo chairman. Do you know anything about him?"

"You could say that," Stone replied.

"I'm actually getting interested in the whole Navajo Nation over the last fifty years. It seems like they were totally exploited. I thought I would look at the old case against Benallie. Seems like an example of the conflicting myths about the Indian, you know, the 'noble savage' and tribal leader versus becoming corrupt and greedy just like the white exploiters."

Stone didn't answer right away, as if deciding how much to reveal to the young man sitting across from him.

"I had quite a bit of involvement with the Navajo Nation over the years. Especially when I was a prosecutor."

"Were you involved in his case?"

"I was. I was one of the prosecutors," Stone said.

Sam looked expectantly at the lawyer. Stone sounded reluctant when he spoke again.

"My involvement with former chairman Benallie and the Navajos is a long and complicated story. I agree that he was a character who encompassed many of the myths that we European descendants have created in our minds since the seventeenth century. It's probably worth attempting to understand if you're interested in Navajo country."

"I was talking to someone that said he was a hero in World War II. Do you think that's true?"

"Who knows? To me, Benallie was just another white collar criminal; he just happened to grow up on the Navajo reservation. As far as I'm concerned, he turned his back on the values and ways of his tradition. He went for the good old American dream of political power and mapped out a quest to become as wealthy as possible."

How different from Nina's account, thought Sam. But he could not wish away Stone's experience and apparent knowledge of the facts. "So I guess you don't go for the concept of Benallie as the noble warrior?"

"Personally, I would seriously question Benallie as any sort of model."

"So you prosecuted cases out near Gallup?"

"That's right. That's where I began. Prosecuting criminal cases and later corruption cases."

"So in the end, which do you consider yourself, a prosecutor or a defense lawyer?"

Stone leaned back. More client uneasiness to deal

with. "You need to understand something about lawyers, Sam. We're here to advocate for our clients. When you're a prosecutor, the client is the state of New Mexico, and you're representing the citizens against people accused of breaking the law. When you're a defense attorney, the client is the defendant. What's important—in either case—is understanding the system, knowing the facts, and applying the law."

"Well, I guess it's to my advantage that you've been both. I'll just sit tight and wait for you to tell me what to do. "

"Good thinking," Stone said and then added with a slight grin, "Another thing you should know about me. I hate to lose. Period."

Sam felt an immediate sense of relief and half smiled.

"I'm glad you said that. To be honest, thinking about this case is sort of driving me crazy. I mean, if I end up with a conviction, especially a felony conviction, I'll never get a decent job, I won't be able to vote, I won't be able to own a gun, nothing. I mean, I'll be a felon for the rest of my life."

"Calm down, son. Let me take care of it."

Sam stood up, and they shook hands. "Well, thanks. When should I come by again?" he asked.

"I'll give you a call."

Just as Sam was walking through the door, he heard Stone's voice. "Wait."

The lawyer had picked up the phone, but he hung it up. "Look," he said quietly, "if you want to get your mind off your troubles and look into old cases, maybe you should dig into the Blair homicide case."

Bingo! An image of Tua's gleaming smile and gentle laugh flashed across his mind, even as he took in Stone's strange, almost sad, expression.

"You should take a close look at the Blair case. Especially the trial," Stone repeated more emphatically. "Yes, look at that case if you want to learn something about justice."

"What is so special about it?"

Stone appeared torn on how much to say. "I'm not at liberty to talk about the case in any detail. All I'm saying is that you'll learn a lot by looking into it."

"I understand. But what's the best way to learn about the case? Can you tell me that?"

Stone looked up at the ceiling fan, which was turning slowly.

"You should talk to Rio Polo."

"Who is he? And how do I get in touch with him?"

Stone pulled out a piece of scrap paper, looked in his Rolodex, and scribbled a name and number. "Rio Polo was an investigator. He retired from the police department and works for the Racing Commission now. He lives in Albuquerque. I put down the number of the Commission office. He's easy to recognize. He's Hispanic, fairly short, and bald."

Sam took the piece of paper and put it into his shirt pocket. "And you told me you represented one of the defendants, right?"

Stone looked directly into Sam's eyes for a lingering moment. "Yes, Trent Hurley," he said and then quickly looked down at his desk and picked up the phone again. The conversation was over.

CHAPTER 16

That Saturday, as the professor's motorcycle brought him to the outskirts of Albuquerque yet again for his meeting with Rio, Sam was thinking about his strange conversation with Stone. Stone had represented Hurley, so he couldn't talk about the case. "But what does he want me to find, and what was all that talk about 'justice?'"

Sam had contacted Rio at the Racing Commission, and they had agreed to meet for lunch at a little burrito place called El Puerto. Sam found it with no trouble. A couple of cherry bombs left over from someone's Fourth of July celebration went off nearby as he walked to the door. He noticed a light blue Chevrolet parking about twenty yards up the street. "This must be him," Sam said to himself, recalling Stone's description.

The man stepped out of the car and placed a beige-colored cowboy hat on his suntanned head as he walked down the sidewalk. He spotted Sam and put out his hand. "Hello, you must be Sam," Rio said confidently. "Just call me Rio. Let's get something to eat. I'm hungry."

Inside, they found an empty booth in the back and ordered two lunch specials.

"So, I double checked, and Stone tells me he told you to contact me about the Blair case," Rio said. "Tell me again how you know Mike Stone."

Sam noticed how dark and leathery his skin was.

"Part Hispanic, part sun," Sam thought to himself. He was clean-shaven, and his friendly eyes put Sam at ease. "I'm surprised that Mr. Stone didn't tell you he's representing me on a little case. I'm in school back East. I'm just here for the summer doing legal research for a lawyer up in Santa Fe. I really don't know Mr. Stone all that well, but he suggested that I look into the old murder case. And this will amaze you, but he wasn't the first person to ask me that. So did Tua Dumay, Professor Blair's daughter. I got to know her in Providence, Rhode Island, where I go to school. When she found out I was coming out here, she gave me her father's motorcycle to ride out, as well as a cryptic note asking me to try and fix some mistakes she'd made. I can't believe she wasn't talking about the murder case. Tua referred me to Mr. Stone, but I haven't had a chance to tell him about the note yet. And for the record, I've already talked with Tom Smith, the reporter, and the decision in the Blair case doesn't sit well with him either."

"A good man, Smith. And Tua Dumay...after all these years."

"Unfortunately, she died late this spring, so I couldn't ask her what she meant."

"I'm sorry to hear that. She had more than her share of adversity in life."

"I'm beginning to understand that."

"Mike didn't mention that he represented you, but, of course, he usually doesn't disclose who his clients are. I'm glad you told me that." Rio took sip from his glass. "I presume from the fact that you're not in jail that it's nothing too serious."

"Right," Sam said in as confident voice as he could muster.

"Sounds good. I sometimes think it would have been nice to be a lawyer. You know I was a cop here and then in Santa Fe for fifteen years, and then went to work for the Attorney General and later the Racing Commission. I'm semi-retired, and now I only get called in on special projects."

Sam nodded. This man knew his way around. "So how do you know Mr. Stone?"

"I met Stone about thirty years ago when I worked as an investigator for the AG. We have a good relationship, and he calls me in every now and again if he needs a private investigator."

"Thirty years is a long time. I gather you were on the Blair murder case back then."

Rio took a large bite of his burrito and chewed on it for a moment. "Yes. I was the lead investigator. Normally the local police and prosecutor handle a case like that, but it was high profile. The Attorney General wanted it, and the local district attorney was happy to unload it because of some complications involving witnesses and evidence." He paused to see if Sam was following him before he continued.

"Stone had been handling big, white-collar fraud cases at the time. He was good, of course, probably the best there is. Always politics involved, though. The Attorney General was getting a lot of good anti-crime publicity, but Stone ran afoul of the AG on one case and got sacked. To everybody's surprise, he ended up at the defense table in the Blair case."

Sam needed Rio to know he had done his homework. "Trent Hurley, right? I found out he got a plea bargain and testified against the other kid, who got convicted and went to prison. Funny thing is that I keep thinking there's more to it, the way people are acting."

"Basically it looked like a random break and enter. Two kids, probably on drugs, panicked and shot the professor when he confronted them."

"So, do *you* think that's all it was?" Sam asked cautiously.

Rio was silent and looked over Sam's head.

"I really don't know," he finally answered. "I always thought that the murder was somehow related to Dr. Blair's work. So did Mike. But it was just a hunch. We couldn't prove anything. But I'll tell you something—that Stone was a bulldog and would have dug into everything if his client hadn't confessed. I know Mike always felt badly for Dr. Blair's family. His wife died shortly afterwards."

"Well, I'm really interested to learn more. I was wondering about Josh Metcalf, the one that got convicted. I understand he's in prison just outside of Santa Fe. Do you think it would it be possible for me to go talk to him?" The idea frightened Sam, but it was the only practical step he could think of.

"No reason why not. The place still gives me the creeps, though. The riot in the max security section of the prison in 1980 was one of the most violent prison riots in American history. Thirty-three inmates died, and more than 200 were wounded. It was a miracle that none of the twelve officers taken hostage were killed, although a number were beaten and raped."

Sam's fear of incarceration raised its ugly head. "That sounds horrible," he said. "What caused the riot?"

"Major overcrowding, cuts in educational and recreational programs, inconsistent policies, poor communication—you name it. It lasted 36 hours. The inmates became animals, even broke into the separate unit where the snitches were held and killed them with hatchets and blowtorches. In the end, they surrendered. Some got prosecuted, but not many—it was too hard to sort out who exactly did what. It was a mess. I was involved in the investigation. No one involved ever really got over it."

Polo saw that the color had left Sam's face. "Some good actually came from the riot," he added. "The government and the Correction Department instituted systematic reforms that led to the modern correctional system in New Mexico. But to get back to your question, sure, go see Metcalf. I'll get you an expedited Special Visit permission as a legal researcher, which after all you are, and we'll have to hope that Metcalf signs it. In the meantime, I'll see what I can dig up."

"Great," Sam replied. "I'm especially interested in the gun that was used, the one the police never found."

"You've done your homework, I see. We looked high and low for that gun, but it never turned up. It's always hard to get a conviction if you don't have the murder weapon. In fact, that's why Stone's client, Trent, was so important. The trial really came down to his testimony against Metcalf."

"I keep hearing about Trent's confession. How did it

happen? I mean, did he just come in to the police station and start talking?"

"No, not really," Polo explained. "As part of our investigation we talked to everyone who might know the professor or his house or family. Routine stuff. Anyway, we discovered that Trent and Josh were friends with the daughter's kid, Felix, who had some mental problems or something. The two of them had been to the professor's house several times. That's how we found out about them. We brought both kids in to talk to them. The one, Josh, asked for a lawyer and wouldn't talk to us. Seems he'd had a couple of previous run-ins with the law for minor stuff—truancy, shoplifting, that sort of thing—and his instinct was to hunker down."

"And Trent did talk to you?"

"That's right, even though he had more petty stuff on his record than Josh."

"Did you do the interrogation?" Sam asked.

"No. Not me. It was Detective Phillips. He talked to him for hours, and finally Trent told him what had happened."

"Just like that?"

"No, it doesn't really happen that way. What usually happens is that the detective plays the facts of the case against the suspect, to show that he, the detective, knows what he's talking about. In this case, Phillips kept laying out what he believed the facts were to see if he could get Trent to agree to talk."

"And that worked?"

"Yes. As I recall, Trent was a bright kid, the sharper of the two. It turned out that Phillips had it pretty much right, that the two went over to the professor's house to steal some stuff and the professor woke up and confronted Josh."

"Then what happened?"

"Josh panicked, probably, and in any event he shot and killed the professor. Trent was acting as lookout. He heard the shots, and Josh came running out. They were both freaked out. Trent said he saw Josh with a small handgun, but he didn't see what it was. They both took off running and he didn't see what happened to it."

"So tell me again why the gun was so important if you had Trent's testimony."

"It's not necessary to have the physical evidence to get a conviction, but evidence helps to corroborate the facts of the case, to back up the confession. Remember, Josh refused to give a statement. It's a statement that convicts 90% of defendants—that's why police are trained to get confessions. And then at trial, the defense lawyer attacks the testimony of the other witnesses, especially if the confession came from one of them. In this case, the lawyer attacked Trent's testimony, inferring that he said what he did to get a sentence reduction."

"Well, that's true in a way, isn't it?

"Yes, of course. But they're also supposed to be telling the truth. It is up to the lawyers to make sure witnesses at trial can explain why they're testifying, and Mike Stone is nothing if not a good lawyer. Usually good witnesses admit that they hope to get a reduced sentence but that they have to testify truthfully for that to happen. It sort of ends up adding to their credibility. Metcalf's lawyer went after Trent, but Trent kept repeating that he would benefit only if he told the truth."

"Hmmm. I see how that could be effective."

"Like I said, everything was more up in the air in this case because there was no gun to link the murder to Josh Metcalf. When he testified, he said he had nothing to do with any burglary or murder. He even cried on the stand. But he had no good alibi. He testified that he'd been out with Trent that night and went home late, after his parents were asleep. Trent was a really good witness, and his testimony was totally consistent with what Detective Phillips put together with his investigation. That was critical. The jury didn't believe Metcalf and convicted him. He got a life sentence, and public opinion was satisfied."

"And Trent got seven years." Sam thought ruefully about his own case and the statement he had given the police officer.

"Yeah. He ended up pleading guilty to the burglary and being an accessory to the shooting. And with good time, he only had to serve 85% of that, about six years."

"Even that sounds like a lot."

"It's a hell of a lot better than life in prison," Polo replied. "He was sent out of state to do his time in a minimum security facility. Metcalf is still doing time in a maximum."

There was silence as the two finished their lunch. Somewhat startled that he was actually engaged in Tua's quest, Sam picked up the check. When they were outside, Sam saw Rio start at the sight of something off to the right.

"That the motorcycle, isn't it?"

Sam nodded. "Yeah, the one Tua gave me."

"You weren't just kidding, were you? Neither was she, apparently. My God, what a small world! Like everyone around town, I knew the professor," he added, turning to Sam. "He was a sight—an old guy on an old bike. He did enjoy it, though. He used to show up at town hall meetings on that damned motorcycle." He smiled. "Mind if I take a look?"

"No problem."

When they got to the bike, Rio ran his hand on the tank and along the seat. "Yeah, this is the one. It's still in good shape. All the more motivation for me to dust off the files on the case. Where can I get in touch with you?"

"You'd better use my private email address or call me on my cell. Here's my home address as well." Sam scribbled the bits of contact information on the back of a Fisher business card. Then he put on his helmet and started the engine. When it settled into a quiet purr, he reached over and shook Rio's hand.

"I'm really grateful for your help. It's been great talking to you."

"You should get your visit approval in about ten days. Tell Stone to give me a call."

CHAPTER 17

Sam's worst nightmare as a young, white male was serving hard time in a state prison. The idea of the strong preying on the weak on the inside was a staple of TV and movie plots, but there was probably a good amount of truth in it, he thought to himself as he pulled into the parking lot of the New Mexico State Penitentiary after the ten-mile ride from Santa Fe.

His stomach knotted up as he walked into the windowless main building, made of cinderblocks and cement. Tall walls connected it to the prison complex, and all the doors were made of reinforced steel. A double row of sharp, glinting razor wire spiraled along the top of every outside wall and fence.

Once inside, Sam noted the video monitors in the two upper corners of the large open room and saw the shadow of a guard sitting in a small room behind darkened bulletproof glass. A large sign warned that metal objects, contraband, and weapons of any sort were strictly prohibited under penalty of law anywhere in the facility. It also notified visitors that they would undergo electronic and body searches before entry and at any time afterward as well.

Sam approached the guard behind the glass, who pointed to a sign above that instructed him to hand over his identification. Then he pointed to a bank of lockers against the wall. Sam went over and placed his wallet and belt in a small metal locker. As he turned, several guards entered the facility to begin their shifts, and Sam remembered Stone's warning that it was best to refer to them as "correctional officers" rather than "guards," which they considered degrading.

"How could anyone be willing to work in a prison?" Sam asked himself. "How is it possible to voluntarily spend one's working life confined in a locked facility with hardened criminals?" He saw that each of the guards, "correctional officers," Sam corrected himself, had to go through the metal detector as well. It dawned on him that the prison trusted no one, not even its own employees, not to smuggle in contraband. A streak of apprehension traveled up the back of his neck as he went through the metal detector and was patted down by a large officer in a gray uniform while a drug-sniffing dog nosed about his legs.

Sam had received approval for a "non-contact" visit, so he would be talking to Metcalf through bulletproof glass via telephone. Good thing he was a "special visitor"—no one with a felony charge, let alone a conviction, could get regular visiting privileges. The guard in the booth reviewed the letter officially approving the visit and waved him to the dark green metal door next to the booth. Sam stood in front it, and a second later, with a buzzing sound, it slowly slid open, exposing an outdoor corridor of metal fencing which led to another green door twenty-five feet away.

Sam walked in bright sunlight to the solid metal door. As if by magic, it slowly rumbled opened, and he stepped into a small florescent-lit room with another booth and another guard, who waved Sam to yet another door. It too slid slowly open, exposing a larger reception area. To his left, Sam saw a row of booths with small metal partitions between them. In one, a heavy Spanish-speaking woman was talking on the phone to an inmate, a small child in her lap pulling at the phone. An older man sat in the next one; next to him stood a younger woman in blue jeans clutching the phone with one hand, with her other pressed, mirror-like, against her husband's or boyfriend's on the other side of the thick glass.

The next booth was empty. Sam made his way there and sat down on the metal stool bolted to the cement floor. Everything was either cement or plastic and was painted an almost colorless light green. On a small shelf in front of him, a phone handset dangled from the wall by a short metal cord. He thought about the dozens—hundreds—of people who had gripped that phone, desperately talking to a boyfriend or family member locked up like an animal on the other side. He felt almost nauseated as he picked up the smooth, black, plastic receiver and turned it over in his hand. Just then a muffled ringing sound was succeeded by a buzz and the sound of the metal door moving on the other side of the glass. Sam looked up, and a small, thin man in an orange prison jumpsuit entered and sat down opposite him, behind the glass.

Josh Metcalf sat motionless and stared at Sam, who put the phone to his ear and smiled pathetically back. Sam had never seen a convicted killer before. Metcalf was very pale and had thin brown hair, black beady eyes, and a nose that seemed too large for his face. He wore dirty

143

long underwear underneath his prison garb, to fight off the cold of the air conditioning. Although he was probably in his early forties, he looked much older. A long sentence in this place would make anyone look aged.

Finally, Metcalf picked up the phone. "Who are you and what do you want?" he demanded with a glare.

"I'm, I'm Sam Shelton," Sam stuttered. He took a quick breath and spoke quickly, fearing Metcalf would hang up the phone and call the guard. "I'm a college student working for a Santa Fe lawyer this summer, and I'm doing some research on your case."

Metcalf rolled his eyes but did not hang up. "Research? What kind of research?"

"On the Blair investigation and your trial. I'm trying to see what happened and if some mistakes were made."

Metcalf continued to stare. Finally, in an angry tone, he spoke again. "Of course mistakes were made, plenty of them. Just look at me. I'm sitting here for something I didn't do. Yeah, there were plenty of mistakes made, but it's too late now."

Sam leaned forward. "But maybe not. Maybe not," he repeated. "Not if I can find some new evidence."

"I've heard that before," Metcalf said. "My court-appointed lawyer said I would win the case, and he was wrong. Then the court-appointed lawyer doing my appeal said I would win my appeal, and he was wrong. Then the lawyer on my writ was wrong, and here I am." Metcalf shook his head in disgust.

"What's that? The 'writ,' " Sam asked.

Metcalf let out a sigh. "My petition for writ of habeas corpus. You know, the petition where you tell the court that you have a constitutional right to a decent lawyer and that you are in prison because of crummy representation. I mean, my lawyer really screwed me over, but the court didn't care. They said he may have made mistakes, but it didn't make any difference. The system is there to protect the lawyers, that's what I mean."

"Yeah, but if there's some newly discovered evidence, you can get the case reopened."

Wondering who or what the visitor might know, Metcalf answered cautiously, "I've read the law books. I mean, I've been here for a long time. There is the 21-day rule. The court won't consider newly discovered evidence that is discovered after 21 days past the final sentencing order. Period." He paused. "And it's been a hell of a lot longer than 21 days since the court sentenced me to life in prison!"

Sam nodded to show Metcalf that he understood and was sympathetic. "But the law changed recently, and there's an exception to that rule."

Having not talked to a lawyer for several years, Metcalf looked at Sam. "Yeah?"

Sam remembered what Stone had told him about criminal appeals and continued, "Yes. The courts will sometimes reconsider scientific evidence that wasn't available at the time of the trial if it proves the defendant is innocent."

"You mean DNA evidence?" Metcalf asked. "Yeah, I've read that too. But no one has mentioned finding DNA evidence. I mean, they didn't even have the gun, and the jury still convicted me." He paused before adding, "Goddamn lawyer."

"I heard about the trial. I guess it was that other guy, Trent Hurley, that testified against you."

Metcalf leaped to his feet. "Don't even mention that name around me!" he shouted into the phone as he took the earpiece away from his head.

Sam stood up too and spoke as quickly as he could into the phone. "I'm sorry. I'm sorry. I won't mention him again. I just want to help." Sam slowly sat down, keeping the phone to his ear.

Metcalf sat back down and brought the phone up to his head again. "OK, look, I get pissed. I mean that son of a bitch testified against me knowing he was lying. It was his testimony that convicted me. I mean, why would he do that?" Metcalf shook his head and continued, "I know why he did it. It was to protect his own hide, that's why. He said I did it so that he would get the deal. Man, if I ever get out, I'll teach him a lesson for setting me up."

Before this moment Sam could only imagine the rage of an innocent person wrongfully convicted, but as he looked at the broken man on the other side of the glass, he could feel it.

He spoke with new energy. "Look, Mr. Metcalf, I believe you. All I'm saying is that I'm looking over everything in your case. The gun, for example. If by some miracle I can find it, there could be DNA that could help prove that you're innocent. They can pick up DNA from just about anything now. I mean, like a drop of sweat or even a little spit." Then, suddenly contemplating the real possibility that this man was not so innocent, Sam sat back. A bit more guardedly, he added, "I figure it's at least worth a shot."

Metcalf listened intensely and then spoke slowly, cautiously. "I can tell you, like I've told everyone else, I did not do that crime. I'm not saying I was a perfectly nice guy, never have been. And in fact I had been in the professor's house before that night. I mean, I knew his grandson." He began to speak more quickly and louder. "But like I told my lawyer and like I told that damn jury, I wasn't in that house that night. I didn't break into the house, I didn't rob anyone, and for sure, I did not shoot anyone!" He paused again and took a deep breath. "Look, if I had any idea where the gun was or even what kind of a gun it was, I would have told my lawyer. I told him that, but he just didn't seem to care. He probably thought I did it, or maybe Trent Hurley convinced him, too."

"The expert at the trial said it was a target pistol or maybe a derringer. Did you ever see anything like that?"

Metcalf appeared to be getting impatient. "Look, I've been through all this before. Why don't they ask Trent Hurley? All I can say is, I didn't take anything, and I didn't shoot the professor."

"So you have no idea what happened that night."

Metcalf first looked mad and then just sighed. "Look, Sam or whoever you are, I've told everyone that I'm innocent, and no one has ever believed me. If you can get me out of here, that would be great, but I'm not holding my breath. It's too painful to even imagine freedom."

Sam saw a tear form in the older man's eye. Touched by this involuntary sign of emotion, he continued, "Mr. Metcalf, all I can say is, there is, and always has been,

147

something wrong with this case. If it's OK with you, I'm going to go through all the trial transcripts again and see if I can figure out if the police overlooked something. About the gun, for instance."

Metcalf looked suspiciously at Sam. "How are you going to do that? The police looked all over for that gun and couldn't find it. Do you know something that you're not telling me?"

In the back of his mind, Sam was becoming convinced that his strange connection with Tua, and now her son and her father, was important and related somehow to solving the whole Blair case. He was not sure what the next step would be, but he wanted to be able to talk to Metcalf again if he needed to. On the other hand, he didn't want to give too much away. "All I can say is that I'll take a look at everything I can."

Metcalf asked, "So who's the lawyer you are working with?"

Sam hesitated for a moment and, thinking about the inmate's reaction to Trent Hurley's name, elected not to mention Stone. "Walter Fisher. He's a lawyer in town."

"Fisher? That name rings a bell. I think maybe Hurley's father or mother did some work for him, or something like that. It's been a long time, so I'm not sure. Anyway, maybe he can help, who knows."

With that, Metcalf stood up and rang the buzzer to notify the guard that the visit was over. Sam sensed that it was important for him not to raise Metcalf's hopes, and so he stayed noncommittal.

"Thanks for meeting with me, Mr. Metcalf. I'll let you know what I find out."

Sam put the plastic phone back into the receptacle and watched as the metal door opened and the guard began to escort Metcalf out. Just then Metcalf turned and shouted, "Call me Josh."

Sam nodded and felt himself smile. The metal door shut with a bang, and Sam turned and began slowly retracing his steps. In blinding sunlight, with the cold cement and steel of the prison behind him, he took a deep breath and felt the warm air rush into his lungs. "Oh my God," he said as he exhaled. "It's so good to breath fresh air. It's so good to be free!"

CHAPTER 18

Sam felt a gray cloud hanging over him; he was having trouble shaking the images of the gray walls topped with spiked wire, the coldness of the steel and concrete, and the look in Metcalf's eyes. Sam figured Metcalf had developed a tough outer shell for self-preservation, but Sam had seen another side of the man, his trapped-animal look. It also depressed him to think about himself in that situation.

Seeing Nina would get him out of his funk, and she could tell him more about yesterday's big rally in the Plaza, the one on the Church Rock anniversary. He could visualize the bright clothing she wore, her soft lips and tanned skin, and the sparkle in her eyes. Sam dialed her number and felt a familiar buzz when he heard her voice.

"Hey Nina, it's Sam. Good work yesterday. I saw the headlines. Why don't we celebrate? I was thinking of riding out to Chimayo for dinner."

"Sounds great," she responded in a cheerful voice. "I could use a change of scene. I can be ready by seven."

"See you then." Buoyed by the prospect of a ride and dinner with Nina, he picked up the stack of papers Schiff had asked him to take to the courthouse and left the office.

Mike Stone was leaving the courthouse just as Sam arrived.

"Mr. Stone! What a great coincidence. Do you have

a minute? I talked to Josh Metcalf last week," Sam said to him. Stone had been at the courtroom on a misdemeanor case and at first seemed in a hurry, but at the mention of Metcalf's name he stopped. "Let's grab a cup of coffee," he said, and signaled to the stairway leading to a little sandwich shop in the basement.

Seated on a plastic chair at one of the little tables, Sam poured milk and sugar into his styrofoam cup. "I've never been in a prison. I found it was really depressing, especially after hearing about the riot back in the '80s."

Stone nodded. "That shook up even the most experienced prosecutors. So what did Metcalf say to you?"

"He kept saying he was innocent and that Trent Hurley testified against him to save his own skin. I don't know too much about this kind of stuff, but I believed him."

"Go on."

"Well, it got me thinking about Trent Hurley. I mean, I know that you represented him, so I figure you can't really tell me anything about what he did or what he said, right?"

"That's right. A lawyer is bound not to disclose discussions he had with a client, past or present. I probably shouldn't even confirm that I represented him, though I'm not disclosing anything, really, since it's a matter of public record."

Sam hardly knew how to word what he wanted to say without making Stone look bad. "It's my understanding that a lawyer is not allowed to let his client lie on the stand."

"If he knows it."

"What?"

"A lawyer is not allowed to let his client commit perjury. That basically means lying on the witness stand. He's not allowed to let his client lie if he knows the client is lying."

"Well, how would you know for sure if he's lying or not?"

"Basically, you can't," the lawyer explained, "unless the client tells you one thing during an interview or meeting and then testifies to something different at trial."

"Well, doesn't that happen all the time?"

"The rule is that if your client tells you he did the crime before trial and then at trial he takes the stand and testifies he didn't do it, the lawyer can't allow that. But usually a client says from the get-go that he didn't do the crime, that is, if he hasn't confessed it to the police already, in which case the lawyer's job is to reach a decent plea bargain."

"But what happens if the client says he did it? What do you do then?"

"I'll tell you this. As a defense lawyer, when I interview my clients I don't ask them if they did it or not. I ask them what they believe the police said happened or what they believe the evidence will show. I really like to gather all the facts first. Remember, once the client tells you something, you're stuck with it."

"Wow." Sam thought about that. "But how do you defend a murderer or a big drug dealer if you know they're guilty?"

Amazingly, Stone's patience was not wearing thin.

"Look, not every one is guilty. And nine times out of ten, if the person did the crime, they either confess or the evidence is overwhelming. Mostly it's a matter of reaching a plea bargain. The prosecutor tends to stack a bunch of charges on a defendant, and the defense lawyer works to bring it down to one or two charges, where the case should have been in the first place. It all works out. In the meantime, people plead not guilty, and some are innocent and some are guilty. That's what trials are all about."

Sam thought of his own situation. "But how about me? I mean I'm guilty, technically. How are you going to defend me?"

"Well, a couple of things. First, the law says you are innocent until proven guilty beyond a reasonable doubt."

Sam smirked. "Yeah, well that's not how I feel."

"Exactly," Stone agreed. "I tell my new clients it's really just the opposite. Once you're charged, everyone presumes you're guilty. It's like being in a big hole and having to dig yourself out."

"My sentiments exactly."

"But that's the good thing about lawyers, that outweighs all the lawyer jokes." Stone said with a chuckle. "They're there to fight for you, the client, and as I told you before, I like to win my cases."

"But, how are you going to do it? You just said I can't get up on the stand and say that fake ID wasn't in my wallet."

Placing his cup on the little table, Stone said, "Well, if you can't win on the facts, then you win on procedure." He paused. "Or a combination of the two. In your case, I think we'll focus on the search and the statement you gave the police. If we can uncover something improper about how they got into your wallet, or if you were coerced into giving the statement, then we might have a shot. I still need to interview the officer and the paramedic."

Stone looked at his watch, so Sam tried to wedge in one more question. "So, getting back to my meeting with Metcalf, maybe Trent told you he was innocent, but maybe he wasn't. Is that possible?"

Stone gave him an impatient look. "I told you before, I can't talk to you about Trent Hurley."

"But you did tell me to look into that old case if I wanted to learn about justice," Sam shot back. "Why? And why did Tua Dumay tell me the same thing? She enclosed a note with the title for the motorcycle, asking me to try to right some wrongs when I got here."

At the mention of Tua's name, Stone sat back in his chair and the anger left his face. "Oh God!...That means that all these years she's been bothered by the outcome, even though it brought closure." Looking down at his coffee, he added, "She suffered so much at the time. To be honest, that was almost the worst part of the case."

"And I heard she had a mentally handicapped son. Metcalf mentioned him. So did Rio Polo. In fact I should have thanked you right off for putting me in touch with Rio. We got together last week in Albuquerque. Did *you* meet Felix too?"

There was a long silence. "Yes, I knew Felix. I read that he was killed in a hit-and-run a few years back. Tua must have been told, but she left after the trial and never came back, as far as I know."

"I can't figure out if the police talked to him about the case. He was never a witness or anything like that, was he?"

"No, even though he was spending the night with the Blairs at the time of the murder. He was really agitated after his grandfather's death, and Tua persuaded the police not to question him. Then, as you probably found out from the media, my client confessed to being involved and told the police what happened. After that, the investigation closed down pretty quickly."

Stone stood up and picked up his brief case. "Well, I'm not sure where it will take you, but I still encourage you to research the case, if for no other reason than to find out what Tua Dumay was talking about. And if you want to help Josh Metcalf, you need to find the gun."

Sam pushed his chair back and stood up too.

"Look for the facts," Stone said, as he shook Sam's hand. "Always look for the facts."

Sam was still mulling Stone's injunction when he arrived to pick Nina up. She gave him a smile and a hug. "Good to see you. Let's go, I'm starved. It's too bad we don't have time to continue on to Taos."

They mounted Pegasus and headed north on Rt. 285 until they hit Española. Sam turned east towards Pojoaque at the red light at Rt. 76, Santa Cruz Road, and they passed a brightly colored Pontiac. Pointing at the car's body, which rode about four inches from the ground, Nina shouted, "Española is the 'Low Rider' capital of the world." Sam nodded as he accelerated along the tree-lined road that followed the small river.

Two miles later, a pick-up truck coming up behind them accelerated to pass. "You're crazy!" Sam shouted as they approached a curve and the truck began to force them off the road. He slammed on his rear brake and felt Nina's body pushing into him from behind. She shouted something he didn't recognize as the truck sped off.

"Are you all right?" Sam turned his head to check on Nina.

"I'm fine," she said. "Let's keep going."

"A good reminder to watch out for crazy drivers on winding roads," he said to himself. They followed the road as it crested on a rise and forked to left, heading north. With no stream nearby, the trees quickly disappeared and the landscape became the more typical dirt and rock spotted with small, bush-like piñon trees. With Nina holding on to his waist as they made their way up and then down into the arroyos, Sam turned his head and shouted to her against the wind, "This is what I was dreaming of when I was riding through the Great Plains in a straight line against the wind."

Nina laughed. "This is why they call this the "land of enchantment."

Cresting a long hill, Sam could see the road wind down into the little town.

Nina pointed. "There's Chimayo. It's famous for the chapel with the healing dirt." Sam pulled over to the side of the road just before the final descent. "Every year," she continued, "there's a huge pilgrimage, and the locals walk here from all over the state, carrying crosses. They even hike up from Albuquerque, along the highway."

Sam pointed to the building next to the church.

"There's where we're having dinner." He put the bike back in gear, and they descended into the little village, took a left onto the gravel driveway of the restaurant, and parked on the grass.

A waitress led them to the outside patio, with its multi-colored umbrellas and white tablecloths. Seated at a table along a high stone wall, they watched the water in the fountain cascade from the upper level of the patio to the lower one. The waitress brought the two margaritas they had asked for, and Sam began to relax.

"It's nice to get away from town," he said after the waitress took their orders and dropped off two sopaipillas. They each took a drink from their ice-covered glasses.

"These are like pillows," Nina said, as she tore open the puffed-up fried pasty and poured in the honey that sat on the table. "I love them."

Sam took another swallow. He could feel the tequila moving through his veins, and without thinking about it, he heard the words coming out of his mouth. "Nina, I just have to tell you..." He could see Nina looking over at him with a noncommittal expression in her eyes, but it was too late to stop. "I just have to tell you how beautiful you are."

Nina laughed. "As militant as I am, I guess I can accept a compliment. Thanks." She paused, then added, "It seems like you have something on your mind. What's up?"

Sam had planned to keep his jail visit to himself, but he trusted Nina and decided to unburden himself. "Well, I went to see that guy in the New Mexico penitentiary, Josh Metcalf, the guy who was convicted of the Blair murder. For some reason I really don't think he did it. I think he was wrongfully convicted."

Nina put her glass on the table. "Hmm. Well, may yes, maybe no. I mean, you wouldn't be the first person to fall for a convicted man's cry of innocence," she said.

"Believe me, I've thought about that too, but you know, the facts in the case just don't add up. And besides that, there was something about how he talked." Sam recounted his whole visit, evoking the sights, sounds, and emotions as best he could.

He played with his fork for a moment and then continued, "So in the end, what I'm saying is that in Mike Stone's first case as a defense attorney he represents Trent Hurley, the other guy charged with the murder. And because he was Hurley's lawyer, he can't talk about the case, but I think he wants me to look into it because he knows something about it stinks. Just like Tua."

Nina frowned. "What are you saying Sam? Are you saying that Stone knows that the wrong man was convicted and he didn't do anything about it?"

"It's not that simple. Stone never asks his clients if they're guilty, and if Trent Hurley was smart enough to fool both the police and the prosecutor by confessing to part of the crime and going along with what the police figured had happened, then he was probably smart enough not to tell his lawyer that he did it, the actual murder that is."

"This sounds crazy to me," Nina told Sam. "Look, the jury heard all the evidence and convicted this guy Metcalf. Maybe you should leave it alone. I mean, what does all this say about Stone?"

"From what I understand, the trial came down to the jury believing Trent Hurley and not Josh Metcalf. I believe Stone is an honest guy, I really do," Sam said adamantly, "and he has a reputation for being a topnotch lawyer. I can see the situation where he doesn't necessarily know for sure that his client did the crime, even if he may suspect he did. In that case, he goes along with the story his client has told him. Especially if that story and his subsequent testimony at trial help his client get a good deal."

"But how does he live with himself?" she replied angrily. "Especially if he thinks an innocent man is getting convicted?"

Sam didn't have a good answer. "If that's what happened, I feel certain that he had a reason, a reason we don't know yet. All I know is that Stone wants me to dig into the case. Maybe he had second thoughts. I guess he figures if I, or we, can figure out what really happened, then maybe we can right the wrong."

"I must admit I don't see much justice in the system. It certainly hasn't been there for my people."

"It's weird to have both Mike and Tua telling me to right a wrong."

"By the way, I meant to tell you that I've thinking about that note. At least some of those words at the end are Navajo words. They're beyond my ability, but maybe we could take it to my mother or even someone like Peter Benallie and see if they can make any sense of it."

Sam had almost forgotten about the words at the end of the note. "Wow, what a good idea! It would make sense, too. Tua's father was working at Church Rock on behalf of the Navajo, and she was really familiar with Navajo weaving. Maybe she picked up some of the words. There are so many coincidences in this case, they don't feel random any more."

Nina nodded. "Well, at least that's something we could do. We could try and figure out that note."

Just then, the waitress appeared with their dinner.

"You've been great to listen to me rant on and on, especially when you had such a big day yesterday," Sam told Nina as they began to eat.

"Well, this case is obviously important to you. What's our next step?"

Gratified by her references to the two of them together, Sam answered, "As you suggested, to find out what that note says. But tell me about the rally."

"Well, imagine 'your' rally with twice the people and none of the roughhousing. It was terrific. A lot of Anglos showed up—some in groups that we work with, but a lot of individuals as well. A couple of legislators spoke, and a really good guy from the NMELC."

"That's the Environmental Law Center, right?"

"Yes. But the real draw was Joe Shirley, the president of the Navajo Nation. That kept everyone on their best behavior. I really feel this thing coming together."

"And you've done a lot to make it happen." Sam raised his glass.

"Thanks. I'm bushed, and I still have the big one to go. It's great to be able to relax tonight."

After dinner, the two sleuths left the restaurant and walked through the metal gate into the adobe courtyard that surrounded the famous chapel. Inside, Sam eyes adjusted to the muted light, and they sat down in one of the old wooden pews.

"It's such a different esthetic—not like anything I've ever seen before," he said, taking in the dark wooden ceiling, the fresh white walls, and not one but five altarpieces distributed around the walls, with skilled but somehow primitive paintings of saints.

"They're called 'retablos,'" Nina said. The one behind the altar also enclosed a carving of Christ on a wooden cross.

"You know, these Catholics are a serious lot," he whispered to Nina. Nina's smile, in response, seemed to lighten up the place.

After a minute, they walked to a small, windowless, stone room to the left of the altar, lit only by candles. Behind wooden barricades about two feet high on either side of the room were piles of discarded canes and crutches. At the front, another wooden barrier isolated a small dirt area surrounded by stones. Sam walked over and read the sign stating that this was the "healing dirt," the red, dusty prize sought by all the pilgrims who had come to this place through the centuries. Instinctively, he reached down and grabbed a handful. He was not a big believer in such things, but as he felt the red, grainy dirt sift through his fingers, he turned to Nina.

"I think we need some miracles too. I merely want to heal an injustice—you want to heal the whole Earth."

CHAPTER 19

That weekend Nina's Subaru headed not north to Taos, but west. It left I-40 at Flagstaff and turned north toward Navajo Nation lands that straddled three states. Near Kaibito, the car turned right onto a dirt road heading east, back towards New Mexico and the mountains, churning up clouds of dust as it went. Peter Benallie had agreed to take Nina and Sam to the reservation and sat in the front seat. In the back, Sam looked out the side window and noticed a battered old Chevy pickup truck parked on the side of the road. As the car slowed down and pulled to the side of the road, an old man pushed open the driver's side door and waved.

"It's Atsa Chee," Nina said. "He's a medicine man, at least 85 years old."

Chee stepped out of the truck and walked toward the car as the dust settled around them. Sam noticed his dark skin and deeply lined face and neck. Wisps of white hair escaped from a weathered cloth hat. He wore a black-and-white checkered shirt, blue denim pants, and tennis shoes.

The two older men embraced and exchanged greetings. The medicine man, keeper of the ancient ways of the Holy People, and the *naat'aanii*, four-time chairman of the Navajo, were obviously moved to see each other again. The old man blessed his visitor with corn pollen.

Nina and Sam stood back. "Chee lives according to

the Beauty Way of the Diné that my mother told you about," Nina said. "He 'walks in beauty,' living in harmony between the four sacred Navajo mountains, under what our people call *naats'eelit*. The word means 'the rainbow that stretches over us and protects us.' "

"That's so elemental," Sam said, moved by the mythical language of the Navajo traditions.

Nina continued, "It also means 'sovereignty.' "

Chee turned to Nina and Sam. "Chairman Benallie has always protected our land. He is a great leader to our people."

Sam tried to reconcile this with his research about Benallie after his conversation with Stone. He knew from further reading that Benallie had been stripped of his power by his own tribal council and charged with more than a hundred criminal counts by a special tribal prosecutor, and then faced indictment by a federal grand jury. Sam looked at the old man and thought about how he had once been the most powerful Indian in America. Now he apparently found solace in the unshakeable faith of his most traditional followers—people like Atsa Chee, who saw him as the keeper of *naats'eelit*, the guardian of sovereignty, someone who, in their view, understood the old ways far better than a younger generation of Navajo leaders.

Benallie turned to Nina. "This is Nina Lapahe, Henrietta's daughter," he said to Chee. "And this is her friend Sam."

Chee nodded his head and smiled. "You are fortunate to have met Chairman Benallie and to have him show you our land," he said. Turning to Sam, he continued, "I understand that you are interested in the man who loved rocks. I knew the doctor. He was very interested in the earth, the mountains, and especially the rocks. He used to come here in his truck and spend days in the mountains. He was a very smart man."

"That's what I understand. I knew his daughter, and she asked me to find out what he did while he was out here."

The old man squinted his eyes against the sun. "He worked for a big university, that I know. He used to come out here to do studies. Sometimes with students and sometimes alone. I met him, and we became friends. Sometimes he would stay with me and my family. But he was most concerned about the big mine over in Church Rock."

"Do you know why he was so interested in the uranium mine?" Sam asked.

"He was afraid that the big ponds would not hold," Chee said. "Many Navajo worked at the mine. It was dangerous work because of the chemicals and poisons there. The company made big storage ponds to keep the bad water. The doctor was afraid that the dam would not hold and that the water would poison the land."

"So you knew about that. Why didn't he do something about it or tell someone?"

"He was a very careful man," Chee explained. "He wanted to do some more studies, I am sure. I am not positive, but I think he did warn the company. He was shot and killed at about that time. Did you know that?"

Sam nodded. "Yes. His daughter, Tua, is the one who told me to come to New Mexico and see if I could find out what happened. Do you know if he warned anyone else?"

"He told me he was concerned about the poisons and that he was afraid that the dam would not hold," Chee repeated. "That's all I am sure about."

"So no one from the tribal council and no federal authorities came to talk to you about the dam."

Chee looked over at Benallie. "No one came to talk to me. A lot of things were going on at around that time. We were mostly hearing what was happening with Chairman Benallie. We were told that the doctor got killed. Of course, we were saddened by that news, but many people die, for different reasons."

Sam stepped back. "He must have been investigating the dam at Church Rock just before it let go."

Nina turned to Sam. "You have your suspicious look, Sam." Chee and Benallie chose this moment to excuse themselves. They turned and walked slowly down the road.

"I can't help but feel that the two things are connected," Sam said to Nina. "I mean, he's killed just as he's looking into what becomes the worst radiation release and contamination disaster in American history. Do you think that's just coincidence?"

"Sam," Nina pointed out, "You've told me that all the evidence showed that those kids were breaking into his house and he was killed during the struggle, or something like that."

Sam stuck his hands into the front pockets of his blue jeans. "Yeah, I know all that. But don't you wonder why they were breaking into the professor's house in the first place? I mean, maybe they were looking for something in particular. Maybe someone sent them in to look for something."

Nina looked up at the hot sun baking the shadeless landscape. "I think maybe you've been in the sun too long. Who would have them do that?"

"I don't know. I'm just thinking out loud. It just seems like such an odd coincidence."

"Why don't you ask your lawyer friend, Mike Stone?" she asked.

"I've thought about that. But he can't and won't talk about the case."

The two old friends had turned around and were walking back in their direction. Sam suddenly remembered the wrinkled yellow note from Tua burning a hole in his wallet—the main reason they had come all this way. "Nina, hang on! I almost forgot to ask Benallie and Chee if they could tell me what the words on the note mean."

When the men arrived at the car, Sam explained his need and handed the note to Benallie, who looked at the words scribbled along the bottom. After a minute, he shook his head "They are Navajo words. 'Mae' is fox, 'dzeh' is elk, 'dibeh yazzi' is lamb, 'tkin' is ice, 'al an as dzoh' is cross, 'lin' is horse, 'be' is a deer, 'dzeh' is elk, 'klizzie' is goat,' no da ih' is ute, 'nesh chee' is a nut."

"The words are a bunch of animals and nuts?" Sam asked. "That doesn't make any sense. I mean, why would Tua write an enigmatic note and then put down a string of animals?"

Just then Chee interjected, "Say that again."

Benallie repeated the words. "Mae dzeh dibeh yazzi tkin al an as dzoh lin tkin be klizzie no da ih nesh chee."

"I can tell you what that means," the old medicine man said. "When I was young, I joined the Marines during World War II. I was part of a group called code talkers. We used the Navajo language as a code to send messages to our troops, because the enemy had figured out all the regular codes. You use the first letter of each word. No one knew the Navajo language so no one could break the code."

"You were a code talker? Sam asked. "I've heard they were part of every assault conducted by the Marines in the Pacific!" Realizing he was talking to an actual soldier, he looked at the deep wrinkles in the old man's leathery face and added with heartfelt admiration, "You were known for your bravery and for how important you were in winning the war."

Chee shrugged his shoulders. "I was young, and we all put our differences aside. Lots of us joined the Marines."

"What does it mean?" Nina asked.

Chee said simply, "Felix hid gun."

"Felix hid gun?" Sam was so stunned he took a step backwards and turned partially away from the others. "Oh my God! Mike said to look for facts," he said more to himself than to them, "but this one changes everything."

"I must go," Chee announced and moved toward his truck. "Nice to meet with you," he said as he raised his hand to say goodbye. Sam quickly recovered and chimed in, "I'm honored to meet you. Thank you for your help."

Chee climbed in, started the pickup, and headed back in the direction he had come from, covering them with dust.

Later, sitting in the car pondering the message, Sam's thoughts returned to the old chairman in the seat in front of him—all he had done for the Navajo Nation and all that he had endured from the criminal justice system. A thought occurred to him. "Chairman Benallie, I hope this question will not offend you, but wasn't Mike Stone involved in your prosecution?" he asked.

"I remember that name, Stone. I think he may have been part of those that brought charges against me. Why do you ask?"

"I know him," Sam said. "He stopped being a prosecutor and now defends people. Back then I think he also tried to bring charges against the uranium mine about not complying with some of the regulations, after the dam broke at Church Rock."

Benallie nodded. "That could be."

"And he got fired, and his first client as a defense attorney was Trent Hurley, the man accused of shooting the professor. I wonder who paid Stone to represent him...." Then Sam voiced his question more pointedly.

"Do you know, by chance?" he asked. "Do you know who paid Stone to represent Hurley?"

"I do not know for sure," Benallie replied, "but I do know that the attorney who represented the mine was Walter Fisher. Everyone knew Fisher back then. He used to be the District Attorney for Rio Arriba County. Then he became the County attorney and later the advisor of Emilio Romero, the local strongman. The headquarters of the mining company was in Rio Arriba, and I am sure he was involved with it. I know he had clients in McKinley County and Mora County. We used to see him over in Gallup and in Window Rock as well."

"What's going on, Sam?" Nina could see that Sam's face had suddenly lost all its color.

Sam's mind was racing. "Well, if Fisher knew something was up, and if he thought that Hurley was involved in maybe stealing something that the professor had found, then, as a lawyer, he would obviously know that once Stone was Hurley's attorney, he wouldn't be able to disclose anything Hurley said to him from then on."

Nina looked quickly back over her shoulder. "Sam, I think you're putting too much into all this. I mean, there is nothing to prove what you're thinking."

After dropping the chairman off at his modest house in Window Rock, Nina and Sam continued on to Santa Fe, puzzling over the new clue.

"It's really two facts, when you think about it: Felix hid the gun, and Tua somehow discovered it," Sam said. "But where do we go from here? And why on earth couldn't Tua have just told me what was on her mind without turning everything into a riddle?"

CHAPTER 20

"Felix hid gun." Sam repeated himself. "Felix hid gun. What happened that night?"

Nina had just taken a bite of her chicken salad sandwich and looked at Sam with exasperation. After washing it down with diet Coke, she said, "I'm getting tired of you talking to yourself—you've been saying that non-stop since we saw Atsa Chee yesterday. We need to stop talking and start looking."

"But where? The professor's house and the place Tua and Felix used to live probably won't do us any good— the police scoured them at the time, and I bet they've changed hands a few times in the last thirty years."

"Maybe our best bet is to head over to her weaving shop on the Plaza and see if anyone can tell us more about Felix."

"Good idea," Sam replied. "I still have some of my lunch hour left. The shop's at La Posada."

As one of very few hotels in a prime location at the center of Santa Fe, La Posada was a destination for thousands of tourists, especially during the summer months and Indian Market Week in early September. Sam and Nina walked into the dark, air-conditioned interior of the large adobe building and down the main hallway. They passed a restaurant on the right and soon came to a junction. To the left were several shops selling souvenirs, art, or western clothing.

"There it is. Handwoven Creations."

Inside the small shop, the walls were covered with colorful sweaters, scarfs, and exotic-looking articles of clothing. Wood and glass display cases on the floor and against the back wall exhibited Southwestern-style jewelry, art nouveau boxes, mirrors, and other trinkets. An extremely thin woman in her mid-thirties or forties sat behind the high counter in the corner, next to the doorway. She wore silver hoop earrings and bracelets, a loose turquoise-blue blouse, and a long red skirt.

"Can I help you find something?" she asked pleasantly.

Sam nodded. "I wonder if I could ask you something."

The woman nodded. "Sure. What can I help you with?"

"My name is Sam Shelton, and I'm here for the summer. Back East, I knew a woman named Secunda Dumay. She used to work here, I think. We were wondering if you ever knew her."

The woman looked blankly at Sam and then at Nina. "Secunda Dumay. Hmm. Secunda Dumay...No, that name doesn't mean anything to me."

"She had a nickname," Nina interrupted. "Her friends called her Tua. She was a weaver, and it's our understanding that she started the store years ago with some friends."

The woman sat up straight. "Oh, Tua. Yes, I recognize *that* name." She paused for a moment. "Well, actually, I should say I've heard the name. My mother started the shop with her."

"Fantastic," Sam responded. "Could we possibly talk with your mother? Is she around?"

The sales clerk looked silently at the two strangers, as if to size them up, and after a moment she voiced her decision. "Sure, let me give her a call."

She picked up her cell phone and hit a button. Her mother answered right away. "Hey Mom, I have two folks here who say they're friends of your old friend Tua Dumay." After listening for a moment, she spoke again into the phone. "Do you want to speak with them? I can put them on if you want." Then, to Sam's chagrin, she hung up.

"What did she say?" he asked.

The woman smiled. "She said she's coming right down to meet you. She should be here in about twenty minutes."

"Super. We'll walk around a bit and come back in fifteen. Thanks so much for your help."

"Sure thing," she said, as she turned to attend to three large, middle-aged women sporting turquoise jewelry and Texas accents.

Sam and Nina had just returned from their stroll when a woman in a bright blue work shirt and blue corduroy pants bounced into the store and looked around with a proprietary air. Sam stepped forward.

"Hello. I think maybe you're looking for me. My name is Sam Shelton, and this is my friend Nina Lapahe. Thanks for coming to meet us."

"Hi there. My name is Joy. I was good friends with Tua. It's been years since I've seen her. How's she doing?"

It fell to Sam to tell her the bad news. Joy teared up, clearly upset. "She was a truly great person. She was always such a good soul and friend. She loved to weave and, my Lord, she had a gift for colors. She was always laughing at odd things, and we had such a good time together."

Sam and Nina both nodded. "We've been finding she meant a lot to different people," Sam replied.

"She was tall, thin, and so beautiful. And with that long black hair and tanned skin, all the rich tourists thought she was half Navajo and would buy anything she suggested." Joy laughed to herself at the memory.

"I understand that she left after her father was killed," Sam said.

"Yes, it was a real tragedy. She had some rough breaks, first the problems with her son, then her husband leaving her, and then, like you said, her father getting killed." Joy sighed. "But through it all, she always kept weaving. She loved the colors, the symmetry, the artistry, the rhythm of it. It gave her peace."

"I can see that," Nina added. Almost as an afterthought, she asked, "Did she like to do puzzles, do you know?"

Joy looked a bit startled. "Funny you should ask that. But yes, Tua was fascinated by puzzles. She was always doing crossword puzzles, jigsaw puzzles, math puzzles, just about anything where you had to figure things out. I swear, sometimes you could hardly get a straight answer from her."

"I wonder where she got that from?" Sam asked.

Joy laughed. "Who knows, maybe from her father.

He was a scientist, you know. Anyway, she was always a joy to have around. I miss her."

"We heard her son died, too," Sam said.

"That's right. With Dr. Blair gone, Felix became harder for Tua to handle. He loved his grandparents, and his grandfather had been particularly patient with him. He was mentally retarded, you know. After the trial, she got no help from her no-good ex-husband, and she decided to send Felix away to a special school. Then she decided to leave Santa Fe too. She sold me her share of the shop and went East. I thought in my heart she would move back, but she never did. She came back a couple of times a year to see her son. We would get together for dinner at the beginning, but it seemed like we saw each other less and less over the years."

"And do you know the details of her son's death?" Nina asked.

"No, not really. Only what I read in the paper. He was killed a few years back in a hit-and-run accident up in Española. I think there was alcohol involved. It was too sad."

"Do you know if there was an investigation or any legal proceedings?"

"Hmmm. No, I don't. But there's a lawyer up at the Attorney General's Office who might know the details. He's a Sikh. His name is Guru something."

"I'm sorry?" Sam was confused.

"A Sikh. You know, they're the ones you see around town wearing white turbans on their heads. They have an ashram, a kind of commune, up in Española. They've lived around here for decades."

"I know about the ashram, but why would they be involved with Felix?" Nina asked.

"Tua used to go up there from time to time, and after Felix finished school, she enrolled him in one of their workshops to help him learn some employment skills. They're very accepting of all sorts of people, you know. She told me that he really liked it there, and the people seemed to accept him. When she was thinking of what to do with him after the special school, he asked if could stay there."

Joy looked over toward the door as two more women walked in. "The Sikhs said yes, and so that's what happened. Felix moved into the ashram and worked at various menial jobs. Tua told me it was a good situation and that he seemed happy. It did him good to be more independent. That's why she felt she could leave. Of course, she came back from time to time to see him."

"You said there's a man we should see at the Attorney General's office."

"I'm not sure what his name is. It's an Indian name—Indian from India—but everyone calls him GT. He must still work there—I saw him downtown just last week. You can't miss him. He is very tall, with a gray beard and gray hair, at least the little bit you can see outside the turban. He always seems to wear a gray suit as well."

"And you think he may know something about Felix?"

"I would think so. It's a very close-knit community up there. And he's a lawyer, after all, and he's been here for a long time."

Sam looked over at Nina. "Looks like he may be our next stop." Turning back to Joy, he added, "It's hard to imagine Tua's distress when Felix was killed."

"I don't think they ever caught the person who did it. It was probably some stoner or drunk Indian."

Sam felt Nina step on his foot and took it as a signal to leave. "Joy, thank you so much for coming to meet us, and thanks for the advice."

Outside in the sunshine again, Nina blew her top. "'Probably a drunk Indian,' she says. That really pisses me off. It's always the same old assumption. I mean, why doesn't someone assume it was just an accident—someone taking a curve too wide or someone getting a thrill trying to give Felix a good scare?"

"Wait!" Sam stopped in his tracks. "Maybe it wasn't just an accident."

"What?" Nina asked.

"Well, you just said it. If my crazy theory is right, then maybe someone sent Trent Hurley into the professor's house to find something. We know that Felix knew both Hurley and Josh Metcalf, and that Felix hid the gun, and then all of a sudden he's sent away to boarding school after the trial."

"What are you getting at, Samuel?"

"Well, if Felix knew something or had done something, maybe Tua wanted him out of harm's way. Later she thought the ashram would protect him too. But it didn't work. Felix was killed after Hurley was released from prison. We saw ourselves that it wouldn't take much to force someone off the road up there."

"OK, I see what you are saying," Nina said. "But

like the rest of your theory, there's absolutely nothing to back it up. You're just going on a hunch."

"Yes, but it's more than a hunch to me," Sam explained. "It's sort of like a Navajo vision. I'm getting all sorts of signs that something else was going on."

They reached the motorcycle, and Nina put on her helmet. "Well, we still don't really understand what 'Felix hid gun' means. Maybe you should get a vision for that."

"I don't need a vision right now. What we need is to find GT and talk to him. Schiff will just think I'm at the library, and I can always go in to work early to make up the lost time." He located the number of the Attorney General's office, already in his phone. They were in luck; Taran Singh agreed to see them right away. Sam brought Pegasus to life.

Within minutes, the two were on Galisteo Street at the restored Villagra building. They headed down the main hallway towards the stairway to the second floor, where they were greeted by the Hispanic receptionist.

Sam spoke up. "We're here to see Mr. Taran Singh. He's expecting us."

The secretary smiled. "Yes, he told me. Have a seat, and I will let him know you are here."

A minute later, the tall, distinguished-looking lawyer arrived.

"I'm Guru Tarn Taran Singh, but you can call me GT," he said with a smile. "Please, come back to my office."

The three walked through a doorway on the left and down a narrow hallway with small offices on each side, each with a lawyer on the phone or at the computer. GT opened the door at the end of the hall and waved them into a large, sunny office with a big wooden desk. A blue ceramic bowl on one side of it was filled with ripe bananas. The rest was covered with neat stacks of paper.

The lawyer hung his jacket on a hanger behind the door. As Sam glanced around he was immediately drawn to the large oil painting of a lion hanging behind the desk. "The lion is an important symbol for Sikhs," GT said, noticing Sam's interest. "Courage and ferocity. These are important qualities for warriors." He motioned to them to be seated.

"I see," Sam said. "From what I understood about the Sikhs, I might have expected a more peaceful symbol."

"Yes, many people get confused. 'Sikh' means simply 'seeker of truth.' Our mission is to serve humanity, but that does not mean we should not be warriors as well."

"I stand corrected. And I want to thank you for seeing us on such short notice. As I mentioned on the phone, we are looking into the death of Felix Dumay about twenty years ago. I got to know his mother this past year. We understand that he was a member of your commune."

GT nodded. "That's correct. Felix did live at Hacienda de Guru Ram Das. But if I may venture to correct you again, it's not really just a commune. We refer to it as a spiritual community, where spiritual seekers join together to study, grow, and excel."

"I see. How long has it been in Española?"

"Since 1971. We started in Santa Fe with just a few people, but over the years it grew, and we finally moved to Española. We have about 350 people living there right now. Of course, there are many thousands more around the country, and millions around the world."

Nina interjected, "And at the same time, you're a lawyer here at the AG's office. What type of law do you practice?

"I've participated in most areas of the law, but for the last fifteen years I've acted as legal counsel for the state of New Mexico in civil matters." Turning to Sam he continued, "I was interested to receive your call. It's been quite a few years since Secunda left Santa Fe."

"She gave me her old motorcycle several months ago when she learned I was coming to Santa Fe. I believe she wanted me to look into her father's murder and find out more about her son."

"Really."

"Unfortunately, she died this spring, which makes her directive feel even more urgent. I'm working with the Fisher law firm for the summer, and with Nina's help, I've been doing some research on Dr. Blair's murder and the trial that followed."

"Go on."

Glancing over at Nina, Sam continued. "To be honest, the more we've learned about the trial, the more interested we've become in Secunda and her life in Santa Fe. An old friend of hers from the weaving shop she helped start told us that Felix lived at the community with you in Española. I understand that he was somewhat mentally handicapped but was happy living there. Then he was killed."

GT said nothing for quite a while. To Sam he appeared to be sizing them up. His voice, when he answered, was slow and calm.

"Yes, that is pretty much what happened. We embraced and worked with Felix for some time, and he fit in well at HGRD after his return from boarding school. We were happy to accept him into our family. Felix had difficulty speaking, but he was well loved. It was a tragedy for everyone when he was killed. He was a nice person with a wonderful, giving spirit."

"Do you know if anyone was ever prosecuted?" Nina asked.

"The police were never able to find out who hit Felix," GT responded. "To this day, it remains a mystery."

Nina asked, "Did anyone gather his belongings afterwards?"

"Yes, of course. In the Sikh tradition, with his mother's consent, he was cremated. He did not have much, but all his worldly possessions were burned with him."

"So you didn't find a gun in his room, for example?"

"A gun?" GT was genuinely surprised. "No, he certainly did not have a gun! Why on earth would you think he had a gun?"

"We're trying to account for a missing gun, and we're looking at all possibilities, even improbable ones. We didn't mean to offend you."

"Felix was a gentle person," GT responded. "He hardly ever spoke, but he was always pleasant and giving.

He never had a gun at HGRD, that I know."

After a moment of silence, Sam looked over at Nina and nodded. The two stood up to go. "Thank you so much for seeing us. You've been very helpful," he said.

But that was not what he was feeling, unless arriving at a dead end was progress.

CHAPTER 21

What did those numbers mean? All day at work Sam had been thinking less about the lease forfeiture he was working on than about Tua's note and the numbers on the motorcycle. Now he was pacing back and forth in his kitchen, waiting for Nina to return his call.

When the phone rang, he picked up immediately.

"Hi Sam, it's Nina. You sounded pretty frantic. What's up?"

"Nina, thanks for calling me back so quickly. I need to talk to you about the numbers on Pegasus." He paused to let her answer but then said impulsively, "I think I should tell you in person. Can I come over?"

Sam was on Pegasus in two minutes, heading up Garcia towards Nina's place at the top of the hill on Don Miquel. He pulled up in the small driveway in front of the adobe house where she had been staying for the summer, leaving his helmet and jacket on the seat. The house was surrounded by an old adobe wall. He walked through the arched gateway and knocked on the solid wooden front door.

Nina's warm smile greeted him. "Come on in," she said.

Sam had never been inside the house. He walked into the living room and sat down on the couch against the far wall. The house was a refinished adobe house with a cool slate floor in the living room. He glanced at the kiva fireplace in the corner between the paned windows embedded in the adjacent walls. A stone mantel was built into the curved chimney.

The ride over had calmed Sam down. "I really like your place. I love how the windows sink into these thick adobe walls. In fact, I like everything about adobe walls and how they curve around things."

Nina sat down next to him on the Navajo blanket that covered the couch.

"It's been a great place for the summer. I lucked out that my boss knows the owner, and she wanted a responsible house sitter rather than a tenant." Nina pointed to the stairs going up to the second-floor addition. "And the second floor is just as nice." But she knew that Sam had other things on his mind. "So tell me what you're on to. You sounded really excited over the phone."

Sam leaned forward. "It's about the numbers on the motorcycle," he began. "You know I've been trying to figure out what they mean since before I got here. I knew they had to be some kind of a code—two are the right length for social security numbers—though I didn't know how I'd find out whose—but they're all too short for phone or credit card numbers or most bank account numbers."

Nina sat back and crossed her legs. "So what's your new theory?

"Well, when I first saw the motorcycle in Tua's garage, it was covered with a Navajo blanket. And she herself was a weaver: in fact, I'm beginning to think of her like Spider Woman in your mother's story, only weaving a web of clues. The Navajo words on the first clue made it a challenge, but it wasn't that complicated in the end—just a basic alphabetical code."

"Go on," Nina said.

"Then it really hit me that the numbers could be one too, and all this time I hadn't even tried to crack it!"

"Did you try?" she asked.

Sam stood up and reached into his pocket. "You won't believe what I found. I got so excited I didn't trust myself to finish it, and besides, I wanted you to share in the discovery," he said with a grin as he put a piece of paper on the table in front of her. "Here are the numbers on the bike."

192015145
81512419
208511525

Nina stared for a minute. "How would you know where to split them up?"

"Well, if we're talking about the English alphabet, then even a double digit would be less than 26, right?"

"Yes...but even with that, there are combinations that make different numbers."

"I tried it using combinations of just single and double digits. I'll show you."

Nina got a piece of paper from her backpack and made a list of the letters of the alphabet, and next to each she wrote the corresponding numbers from 1 to 26.

"OK, you say what each digit or combination of one or two digits under 26 gives, and I'll write it down," she told him.

"Well, 1 or 19 would be either A or S. Next is either 9 for I or 20 for T, but it has to be T, since zero doesn't stand for anything by itself."

Sam guided Nina through the first number, Nina writing down the single and double letter equivalents in two columns. Of the eight single digits, all but one yielded vowels, but the first four pairs of numbers read STON— STONE with the addition of the final 5=E. No other word emerged when they substituted the other vowels. Nina looked at Sam in disbelief, her heart racing.

"That's got to be it."

"OK. Let's not get too excited, or we'll screw up," Sam said as they attacked the second sequence. "8 has to be H, because 81 is too high. Here we go again with the vowels. 1 is A and 5 is E..."

"And together, they're O. Every time we had a 1 in the first string, it was part of a pair."

"41 is too high, so 12 is either AB or L. 24 could be X—unlikely."

"Let's say it's L. Then 4 could be D, and 19 isn't AI but S."

"HOLDS!"

They raced on. "20 is clearly T, because of the zero, and 8 has to be H, because 85 is too high. So is 51, so the 5 has to be E. THE. Two separate 1's don't work, so 11 has to be K," Sam said.

"That leaves 525. That's EBE if they're singletons. 52 is too high, so 5 is E. KEBE? No way. 25 is Y. KEY. STONE HOLDS THE KEY." As excited as she was, Nina read the deciphered message quietly, with awe.

Sam was less restrained. He pulled Nina up and

enveloped her in a huge bear hug. "We did it! We cracked the code!" More soberly he added, stepping back, "But what does it mean?"

"Could the two messages be connected?"

"You mean like "Stone holds the key" is a clue about Felix hiding the gun? Let's think about it," Sam replied. "Tua found the gun—everything points to it. She probably found the gun with Felix's belongings and thought that somehow he was involved."

Nina nodded slowly. "She thinks her only son may have been involved in the murder in some way and, of course, she saw how upset Felix was and what happened to Josh Metcalf when he tried to say he had nothing to do with it. Yes, I can see that...I can see her finding the gun and then hiding it again so the police wouldn't come after her son."

"Right," said Sam. "We know that Tua stepped in so that Felix wouldn't be interrogated by the police. She had to protect her son, even if she was dead sure that he was innocent. If I'm right, 'Felix hid gun' means just that: he did Hurley a favor when Hurley asked him to hide the gun and keep it a secret."

"Poor Tua," Nina said. "So you think she hid the gun and lived with her secret for all those years?"

Sam nodded. "And to compound the tragedy, it didn't save Felix in the end. She probably planned to tell someone but never figured out how. It drove her crazy. Then I showed up, so she started making the clues. From what I've learned about her, I'm sure she wanted the truth to come out, and we've just discovered something that might make that happen."

"You have to talk to Stone."

"Yes, but what do I say? He's made it clear he isn't going to talk about Hurley, and I think he's really fed up with my prodding him about the case."

"Look Sam, you told me you're thinking of becoming a lawyer, and that's what lawyers do. They advocate for their clients and that means being pushy and confronting people. Trust me, I know a lot about advocating and being pushy." She looked over at Sam to catch his reaction.

Sam just smiled. "I like the fact that you speak your mind. That's probably why I hang around you so much. But you're good at listening too. Thanks for helping me sort out my thoughts, not to speak of the cypher."

"Listen," Nina rejoined, "we've done a good piece of work tonight, but even though it didn't take a long time, my brain is frazzled. Let's take a ride to cool down." She had grabbed her jacket and was already heading for the door. Sam let out a sigh. He could only follow. His soft front tire wouldn't be a problem if they only went as far as the Audubon.

As they rode up Canyon Road, Nina held onto Sam's waist a bit more tightly than before, and Sam felt a glowing warmth expand from his chest up to his cheeks. A few minutes later, they were standing on the green lawn of the Nature Center staring at the old oak tree where they had first spoken.

"The assistant director told me earlier that it's about twenty or thirty years old," Sam said. "She said oak trees grow about two feet a year, depending on species and environment. They're not indigenous to this region..."

"No kidding."

"...and it was planted as part of their outdoor education program."

Nina nodded as she looked up at the crown thirty-five feet over her head. "I have always loved this tree. It's so different from everything else around here. I love the color of the leaves and how straight and tall it is."

"And for us Anglos, you know, the oak symbolizes strength and endurance. And justice!"

Nina looked out over the adobe wall surrounding the old estate. The sun was setting behind them, bathing the old city in amber light and lengthening its shadows. "It really is beautiful up here. This has to be the most romantic spot in the whole city."

Sam stopped staring at the oak tree and followed her gaze. "I agree with that," he said. "It'll be dark soon. As long as we're here, let's just enjoy the sunset."

They left the enclosure and found a spot with a bench and a clear view of the Sangre de Christo Mountains. Sam put his arm around Nina's shoulders. As she turned her face to his, he gave her a long, unhurried kiss, and he realized he had not been the only one waiting for this moment. The sky became a fiery orange with streaks of blue. Behind them, the glow on the adobe walls of Santa Fe slowly faded, and its streetlights sparkled in the clear air.

CHAPTER 22

The next day at 12:15, without an appointment, Sam pulled into Stone's parking lot just as his lawyer was walking into the building.

"Hey, Mr. Stone."

Stone turned and waved.

"Do you have a couple of minutes?"

Stone held the door open while Sam caught up. "Sure, come on in. I don't have to be in court until 2:00.

When they got to his office, Stone placed his coat behind his chair and shoved his briefcase behind the desk. Sam sat down across from him.

"So, what's up?" Stone asked.

"Actually, I know it bothers you, but I'm still obsessing about the Blair case."

Stone was surprised. "You know my hands are tied."

Sam took a deep breath and then exhaled. "I'm more convinced than ever that Trent Hurley lied on the stand."

Stone's face seemed to turn white and he sat in silence for what seemed to be an eternity. "Where did that come from?" he demanded to know.

"On the 13th, I talked to Josh Metcalf who told me that Hurley lied about him. Then last Sunday, one of the last of the Navajo code talkers deciphered a note Tua gave me that said that Felix hid the gun."

"What did you just say?" Stone asked. "What did you say about Felix and the gun?"

"Tua's note—just the three words "Felix hid gun"—was written in Navajo code. I'm thinking that Hurley shot the professor and in a sudden inspiration gave it to Felix to hide, so that Felix would be implicated if the gun turned up. When it didn't, he shifted the blame to Metcalf. Felix probably had no idea what it was all about. It looks as if Tua found the gun in Felix's stuff and was scared the police would arrest him."

Sam had to slow down. "But she was profoundly uneasy about her decision. That's why she wrote the note when she knew I was coming here. And that's why she left New Mexico. Her secret was too painful." He hesitated before adding quietly, "She left another clue etched on the motorcycle, one that involves you. My friend Nina and I deciphered it just last night. It says 'Stone holds the key.' "

Stone said nothing, so he continued, "Just as you suggested, Nina and I are still looking for the gun, the derringer. I talked to Rio Polo about it, and he said if we can find it, he'll have it tested for DNA. Rio said Hurley is pretty smart and would have wiped the gun clean, but he says that with the new tests, his DNA would probably show up, especially if he wrapped it up in something. At very least it would get Josh Metcalf out of prison."

Sam saw that Stone's face had crumpled and decided to hold back his hypothesis about Felix's death.

"So you continue to believe that I knew Hurley was guilty and let him testify that he didn't do the shooting?"

"What am I supposed to think?"

Stone loosened his tie. "Sam, I will tell you this one last time. You can believe me or not, it really doesn't matter to me. But I swear to you that my client, Trent Hurley, never told me that he shot or killed the professor. If he had, I would never have allowed him to testify otherwise. I must admit I was suspicious, but the words never came out of his mouth. Later on, when I started to put my own pieces together and my suspicions grew, there was really nothing I could do. To tell you the truth, if I were to talk to you openly about the case, I wouldn't be telling you anything you don't already know. I'm as much in the dark as you are about how I 'hold the key.' "

"So we're all in the same muddle."

"But Rio is right. If you're able to find the gun and give it to him, and the results come back positive for Hurley and not for Josh Metcalf, that would be enough to re-open Metcalf's case and probably to set him free. And you might want to check the court files. They're public documents, and you never know what might turn up."

Sam decided to confide one more thing, even if it was pure conjecture. "I'm also thinking that Fisher may be involved."

Stone stared at him. "Why do you say that? What are you thinking?"

"I've found out that Dr. Blair knew that the mining company's dam at Church Rock was defective. Maybe he notified the company, which was represented by Fisher at the time." A slight smile crossed his face as he looked at Stone. "I mean, we all know how good lawyers are at keeping all information confidential. So, I'm thinking maybe that was why Blair was killed."

"You're saying that you think Dr. Blair was killed because he knew about the dam?"

"Well, it makes sense. If the mining company knew the dam was bad and did nothing about it, and radioactive waste flooded the entire area, then they'd be in big trouble. Maybe they wanted to make sure Blair didn't say anything."

The two sat in silence, absorbed in their own thoughts. Stone finally broke the silence in a low-pitched, raspy voice.

"I may be crossing the line by telling you this, but it was Fisher who paid me to represent Hurley."

Sam's jaw dropped. "Then it's true!"

Stone looked away. "It makes sense in the light of what you just said. He knew full well that once Hurley was my client, I couldn't and wouldn't say anything, and I see now that I walked right into his trap."

Sam slumped back in his chair, affected by the old warrior's distress at being compromised. "I'm so sorry" was all that he could think of to say. Stone leaned his elbow on the desk and put his head in his hand. Then he looked up.

"Sam, I think I should tell you something else. It has to do with Tua."

Sam was taken aback. "What?"

"I got to know Tua back during the time all this was going on. I first met her during the investigation and the trial preparation and then started to spend more time with her." Stone looked out the window. "She was the most remarkable woman, tall and beautiful."

"That's what I have heard."

"She was so full of energy and spirit, it was a joy just to be near her. It's hard to describe, really. She just loved life." He paused and looked back at Sam. "She was an incredible artist, you know. Loved to weave and paint." Stone smiled at the memory.

It was suddenly clear to Sam that his old lawyer, Mike Stone, had fallen in love with Tua.

"We used to meet up at the Audubon Center all the time, but especially in the evenings. She absolutely loved it up there and would often tell me it was her favorite place in Santa Fe. I can still remember watching the summer sunsets with her."

"Geez," Sam thought.

"As you can tell, I fell for her." He hesitated as if deciding how much to say. "It was a difficult situation because I was married."

Sam nodded. His own parents' marriage was still solid, but he had friends whose parents had split up for reasons such as this.

"After the trial, Tua sent her son away. She said she had done something to protect Felix and hoped she wouldn't regret it. I didn't push her and she never told me. I didn't want to get her in trouble. I really don't know what I would have done if she'd told me about hiding the gun."

"And all this time she's been conflicted about telling her secret."

Stone reached into the top drawer of his desk and took something out. "Up at the Audubon, there's a big oak tree she especially loved because it was so different. She said it was a symbol of our feelings."

He held out his palm across the old wooden desk. In it was a two by three-inch wooden box stained a dark brown, with an intricate pattern of an oak tree carved on the top.

"We bought a pair of them when we were up in Taos, when things were so crazy after the trial and she was trying to figure out what to do and whether she could stay in Santa Fe. I gave her one of the pair and she gave me the other. Without our saying it, I think we knew we would have to make do with memories and mementos."

"Can I have a look?" Sam asked, and Stone handed it over to him. Sam gazed with amazement at the wooden box and the picture of a tree in the middle.

"When did she leave?" he wanted to know.

"Almost right away. I never heard from her again. I am sure she was trying to protect me and my feelings." After a minute, he added, "But I never stopped thinking about her. I tried to find her once, but she left no information as to where she was going. It was clear it was over. I wish you could tell her I cherish my box and have kept it safe."

The two sat there, letting the day's revelations sink in. Finally, Sam spoke up.

"Mr. Stone, Tua went to some trouble to etch numbers on the motorcycle that spell out 'Stone holds the key.' Can I ask you to think about what she could have meant?"

"I'll be damned if I know. But give me a couple of days."

CHAPTER 23

Sam arrived early at a restaurant called the Pink Adobe, to bring Nina up to date on what he had learned from Stone. She had told him about the tree growing up through the roof in the middle of the bar. What he didn't expect to see was Tom Smith, seated on a barstool.

"Sam, hello!" he called over rather too loudly. "Let me buy you a beer." The one he was nursing was clearly not his first.

"Hey, thanks, Mr. Smith. I'm meeting my girlfriend Nina. She's an organizer for NAAC. She's one of the people behind the anti-uranium rallies this summer."

"Ah—a girl after my own heart. I hope she has a good slingshot, because she's taking on a Goliath," Smith answered, gesturing the order to the bartender as Sam slipped onto the stool next to his. "FMC—from Virginia, of all places—is worth hundreds of millions of dollars. Trust me, with those kinds of assets they still have a huge influence in the state government. Did you know that in the '60s the owner of the Church Rock mining operation bribed the entire state legislature to pay for a haul road to the mine and then bragged about it for years? Ah, those were the good old days," he laughed sarcastically.

"You know, I still can't get my mind around the Church Rock numbers. Over a thousand tons of solid waste and ninety million gallons of liquid..."

"Well, Church Rock wasn't much to look at—a

scattered community of dirt-poor Navajo families herding their cattle, horses, and sheep and watering them in the Rio Puerco, plus a couple of mine shafts, support buildings, and that uranium mill across the highway. The biggest feature was the pond of contaminated liquid.

"But it was the largest underground uranium mine in the United States," Smith continued, after Sam's beer arrived. "A couple of million tons of ore came out of that mine every year during the fifteen years it was open. You know how it works: at the mill, you grind the sandstone very fine and then let sulfuric acid percolate through it. The acid carries off the uranium, and it gets captured along with some other stuff and stabilized as 'yellowcake.' Mind you, a ton of ore only yielded between one and five pounds of uranium. So you can see there were a lot of leftover tailings, still containing 99% of the radioactivity. And the leaching liquid had residues of elements from every corner of the periodic table, things like radium and thorium. The idea behind the dams was to let the liquid evaporate and then figure out some way to isolate the dry stuff safely. Trouble is—no one to this day has figured out how to do it. It's the leading source of radiation exposure. About 140 million tons of this stuff are scattered all over the West. Navajo miners were at risk in the mines, but tailings exposed everyone—still do—through wind and water erosion. Back then, some families even used blocks of tailing material to build their houses!"

"Nina's father was one of the miners who later died of lung cancer."

"I'm sorry to hear that. She's probably told you how

negligent the mining companies were. That was true at Church Rock too. The pond was supposed to be lined and to have seepage devices and a monitoring well, and it was supposed to be retired after eighteen months, but none of that happened. The Church Rock disaster was no accident!" The reporter slammed his hand on the bar.

"And get this—the mine was back in operation after five months. And then, when the price of uranium fell in 1982, FMC just tidied up a little and walked away, along with mining companies all over New Mexico. No fences, no signs, no nothing, often. The official number of abandoned mines on Navajo lands is 500 or so, plus four mills, but the unofficial one is closer to 1200."

"So the company got away with it, basically."

"They ended up paying a half million dollar fine, but that was pocket change to them. I mean, no one was overly concerned about a few Navajos. Would you believe that the Governor of New Mexico refused to declare the site a disaster area, to get federal help?" Smith smacked his hand on the bar again, and eyes turned in their direction.

"But didn't the feds have oversight anyway?"

"That's where it gets surreal. There were five agencies with overlapping and sometimes contradictory goals—think Nuclear Regulatory Commission and the EPA. Add to that, many gaps in the oversight, ironically, and lax enforcement, plus a patchwork of complicated ownership and land use issues. It took them twenty-five years to get their act together. There were some good people in Washington—but don't get me going."

Sam suddenly had a much better idea of what Nina

was up against. And he decided to bring up his own obsession related to the mine.

"You remember how Tua Dumay asked me to look into her father's murder. Well, I've kept at it since I last saw you, alongside my day job, and I'm coming around to your idea that Dr. Blair's research might have had something to do with his murder."

Smith looked Sam in the eye. "My reporter instincts told me that there was a connection. One of my environmental friends told me later that Blair had been looking at whether the dam's composition and underlying rock formation made it likely to fail. I just never could find a smoking gun."

"I don't know if it's significant," Sam replied, "but among other things, I've learned that Walter Fisher, who represented FMC, hired Mike Stone to defend Trent Hurley."

"Hmmm...caging the tiger. I'll have to think about that."

Nina had appeared in the doorway and was scanning the room. Sam waved to her and introduced her to Smith when she came over. They decided to move to a nearby table.

"Well, young lady, you've got yourself a worthy cause and a powerful adversary," Tom said.

A shadow crossed Nina's face. "Sometimes I get paralyzed with anxiety when I think about what will happen if we fail. Even though Church Rock was finally named a Superfund site, the cleanup is nowhere near complete after all these years, and now they want to reopen the mine. It hardly matters that the Navajo Nation banned mining and milling on our own land—our water would be affected anyway."

"The health effects among your people have certainly persisted," Tom replied. "No surprise, really, when you know that the water had seven thousand times the allowable radiation. I'm so sorry your family was affected. You know, the country has never been up in arms about the ongoing plight of the Navajos in our own back yard," he sighed, "and the various radiation disasters disappear from sight after a few nightly news reports. We never seem to learn from our trips down the yellowcake road. So what's your plan for August 16th?"

"Well, our coalition for that rally includes more than two dozen groups, and people will be here from all over the state and beyond. The head of Earthjustice is going to speak, but the star attraction is the grand old man himself, Stewart Udall. He lives just outside of town, you know," Nina explained to Sam, "and he's still active at the age of eighty-eight."

Smith looked at his watch. "Kids," he said, pushing back his chair, "I'd love to continue our conversation, but you'll have to excuse me. I have to meet my wife at the Plaza. You have a good evening—you might try the apple pie if you stay here for dinner. Nice to meet you, Nina. Keep up the good work."

"Likewise."

"Take care, Mr. Smith. Thanks for the beer."

"He's a pretty intense guy," Nina said after he had left. "I'm glad I got to meet him. But tell me about your visit with Stone."

Sam filled her in, her face reflecting her surprise and

sadness as he spoke.

"Poor man. The murder and the trial are really coming back to bite him—hard," she said finally.

"And as bound up in it all as he was, or is, he has no clue about 'holding the key.' "

"I was thinking, maybe Tua meant it literally. The next time you talk to him, I think you should ask him to look really carefully at anything and everything Tua ever gave him."

CHAPTER 24

Sam jumped out of bed when the alarm went off. It was Friday morning, and he was hoping to get to work early to make up for the visit to GT, so he threw his clothes on and headed out to the bike parked on the street. As he pulled out his key, he noticed that the angle of the motorcycle was not right.

"Damnation!" he said, his eyes homing in on the front tire. "It's gone flat!"

He walked around the bike shaking his head and sorting through his options. "OK, I can pull off the wheel and roll it to a garage, or I can walk to work and then call a garage."

Opting for the latter, Sam walked briskly to the office, his thoughts drifting away from the bike to the riddle of the key. When he got to work, Sylvia was already there. As he hung his jacket on the coat rack by the front door, he sensed a new energy in the air.

"Hi Sylvia. What's up?"

She peered over her spectacles and put down the file she was preparing. "Haven't you heard? Mr. Fisher officially got the entire mining project. We'll be very busy for the next year at least."

"Really? But the politicians haven't actually decided to lift the ban, have they?" Sam started to head up the stairs to his office.

"The actual vote's not till August 17th," Sylvia said

with vigor in her voice, "but we've been appointed as counsel to oversee all the new bids. It's been slow around here with the economy so troubled, so this will really help us."

Sam had become thoroughly uncomfortable with Mr. Fisher's possible role in the Church Rock disaster and his real one in the Blair trial. He needed to know more, so he turned back to Sylvia. "I'd like to get some background on Mr. Fisher's earlier work for FMC. Are there any old files on it around here?"

"Why are you asking?" she shot back edgily.

A bit startled by her reaction, Sam stuttered, "Uh, well, I thought I should be prepared in case Mr. Fisher wants me to look up procedures or precedents for him."

Almost too quickly, she responded, "The important ones are locked up in this file cabinet," she said, pointing to the green one to the right of her desk. "And only Mr. Fisher has the key."

"Oh. I didn't realize," Sam said without thinking. Seeing the look on the secretary's face, he quickly added, "Then I'll count on Mr. Fisher to tell me if there's anything I should look at." He went up the stairs two steps at a time and sat down when he got to his desk. "What was that all about?" he pondered.

Just then, Stephen Schiff walked in. "Well, I guess you've heard about your new chore."

"No. What is it?"

"UPS delivered some boxes of old FMC files yesterday after you left. Fisher wants you to catalogue and index them. They're in the storeroom next to my office."

Sam sat up straight and pulled out a pad of paper. "It sounds like the work will be piling on."

With a sour look on his face, Schiff snorted, "Yeah, that's for sure. And you can guess who'll be handling most of the litigation the mining industry brings in its baggage."

"Well, let me know if I can help you in any way," Sam said in a friendly tone. He knew he only had three more weeks to go, and he had learned that the best way to handle Schiff was to play along when he got whiny.

"Say, Steve, speaking of files...," Sam called out as Schiff was closing the office door. "Sylvia told me our old FMC files of any importance were all locked up and implied that I should keep my distance. Is that right? I mean, I thought I should take a look at them in case I had to do some background research. And now this new stuff has arrived."

Schiff shook his head. "That old lady should mind her own business. She needs to remember she is just a damn secretary. I'd tell her so, but it would piss Mr. Fisher off."

"Really? Why's that?"

"They go way back, those two."

"Like how far back?" Schiff stepped back inside.

"She was Fisher's secretary when he was district attorney in the fifties. He's always had a fondness for her, and for some reason he's kept her with him all these years. He got her a job when he was the Rio Arriba county attorney, and he hired her when he opened this law firm. They must be good friends, because she's only a so-so typist and she takes her time filing anything. It pisses me off because it means more work for me."

Sam could only imagine what Schiff was saying about him if he was that happy to complain about others. But Schiff was in a talkative mood, so Sam decided to venture a bit further.

"So it's probably something personal that makes him so loyal to her...." Getting no reaction, he returned to his first line of inquiry. "All the same, I wonder why she was so touchy about the files. It was almost like she was hiding something."

Schiff paused as if wondering if he should respond or not, but in the end, he only tossed a "Who knows?" over his shoulder and closed the door behind him.

Sam resolved to look at the forbidden files, and a folder in the top drawer of Sylvia's beige filing cabinet would show if any less sensitive FMC file boxes had been stored in the basement. "Nothing to stop me from coming to work after hours," he said to himself. In the meantime, he had another mystery to deal with. He picked up the phone book and dialed the only garage in town that worked on motorcycles.

"This is Anton," the voice announced. "Can I help you?"

"Yes. My name is Sam Shelton. I was wondering if you can fix a flat tire on my motorcycle."

"Sure. Do you need me to pick it up, or will you bring me the wheel?"

"If you don't mind, it would be better for me if you could pick it up. I live here in town, so it's not far."

"OK. What time?"

"How about at lunchtime? I'm at work right now,"

and he gave him the address.

At 12:30, Sam was back with Pegasus when he spotted an old Volkswagen Jetta with a small flatbed trailer behind it. After parking, a tall, good-looking man with thick black hair nodded and walked casually toward them. His grease-covered overalls had an oval patch displaying his name, and a familiar odor of oil and gas wafted from him as he held out his hand.

"Hey, I'm Anton" he said, pulling a wrench from his pocket. "Yeah, I recognize this. It's an old Beemer, of course. I'd say a '63 or '64 R50/2. Nice German bike. Some say it was the best bike ever made. It has those opposed twin cylinders"—with his wrench, he tapped one of the metal cylinders that protruded horizontally from either side of the engine—"and it was one of the first bikes to have shaft drive." He pointed to the black tubular arm that extended from the engine to the rear wheel.

"Nice to meet you," Sam replied. "I came out of my house this morning, and the tire was flat. I think it had a slow leak. I should have brought it to you before this happened."

"No problem. I'll go ahead and bring it down to the garage. I see from your plates that you've come a long way."

Sam smiled and nodded, ever proud of himself for riding cross-country on two wheels. "Yeah, I rode from the East Coast. Rhode Island. I've been working here this summer."

"Do you have any tools for changing the tire?" Anton asked as he rolled the bike onto the trailer.

"I have a few, but to be honest, this is the first flat

I've had. The bike didn't come with tools, so I bought some. I keep them in the saddlebags."

As he cinched the nylon straps to secure the bike, Anton noted, "I'm not surprised about that with a bike this old. But you can be sure it came with a set of tire-changing tools on board when it was new. This is a BMW, and back then flats were much more common." He finished securing the bike. "Nowadays, bikes have tubeless tires, so you can fix a flat with a plug without taking the wheel off and replacing the inner tube."

"Well, maybe next bike," Sam joked. Looking at his watch, he added, "Well, I've got to get back to work. Can I pick up the bike at the end of the day? What time do you close?"

"5:30. I should have this fixed by then. I believe I have an inner tube that'll fit, but if not, I may have to order one from Albuquerque. In that case, it'll be ready Monday."

"Great." Sam was relieved that he probably wouldn't be without Pegasus for long. "I'll call or come by your garage by 5:00."

After he watched his hobbled steed being hauled away, Sam turned and headed down Garcia Street. As he walked, he pried his mind away from Tua's web of clues and imagined he was riding Pegasus home from Chimayo with Nina, as if flying on a cloud.

CHAPTER 25

"There's lots of weird stuff going on," Sam said into the phone.

Nina responded, "That I can imagine. Now what?"

"Yesterday morning I got up and my bike had a flat tire, for one," he said. "Turns out it won't be fixed until Monday. For two, Fisher's secretary is acting very strangely."

"But isn't she strange to begin with?"

"Yes, but more so than usual. She was so defensive about some FMC files in a filing cabinet near her desk, you'd have thought she was a mother bird and I'd gotten too close to her nestlings. Right now I'm cataloging some new FMC files that just arrived, but they all involve pretty recent activities, so here's the thing: I've decided to go in to the office tonight and go through the old files stored in the basement and maybe even see if I can get in the locked cabinet. I know it galls you that I work for the enemy, but it definitely gives us opportunities we wouldn't have otherwise."

There was dead silence. Nina finally asked, "Isn't that illegal, to go through those files?"

"No, it's not illegal. I work at the office. I'm not breaking in or anything. I'm just going in after hours to look at some old files. The only person who told me not to is the secretary, and she doesn't have authority over me. And most importantly, I'm not the police, so I don't need a search warrant."

"But won't you get in trouble if your boss finds out?"

"Could be," Sam answered. "But that's a risk I'm willing to take. I think it's worth it."

Sam waited for a second and then added, "So do you want to come with me? Two pairs of eyes are better than one."

Again there was silence on the phone. Then Nina responded, "Sure."

"Great. Meet me at the library at nine, and we can walk over together. Bring a flashlight."

Later that evening, they slipped through the back door of the Fisher office using Sam's key. The streetlight provided plenty of light as they walked into the main office area, and the headlights of cars coming around the curve on Paseo de Peralta overlaid it with bright, moving swaths of light. He opened the top drawer of Sylvia's desk and picked up the small ring of keys she kept there.

Signaling for Nina to follow, Sam moved back down the hallway toward the kitchen area and unlocked the door that led to the basement. During the course of the summer, he had frequently gone down to the basement to pull old files for Schiff. Apart from a couple of tables, it was taken up with cardboard boxes of retired cases, marked by numbers and stacked in a shelving system constructed of two-by-fours.

"We're looking for files with the numbers 78-009443 to 79-00125," Sam read from a file card he pulled from his shirt pocket. He had taken advantage of Sylvia's lunch break to search the master file list in the beige cabinet. With Nina right behind him, he moved down an aisle against the north wall, using the flashlight to read the descending numbers on each box.

"Here they are," Sam said. "There are five of them. Let me hand them down to you," he whispered. She carried each one to the nearest table.

"So what exactly are we looking for?"

"I'm most interested in anything that shows that FMC had information that the dam at Church Rock was faulty."

"That could be anywhere. Sam, are you sure you've thought this through?"

"All I know is that Sylvia didn't want me to look at any files. She knows something, and I'm sure there's something here," he said with determination. "I'm just not sure what, or where."

Nina sighed. "All right. Let's go through these as quickly as we can. Who knows? Maybe there will be a folder marked 'Church Rock—Dam about to Give.' "

Ignoring her sarcasm, Sam whispered, "Yeah, you never know. But I do know that if we don't look, we'll never find anything. And by the way, look for anything with the name Blair too. He might have written the company about the dam, and the company would have sent it to their lawyer to keep it confidential."

For the next hour, the two sleuths went through the files but found nothing of significance until Sam exclaimed, "Hey Nina, here's a file on Church Rock."

Nina came over, and he handed it to her. They split it up and used their flashlights to go through each folder, but despite twenty minutes of flipping through documents, they came up empty.

"Sam, there's a ton of stuff here, most of which I don't understand, but I can't find anything about any dam or about the professor."

Sam nodded. "Yeah, likewise here."

Nina put the top back on the box. "You know, they'd have to be crazy to put any incriminating evidence in such an obvious place. If there were a lawsuit, some lawyer could surely get hold of this information."

Sam sighed. "You're probably right. If they have any evidence of wrongdoing, they've probably squirreled it away someplace safer, away from interns' prying eyes. Like upstairs under lock and key in a fireproof cabinet." He carefully put the boxes back on the shelves. "OK, Let's go."

Nina led the way out of the basement, and Sam shut the door behind them. "We have one other thing to check out."

Sam went to the green metal filing cabinet that Sylvia had pointed to the day before. It was locked, but having observed Sylvia, he knew the key was on the ring in his hand. The third try was the charm. He inserted a small silver key, turned it, and the thumb latch popped open.

Nina shone her light over his shoulder as Sam slowly slid the top drawer open and began to read the tabs on the folders.

"These are all the accounting documents," Sam whispered. "That's why they keep them here."

The headlights of yet another car rounding the bend on Paseo de Peralto lit up the room, and Sam instinctively ducked his head. It made Nina nervous.

"I thought you said this was perfectly legal," she said

into his ear.

"I said it was legal, but I also said it could get me into trouble with the boss," Sam whispered back. "Anyway, I don't see anything of value here. I guess we should get going."

"I agree," Nina said. "I probably wouldn't fare as well as you if we got caught. I should have thought of that before I agreed to come. The whole anti-uranium movement could be compromised—Watergate, New Mexico style."

Feeling a twinge of conscience knowing she was right, Sam shut the drawer. "OK, let's go....Wait. Hang on just one more second."

"What now?" Nina's voice had an edge to it.

Sam had pulled open the bottom drawer and was fingering quickly through the last files when the headlights from the latest car on Paseo de Peralta disappeared into the office driveway.

"Sam! Someone just drove into the parking lot!" Nina exclaimed. "They just pulled up!"

Sam slammed the drawer shut and locked the cabinet.

"They just turned off their lights. They're about to come in the back door! We have to get out of here now!" Nina said frantically.

Sam moved quickly to the desk, pulled open the drawer, and flung in the keys. "Let's go!" he whispered as he slammed the drawer shut. "Out the front door."

The two moved quickly across the room, carefully opened the front door, and slipped through. Sam made sure the door locked behind them and then pointed down the stairs to the metal gate. As they got to the sidewalk, the light in the kitchen area turned on. A moment later the reception area lit up too.

As they scurried down the sidewalk, Sam peered down the driveway at the Chevrolet Impala that had just pulled in.

"It's Sylvia's car," he said, his heart still pounding. Nearing the corner, they adopted a more natural pace and headed toward the library parking lot where Nina had left the Subaru.

"What's she doing there so late?" Nina asked.

Sam shrugged, "She's slow, so she often puts in extra time. Nights, weekends—you never know."

Nina stopped and grabbed his arm. "Sam, why didn't you tell me that before we went in there?"

"I never dreamed she'd show up on a Saturday night. I'm really sorry."

She shook her head. "The next time you invite me on one of your little adventures, make sure you tell me everything!"

"I will, I promise."

The two had arrived at Nina's car, and she unlocked the door. As she slid into the driver's seat, she said, "Well, all's well that ends well. I'm glad I came along. Too bad nothing turned up."

"Well, actually, I did spot something," he answered, savoring the secret he had bottled up until they were safely back in the car. He turned to her and noticed how the lights of the parking lot backlit her hair, making her look uncharacteristically fragile.

"You did?"

"In the green filing cabinet, in the bottom drawer, there was a file with Trent Hurley's name penciled on it."

CHAPTER 26

Sam's phone buzzed in his pocket just as he took a mouthful of burrito.

"Oh, hi Mr. Stone," he said after swallowing. "No problem. Nina and I are just having a bite to eat at Harry's Roadhouse, down on the Old Las Vegas Highway." After a pause, Sam nodded and answered, "Sure, we'll come on over right afterward."

"Did you tell him to look at everything Tua gave him?" Nina asked from across the small table.

"Yeah, the day after we met at the Pink Adobe. And it looks like you were right–just now he said he's found something very interesting and that we need to go over to his place to check it out."

"No kidding! Where does he live, do you know?"

"I do now because he told me. It's on Calle Loma Norte. It's right at the top of the hill on the north side of town. It will just take a few minutes to get there."

Pushing aside her plate, Nina announced, "Well let's go!"

Sam hesitated for a second and looked longingly at the red and green chili covering his half-eaten dinner. But when he saw the look in Nina's eyes, he responded with a smile. "Yeah, let's go!"

As they rode up Old Taos Highway, sunset colors streaked the sky, and the Sangre de Cristo Mountains to the east basked in a soft light that turned the mountainside dark green. Just before the crest of the hill, Sam noticed the street sign and turned left. The paving stopped after about thirty yards. He took the first right onto a narrow road lined with adobe homes and quickly pulled into a small dirt driveway, where a row of piñon bushes hugged an adobe wall. Behind it, Mike Stone, in plaid shirt, khakis, and bedroom slippers, appeared in the doorway of a small house partially hidden by small fir trees.

"Hey, that was quick," he said as he opened the wooden gate.

"Mr. Stone, this is Nina Lapahe. Nina, Mr. Stone."

"Hello."

"Nice to meet you, Nina. Come on in."

"This is a nice place," Sam said as the group stepped through the front door and onto the reddish brick flooring of the foyer. He noted the simple wooden table and chairs in the dining room. A painting of the Sangre de Cristo Mountains hung on one of the white walls and a framed poster of the Santa Fe Opera on another.

"Thanks. It's small, but it's all I need. Go ahead into the living room and have a seat. I've got something to show you." He went past the tiny kitchen and disappeared into a larger room next to it.

Sam and Nina stepped down into the carpeted living room. It was open and spacious, with several small paintings on the white walls, stained wooden beams across the ceiling, and a rounded kiva fireplace in the far corner. The living room windows offered a panoramic view of the sunset, downtown Santa Fe, and the huge valley to the south. "Wow, what a beautiful view," Nina said as she sat down on the couch. Sam nodded in agreement as he sat down next to her.

Stone reappeared carrying a brightly colored weaving in his arms. He walked in front of the windows to a still-sunny spot and unfurled it, holding it up for their perusal.

"Have a look at this," he said. The weaving, about three feet wide and five feet long, had a reddish background and multiple patterns of diamonds, triangles and squares in gray, white, and black.

Nina stood up. "It's beautiful!" she said, stepping closer to inspect the piece with an expert eye, "...beautifully designed and woven. It respects the Navajo traditions, but it has a modern touch to it. Where did you get this?"

Stone folded the weaving across his left arm so that he could see both Sam and Nina. "After I got the message from Sam about looking at everything that Tua ever gave me, I pulled this out of my trunk." He looked fondly at the weaving. "Tua made this. I put it away years and years ago." He looked at the sunset with a faraway look, not really seeing it. "She gave it to me just before she left and asked me to take good care of it for her."

Silence filled the room. Then Stone unfurled the weaving again. "Look carefully at the cross in the diamond shape close to the center."

Nina stepped closer. "Yes. The diamond shape represents the Dinétah, the Navajo homeland with its four sacred corners. And the cross is the symbol of Spider Woman. Your weaving even has a Spider Woman hole!"

"You have a sharp eye," said Stone.

"Nina learned to weave from her mother," Sam

explained. "But what exactly is a Spider Woman hole?"

"Well, you know the story of Spider Woman," Nina responded. "Navajo weavers who wanted to weave an image of Spider Woman into their pieces knew that she was not of this world and wanted to avoid trapping her spirit within the weaving. The cross is the symbol of Spider Woman, and they would leave an actual hole in one of the crosses to allow her to get out. Sometimes they just used a graphic of a hole, because early twentieth-century traders thought the pieces with a hole looked defective, even though the holes were finished just like the edges of the weaving."

"That's funny," Stone said. "I actually thought this one was defective." He turned the piece over. "There's a small woven patch in a matching color sewn to the back of the hole. I always assumed some threads had unraveled and Tua just wanted to protect the weak spot, so I didn't pay any attention to it. But today when I pressed the patch at different points, I felt something hard and thin."

Sam and Nina looked at one another.

"I didn't dare try to get it out with my clumsy fingers, but I think you could, Nina," Stone said.

Sam squeezed Nina's hand, and her heart beat rapidly as she accepted the weaving and sat down, spreading it upside down on her knees. She took a deep breath, and then she closed her eyes, both to align herself with its balance and harmony and to focus on the importance of the moment.

"I believe the object should come out through the hole, like Spider Woman," she said as she opened her

217

eyes. "Removing the patch would be simple, but it doesn't seem right." Her fingers probed the patch until she had distinguished the shape of the object inside. Holding on to it with one hand, she turned the weaving over. Carefully, she pushed one side of its top through the hole. Then she rocked it back and forth with the thumb and index finger of each hand, on opposite sides of the weaving, pressing firmly to expand the small slit at each end without breaking its binding. From time to time she stopped, to try pushing the rest of the top through. At last, pushing hard against the end already liberated, she gave a shout as the entire top popped through the hole. The blade of the small metal key slid through easily, and she held it up in triumph, then put it in the palm of her hand to display to her companions.

Sam picked it up gingerly and looked it over. "It's smaller than a regular key. Look, it's got a word pressed along the base of the round part on top. It says 'Germany.' "

"Germany?"

"Hmm. I wonder what that means?" Stone murmured.

The three of them sat lost in thought in the living room, whose walls glowed orange in the fading sunset.

"Navajo weavers say that their thoughts are woven into their rugs," Nina said finally. "Tua's been waiting a long time for this thought to be expressed."

CHAPTER 27

Late Monday afternoon, Nina's Subaru turned left into a driveway that opened up into a parking lot for four small businesses. Most seemed auto-related, with cars in various stages of repair inside garage bays or parked in the lot. Sam pointed to a garage door on the right. "That looks like it," he said.

Nina parked the Subaru, and they got out. Both were still excited about the discovery of Stone's mysterious key.

"Thanks again for bringing me," Sam said to Nina. "It's been a pain not having any transportation of my own. I'll be glad to get Pegasus back."

"I'm looking forward to having Pegasus back too, though not because I mind driving you around."

Anton emerged from the open garage, cleaning an old carburetor with a dirty cloth. "Hello, Sam. I've got your bike all done. I'll wheel it out." A minute later he walked the old black motorcycle out into the parking area.

"Glad to see you," Sam said, patting the saddle. "So what caused the flat?" he asked.

"It was a nail or a spike of some sort," Anton replied. "I couldn't find it lodged in the tire, but looking at the tire mark and the small hole in the inner tube, it had to be something like that."

"That's strange, isn't it?"

"Well, you never really know about these things. I mean, you could have picked up a nail and then lost it, I guess. But, normally you would expect to see the nail." Anton had obviously seen lots of strange things over the years. "Unless, of course, somebody is out to get you," he added with a chuckle.

Sam was momentarily startled at the suggestion.

"Anyway," Anton continued, "I replaced the old inner tube with a brand new one. Better safe than sorry, especially on the front wheel of a motorcycle."

"I couldn't agree more. I really appreciate your fixing this."

The mechanic held out the odd-shaped key used for starting the bike. "Here you go." Sam took the key and inserted it into the ignition switch on top of the headlight.

"That reminds me. I have a key question for you. Do you know what this might be for?" he asked, pulling out his key ring and taking off the key from the weaving, that Stone had agreed to loan him. "It says it was made in Germany."

"It's a BMW key."

"What?" Sam and Nina said simultaneously.

Anton took the key and turned it over in his right hand, pointing to its head. "Yup, it's a Beemer key. You can tell by the size and the raised edge along the outer loop of its head, and, of course, the 'Made in Germany.'"

Sam pointed to the top of the headlight, at the domed plastic cover of the spike-shaped key he had always used to start the motorcycle. "But that's the key for this machine," he said.

"You're right. But this one's not for starting the

motorcycle." He walked to the side of the bike, stopping by the oval rubber covering on the left side of the gas tank. He looked at the key again as if to be absolutely sure. "Remember my mentioning a set of on-board tools on Friday? This key is to unlock the tool compartment."

"Tool compartment? What tool compartment?" Sam wondered. Anton pointed to a small circular opening in the rubber covering. It was about half an inch in diameter and all but invisible to the untrained eye.

"It's quite hard to see because of the dirt and grease that have accumulated over the years. These old BMWs, the ones made before 1970, have a little compartment here in the side of the tank. They stopped making them like this years ago because the lock rusted easily." He pointed to the small hole. "You unlock it here."

Sam could see it now. "So the compartment is indented into the tank?"

"That's right. Here, I'll show you." Anton wiped the opening clean with his cloth and carefully inserted the key into the slot. "You've got to be careful with a bike this old, especially if you haven't used this compartment for awhile. In fact, let me squirt something in there to make sure we don't break the key off in the lock." He removed the key and turned and walked into the garage.

Sam and Nina looked at each other in speechless anticipation. A few seconds later Anton came back, squirted some silicone into the lock, and carefully reinserted the key, gently wiggling it until the lock turned.

"There we go," he announced as he carefully tugged down on the rubber-covered door.

As if by magic, the door opened to reveal a rounded,

concave space in the side of the tank, with streaks of rust on its black paint. But it was the item inside that caught their attention: the compartment was filed with something wrapped in a piece of cloth.

"Is this what I think it is?" Sam whispered. He was afraid to touch it. "Anton, do you have one of those pads that absorb oil?" he asked the mechanic.

"Sure, but what do you need that for? It's just the tools for the bike...although the cloth wrapping doesn't fit. The original tool kit by BMW was a water-resistant pouch that held the tools."

"Still, could you get me a pad?" Sam repeated. When Anton returned with it, Sam used it to carefully pick up the wrapped item and lay it on the seat of the bike. He slowly unrolled the old cloth, touching it only with the pad.

For a moment they just stared in silence.

"The gun," Nina said slowly at first and then exclaimed. "It's the gun!"

The small pistol was about 5" long with a gray metal body and wooden grips on the handle. The faded white tee shirt spread out on the dark seat made the dull colors stand out.

"It's an old pistol," Anton pointed out. "I've never seen one like it." He stepped back. "Well, that sure is a surprise." He looked up at Sam and Nina with a quizzical expression. "Although it sounds like you were looking for this."

"Yes, it's been missing for a long time," Sam replied. He carefully wrapped up the gun and tee shirt and placed them in one of the saddlebags. "You're a wizard!"

"Glad to help," Anton said, clearly not interested in knowing anything more.

"You could do us a favor by not mentioning this."

"No problem."

After carefully closing the side cover and locking the compartment, Sam paid Anton and kick-started Pegasus. Turning to Nina, Sam said, "How about if we meet at my place?"

Nina nodded and got into her car to follow him home.

Fifteen minutes later, the two were sitting at the kitchen table staring at the unwrapped pistol. Looking over at Nina, Sam finally said, "I feel like I just found the Holy Grail. It's time to call Rio Polo." He took out his phone.

"Rio, hi. It's Sam Shelton. Yes, I'm in Santa Fe. Nina and I have found what we think is the missing gun. It turned up in a hidden compartment of the motorcycle." During the pause that followed, Sam stood up and grabbed a piece of paper and a pencil, then sat down again and began scribbling notes. At the end, he gave Rio his address. When the call was over, Sam turned again to Nina.

"Well, needless to say, Rio is very excited. He'll be here in an hour and a half. He said he was heading this way to visit his brother in Los Alamos and will take the gun with him to have it tested. The ballistics part will be straightforward, but the DNA is trickier, so we have to be super-careful not to touch the gun or the cloth or mention it to anyone until he gets here. Our test will jump the queue at the lab, since it's related to a wrongful

223

conviction. They can even accelerate the test if the DNA is decent—the results could be back within 72 hours. And get this. Rio had some recent business with the Attorney General and mentioned that the case is being reexamined privately at the request of Dr. Blair's daughter. The A.G. has agreed to an emergency hearing for Metcalf if anything significant comes to light."

"In the meantime, let's at least take some pictures of the gun. It would be good to have a record of it in case anything happened to it."

"Great idea, Nina. I have my camera in the back with my things." They went to work, too excited to notice that dinnertime had come and gone.

When Rio's car pulled into the gravel driveway just before 9:00 p.m., they had discovered their oversight, and the remains of the delivery from Pizza Centro cluttered the counter. The gun still had pride of place on the kitchen table.

Sam was out the door in a flash. "Hey Rio, thanks for getting here so quickly," he said, as Rio got out of his car. The investigator walked to the back of the car, opened the trunk, and lifted out a weathered black briefcase. "Hello Samuel, I'm glad to be here," he said, shaking Sam's hand. "This may be big news."

Sam led him inside and introduced Nina, who was sitting on a kitchen chair pulled away from the table, holding a mug of tea. "Hello, Mr. Polo."

"Nice to meet you, Nina," he said politely, but his focus was on the small pistol on the table.

Rio placed his briefcase next to the gun and opened it. He carefully took out a large black camera and placed it on the table. He reached in again and pulled out a substantial-looking lens, which he attached to the camera with a practiced twist. The metallic click confirmed it was ready. Finally, he retrieved a small cardboard box containing lightweight latex gloves.

"You come prepared," Sam noted, watching carefully from the opposite side of the table.

"That I do," Rio responded cheerfully. He picked up the camera and began to take pictures of the gun from several angles.

As the camera clicked away, he asked, "You haven't handled the gun, right?"

Sam looked at Nina, who was now standing next to him. "That's pretty accurate. I mean when we first found the gun in the bike, we unrolled the cloth by touching it with the oil pad the mechanic gave us, and we were careful not to actually handle the gun itself."

"Good," Rio said. A moment later, he let out a whisper. "What craftsmanship!"

Rio put the camera down and pulled out a pair of gloves and put them on. Then he pulled a pen from his shirt pocket and carefully placed the tip into the one of the barrels of the derringer and turned it over. Then he took more pictures.

"That should do it." He put the camera down, reached into his briefcase, and pulled out two clear plastic bags. Holding one bag open with his left hand, he carefully lifted the gun with his pen and lowered it into the evidence bag, which he closed. Then he pulled out a roll of red tape, tore off a strip, and sealed it, writing his name, the date, and the time across the tape.

"It's interesting to see how the pros do it," Sam observed.

He was surprised to see Rio peel off the gloves and put on another pair to take pictures of the cloth and place it in another plastic bag, sealed and signed in the same way.

"It's important to make sure that the evidence is not compromised or contaminated in any way while in our custody, especially since it will be examined for fingerprints, DNA, and that sort of thing. It's all to protect the chain of custody."

"For when it's used in court, right?" Nina asked.

"That's right," Rio nodded. "By doing this, we can establish if you testify that while we had the items in our possession nothing was done to alter or change anything."

"You said 'testify'?" Sam asked a bit nervously.

"That's right. If this evidence is used in court, and I have to believe it will be, then you may need to appear in court and testify about how, when, and where you found it, and that you did nothing to change, alter, or damage these items while they were in your custody."

Nina gave Sam a confident look and nodded, and Sam saw Rio's point immediately. "Of course," he said.

Rio held up the plastic bags and turned to Sam and Nina. "Boys and girls, I believe we have hit the mother lode!" His smile broadened. "I can't tell you how much I have wanted to find this gun. You two have done a tremendous job!"

Sam reached over and grasped Nina's hand, which she held tightly. "What now?" he asked.

Placing the two pieces of evidence into his briefcase, along with the camera and box of gloves, Rio closed and locked the top. "I'll continue on to Los Alamos tonight, but I'll be back in the morning to deliver these to the Department of Public Safety's forensic lab here in Santa Fe."

"Is there anything else for us to do?" Nina asked.

"Not really. At this point it's up to the scientists, the firearms experts, and the forensic examiners to see if DNA, fingerprints, or some other trace evidence on either the gun or the cloth will shed some light on who shot the professor."

"Sounds good," Sam said with a sense of relief, as Rio picked up his briefcase and turned to leave. "I guess we'll wait to hear from you."

As he opened the front door, Rio turned and faced Sam and Nina. "You guys have pulled off a miracle. The gun would have been an important piece of evidence in this case, and it always bothered me that we were never able to recover it."

His voice became more thoughtful. "You know, I've worked a lot of cases over the years. This crime happened a long time ago, before DNA was used much if at all. I get a feeling about these things, and something tells me that whoever used this gun probably left us a calling card." He shook each of their hands, put the briefcase in his trunk, and was gone, leaving Sam and Nina in the doorway, feeling strangely bereft.

CHAPTER 28

Nina looked at one of their photographs of the gun. "What if we were to talk to Trent Hurley about this?" she said.

"What? Why would we do that?" Sam answered with a touch of irritation. "The guy's a killer. If we told him the gun had turned up, who knows what he'd do?"

By Tuesday night the strain of waiting for the DNA results was getting to them. Finding the gun was a huge breakthrough, but the next evening they found themselves grasping at ways to resolve the other pieces of the puzzle—especially if the DNA test was inconclusive.

"We've heard from all the players in the Blair tragedy except Hurley," Nina rejoined. "You even went to the state penitentiary to interview Metcalf."

"The prison was a very safe place. And what good would it do to see Hurley? What would we say?"

Nina slumped dejectedly over her tea. "I don't know. You're probably right."

She got up from Sam's kitchen table, put her mug in the sink, and picked up her backpack. "All the same, why don't you call Rio and ask if he knows where Trent hangs out these days?"

"OK," said Sam, eager for a compromise. "I could do that much." The next morning, Rio picked up on the first ring.

"Rio, hello. This is Sam."

"No news yet."

"I know it's too soon. I'm calling because I'm wondering if you can tell us where to find Trent Hurley."

"Yeah, there are ways to get that information. I can call you back in a few minutes. But do you want some free advice?"

"Sure. What is it?"

"If I were you, I would stay away from him. I haven't seen him for years, but he's turned into a rough character, if he wasn't one already, and I would watch it. You know, I've been looking through the files the way I said I would, and I couldn't help feel he was manipulating people."

"Really?"

"Not only that. I didn't mention it on Monday, but I've recalled something I learned after the trial. Like all good cops, I had a lot of informants working for me, some of whom did time with him."

"What did they say about him?"

"Well, don't repeat this, and if anyone ever asks me, I'll deny saying it."

"It's a deal," Sam said.

"My source was in the local jail with Hurley before he got sent out of state to do his sentence, and he told me that Hurley said he had gotten away with murder." After a short pause, he continued, "Now, I realize that people talk, and he may have just been jiving to make himself look tough, but if you ask me, it had the ring of truth."

"So why did the jury convict Metcalf?"

"Juries do a lot of strange things. They usually get it right, but sometimes they're swept away by the crime and the strength and emotion of the prosecutor. That was a high- profile case, and the press had people so worked up that the community wanted someone convicted and punished. Jurors aren't the law. They're a bunch of people with emotions and prejudices, some of whom have a sense of what they think *should* happen. And of course, that whole thing about being innocent until proven guilty doesn't always hold water."

Where had Sam heard *that* before?—though he suddenly realized he'd barely thought of his own felony charge all week.

"In my experience," Rio went on, "a jury's natural inclination is to think that if someone has been charged with a crime, he's probably guilty of something....OK, let me make a call down to the probation office. I have a friend who's about to retire but who still works there. I'll call you back in ten."

"Thanks, Rio."

Sam sat up straighter in his chair and took the top file off the stack he had pulled from one of the UPS boxes. Ten minutes later, the phone rang.

"I got the information. Pretty easy, but you need to remember that this is confidential. Any word of where it came from, and my friend gets fired. He owed me favors, otherwise there's no way you'd get this."

"Don't worry. No one will know a thing. And there's a good chance we won't even use it."

"He lives in Española." Rio couldn't see Sam's startled reaction. "He's been up there for maybe a dozen years. I can't, or won't, give you his home address, but I can tell you where he works."

"That'll do fine. If I decide to talk to him, it's probably better to do it in a public place."

"Good thinking, Sam. Like I said before, if it were me, I'd leave this alone. But it seems like you have your own reasons for talking to him. He's mostly doing odd jobs, and right now he's working part time in Santa Fe at a bar called the Blue Light."

"Right. I've seen it. It's right off of San Francisco Street. It looks like quite a dive—not exactly where the fancy tourists go," Sam said.

"That right. It's a biker bar. Not too many reputable places are going to hire a convicted felon who's done time."

"By the way, can you tell me what he looks like?"

"Not really," Rio replied. "I mean the last time I saw him was a couple of decades ago."

"Yeah, I guess that's right. People change."

"I can tell you he was not too big. About five foot ten, and at least back then, he was thin. He had brown hair, a big nose, and bad skin."

"He doesn't sound too intimidating."

"No. But I suspect he's one of those guys who considers himself the smart one and hangs around with other guys who do his dirty work. Now that I think of it, he must have been pretty bright even back then, to talk to the police, pick up on their scenario, and convince them he was telling the truth."

"Thanks Rio, I really appreciate your help. You know where to find me when the DNA results come in."

"No problem. Give me a call anytime. Seems to me you'd make a pretty good investigator."

At 6:00 Wednesday night, after he left the office, Sam headed for the Guadalupe Café to meet Nina, with Trent Hurley on his mind. "Sneaky, manipulative white guy, mid to late forties, works part time at the Blue Light. Not much to go on."

Nina wasn't alone when he arrived at the cafe. Her companion, a Hispanic woman, wore the green cotton shirt and pants of an ER nurse. "This is Grace, she works in the ER at St. Vincent's hospital. Grace, Sam Shelton."

Sam shook her hand. "Nice to meet you. You must keep nice and busy at St. Victim's," he joked.

Grace smiled graciously at the overly used joke. "Yes, always lots going on in the ER. In fact, I have to get back in a few minutes. Nina told me about you. Nice to meet you too." She stood up to leave.

Sam was surprised and pleasantly flattered by the comment. "Thanks. Hope to see you around."

He quickly ordered a plate of burritos and, after catching up on Nina's preparations for the rally, told her he had found out where Trent Hurley worked.

Nina looked at him. "How did Rio do that?"

"Well, I really can't say. Trent seems to be a bartender at the Blue Light, but knowing that doesn't mean that we're going to go searching for him. Rio did provide another interesting piece of information, though. Seems that Trent has lived in Española for a dozen or so years."

Nina's eyes widened momentarily. "I've thought of an excuse to go see him. Didn't you tell me that Metcalf had vowed revenge? We could give Hurley a heads-up and save Metcalf from going back to prison for a crime he *did* commit!"

"Even if we don't know the DNA results yet?"

"Especially if we don't know the results. If they turn out negative or inconclusive, we're back to square one. And it wouldn't put Metcalf in any extra danger, because if he gets a new hearing, it will be front-page news."

They sat in silence. Metcalf's sallow face hovered in Sam's imagination.

"OK," he sighed. "I'll do it, right after I finish eating, before I lose my nerve."

An adventurous spark lit Nina's black eyes. "I'd like to see this guy too."

"That's no place for you. I'm not sure it's even a place for me, to tell you the truth."

"Well, I guess that makes sense. I would probably just draw attention to you. But I could at least walk over there with you and wait outside."

"Well...OK." Sam was oddly comforted that someone would know he was going into the lion's den, but it was comfort laced with panic—it would be harder to back out now.

They ate quickly and were soon walking through the Plaza and down San Francisco Street. Three old Harley Davidson motorcycles were parked on the street in front of the bar, and light spilled out through the swinging doors, mingling with rock 'n' roll from the jukebox. Sam winced, reminded of the old-fashioned bars of Western movies—and the mayhem that often took place inside. Nina spotted a couple of stores where she could plausibly window-shop or browse and squeezed his hand forcefully before crossing the street. He took a deep breath, transferred his backpack to his hand, and pushed his way through the swinging doors.

Inside, dim light, smoke, the smell of beer, and a blurred impression of black leather and muscle momentarily stopped him cold. All eyes had turned to him. Slowly, he got his heart out of his throat and moved to the bar. The closest bartender was a massive bald guy with tattoos covering his arms, as well as a large silver earring.

"Is Trent Hurley working here tonight?"

"What?"

"Trent Hurley. Does he work here?" Sam repeated.

The bartender glanced down the bar. "Who wants to know?"

"My name is Sam Shelton. I heard he works here, and I have some information for him."

The bartender moved down the bar and spoke to the other bartender, who walked back with him towards Sam.

"I'm Trent. Who the hell are you, and what do you want?"

"I don't want anything," Sam managed. "I have some information I thought you should have."

"Ray, take care of things, will you?"

"No problem."

"Come with me," Trent said to Sam. Most of the patrons shifted slightly to watch them walk to a table in a poorly lit corner of the room—miles from the door, thought Sam with rising apprehension. Trent sat down facing the door, no doubt out of habit. Sam put his backpack on the table, clinging nervously to the scenario he and Nina had worked out on their way over. They had agreed he would shoot straight. "Couldn't you use some other expression?" Sam had asked her.

"It has to do with ancient history," he said to Trent. "This summer I rode here on the old motorcycle of Dr. Blair, that I had gotten from his daughter." Sam expected Trent to erupt. Instead, he saw a light bulb go off in Trent's head.

"You're the one I've seen riding it around town. I could've sworn it was the old guy himself, except that people in those days didn't wear helmets."

"Pegasus is like my calling card!" Sam thought to himself. "He won't react so mildly to what's coming next, though."

"The bike needed some work a few days ago," he continued aloud, "and they found a Remington derringer wrapped in a tee-shirt in the hidden tool compartment."

"What's it to me?" Sam saw a flicker of shock in Trent's eyes, but it was quickly mastered. Just as Rio had said, he's smart and he knows it. With dismay, he also saw Trent give a high sign with his head to two men in oil-stained jeans standing in the shadows, whose black tee shirts emphasized the tattoos on their arms. Then he put up his hand, and they stopped at the bar. To Sam's surprise, Trent smiled, pulled out a cigarette, slowly lit up, and took a drag.

"So how do I know you're not making this up?"

Taking a deep breath, Sam reached inside his backpack and pulled out the print of the derringer that he and Nina had made at Fedex Kinkos.

"They're going to test it for DNA."

Hurley looked amused. "What's interesting about

that case is that it's long over."

"You're right," Sam agreed. "I've read up on the case, and this picture of the gun used in the shooting doesn't really matter to you because you were charged and convicted in the crime, so you can't be re-prosecuted. I came by to give you a heads-up that if someone else's DNA turns up on the gun, Josh Metcalf will be getting out of prison."

"What's it to me?"

Sam said nothing.

"This is just a stupid picture. You have no real evidence." Hurley was starting to get agitated. He pushed back his chair and stood up. Then he shook his head slightly, as if to clear his mind, and sat down again. "This is one unpredictable guy," Sam said to himself, baffled and relieved in equal measure.

"That's right. I've done my research," Hurley smirked, "and I know I can't be re-prosecuted for that offense. Even if I shot the old man, there's nothing anybody can do about it. I'm protected by the Constitution. Double jeopardy. I served my time for that, and the State can't prosecute me again. I know the law. I can confess up the wazoo, and nobody can touch me." He tilted his chair onto its back legs, steadying it nonchalantly.

Sam's blood began to boil at Hurley's loathsomeness, but at the same moment he felt himself turning steely. "But you sent an innocent man to prison, and if he's freed, you'll be one of the first people he looks up."

Enjoying Sam's anger and feeling in control, Hurley just laughed. "Look, I did what I had to do. It was him or me, and in this world it's dog eat dog. All I ever did was go along with what the detective was feeding me."

"Like what?"

Hurley's chair landed back on all four legs. "Those cops are so stupid. One cop told me the evidence was clear that there was a break-in and the old man got shot. He said he was sure it was either me or Metcalf, but not both. He told me to come clean and that if I told him what happened, he would talk to the prosecutor about getting me a light sentence. He kept telling me he thought it was probably Metcalf who shot the guy, so of course I went along with that. I didn't have to do much. I mean, they were desperate to get a conviction."

"So where does Felix come in then?"

Hurley fell silent and took a drag on his cigarette. "I used to be friends with that kid. Even had a few chats with him when he lived at the ashram."

"So you heard what happened to him a few years back."

"Yeah, I heard he got hit riding a bicycle up in Española. Too bad."

"So, blame all this on Josh Metcalf if you get caught, and then, as a backup plan, give the gun to Felix, who's mentally retarded. You really pick your victims, don't you?"

Hurley's self-satisfied air disappeared, and he looked at Sam with venom. "I'm not answering any more of your dumb-ass questions. There's no damn evidence that I had anything to do with any of this, nothing."

"Tell that to Josh Metcalf." Sam had thrown caution to the winds.

Hurley slammed his fist down on the table and stood up. "I'm done talking to you! Get the hell out of my sight."

Seeing this was not an idle threat, Sam stood up, grabbed his backpack, stuffing in the print, and quickly turned to go—but stopped in his tracks. Nina had slipped in and was holding off some drunk cowboy type near the door. Adrenalin jolted through his veins.

"Hey, get your hands off her," Sam yelled, moving toward her. He took a deep breath and grabbed the man's arm.

In the same instant, the man turned with fury in his eyes and swung his fist in a short arc, hitting Sam on the jaw. Sam saw it coming as if in slow motion. "Oh crap!" he gasped as he heard the smack of fist against flesh. His head snapped backwards, and his body was airlifted to the floor. Shock dulled his senses. "Not too bad," he said to himself, gingerly testing his limbs. He rolled over and got up on his elbows, then his knees. "I guess I taught you a lesson," he said wryly under his breath. Hurley had followed him and now gripped Nina by the upper arm.

"Sam, look out!" she shouted. Hurley's two goons were converging on him. They picked him up by his arms and legs and threw him head first through the swinging doors onto the sidewalk. Hurley shoved Nina after him, out the still-swinging doors.

"Get the hell out of here, and keep your nose out of other people's business," he sneered after them, "and take your Injun girlfriend with you."

CHAPTER 29

"I mean that no matter how indifferent I act about the files, she's so nervous she even had her lunch at her desk today. I really wonder what's in that 'Trent Hurley' file," Sam told Nina on the phone, after returning from the kitchen with a Coke to wash down his sandwich. "And she's got to be hiding something about old man Fisher's role in Church Rock too. I'm going to have another go at that file cabinet tonight."

The DNA results were still not in, and he was more determined than ever to uncover the role Fisher had played.

"You're sure you're all right?"

"I look OK—that's the important thing, and my sore shoulder and jaw are pretty easy to hide."

"Oh Sam, I was so stupid to come inside," Nina said for the hundredth time. "Sometimes my appetite for risk gets the better of me. I've got to think things through. If I'd gotten caught at your office, it would have hurt the cause, and last night you got beaten up because of me."

Sam wanted to enclose her in a bear hug the way he had the previous night, after they had limped to the Subaru and Nina had driven him home.

"Listen, you had no way of knowing. And you were 100% right about seeing Hurley. I've already spoken to Rio about his mentioning a bicycle, and Rio is going to look at the case file."

"You don't waste a minute, do you?"

"That's the first time anyone has ever said *that* about me," Sam replied.

"I wish I could help you. The meeting at the Navajo Council Chamber to plan the rally is in high gear. I'll probably leave here at about 6:00 to go back to Gallup, and I'll be back in Santa Fe late tomorrow morning."

"No problem. This is more of a one-person job anyway," Sam replied, with more bravado than he actually felt. "Good luck on your rally planning."

"You'll be impressed—and so will the lawmakers, I hope."

Sam felt jumpy when he left the office at 5:30; a ride would calm him down. After grabbing a fish taco at the Tesuque Village Market, he doubled back to the Shidoni Gallery and wandered among the large outdoor sculptures. Too bad the foundry was closed. The first time he had stopped here, two people about his age had been working in blazing heat at one of the kilns. "Probably beats shuffling papers to make uranium mining legal again."

The bronze piece in front of him was an almost life-size image of a cowboy on a bucking horse. How could anyone make such a perfect likeness out of metal? And how free the cowboy looked! Thanks to Pegasus, Sam had an idea how that felt. "And Pegasus has never tried to throw me..."

At 9:30 that evening, Sam slipped in the back door of the office in the dark. This time, if he got caught, it would be easier to explain what he was doing. He moved quickly to Sylvia's desk, pulled open the drawer, and rummaged through it, shining his flashlight. "Oh no!" he exhaled sharply. "No keys! She's taken the keys!"

Had Sylvia seen him and Nina the other night? Or maybe she was simply as suspicious of him as he was of her. Sam stood up straight and looked around the room dimly lit by the street light. A couple of cars rounded the curve on Paseo de Peralta. Sam walked to the green cabinet and pulled on the handle, hoping against hope to get lucky.

"Nothing," he said, just as a car pulled into the driveway. Sam peered out the kitchen window and saw an Impala pull into a parking space. The driver cut the headlights, and a woman stepped out.

"It's Sylvia," Sam said aloud. "Oh, God—twice in a row! It's not possible!" As she ascended the back steps, he moved quickly to the stairs but then stopped. In that instant, he decided he needed to know what she was doing. Taking a deep breath, he quickly ducked into the coat closet in the hallway, not five feet from her desk.

Sound was muffled from behind the closet door, but if he breathed shallowly, Sam could hear her moving around the office.

A few minutes later, a cell phone rang.

"Hello... Yes, I'm at the office." Sam could hear the secretary's voice but had to strain to catch her words. He took a slow deep breath to keep from getting lightheaded. There was a long pause while she listened.

"Where am I going to get that kind of money?" After a pause she answered, "It doesn't grow on trees, that's why." And a few moments later, "You didn't talk to him, did you?"

Then Sylvia's voice rose. "What? It turned up? In the motorcycle? Dear God, they might be able to trace it to you."

More silence. Sam leaned closer to the door. "You didn't say anything about, well, you know, about that other thing," Sylvia said anxiously.

Suddenly she was shouting. "Don't even mention that poor boy's name around me again. Ever! That was your doing, and you'd better hope no one ever finds out."

Sam found he had been holding his breath. He leaned back and ever so slowly let it out, like a balloon leaking air, praying that the woman just a few feet away would not hear. The back of his shirt was clammy with sweat.

Sylvia spoke again. "All right, it's probably a good idea for you to go away for a while, especially if Metcalf is freed." A pause. "I'll see what I can do. I have to talk to Mr. Fisher about it. He'll probably say to write a check for petty cash from the office account."

Silence followed. Then she spoke again. "I'll ask him about that too. In the meantime, I'm going to re-file it under a different name... OK. I've got to go. Let's hope this whole thing just dies down again."

Now drenched in sweat, Sam heard Sylvia bustling about her desk. A file cabinet door slid open, and two minutes later it clanged shut. Her footsteps led to the back door, which opened and closed, and the car backed out of its parking space and slowly moved down the driveway. After waiting another five minutes, Sam carefully opened the door and peered out. Hearing nothing, he walked quickly over to the cabinet and tried the top drawer.

Locked tight. He moved to the desk and opened the top drawer. Not unexpectedly, Sylvia had taken the keys with her.

Sam felt defeated. He turned to leave as well, but crossing the kitchen, he wondered what Nina would do in his shoes. One way to find out.

"Hey Nina, sorry to bother you at this hour. I'm in the office."

"Is something wrong?" Nina asked.

"I was just feeling lonely. No, seriously, the green file cabinet is locked, and Sylvia took the key."

"Look for a second key," she said without hesitation.

"What?"

"Look for a second key," Nina repeated. "Look, Sylvia's got to be at least in her late sixties or early seventies. She must have a backup in case she loses her key or forgets to bring it. I bet you she has a spare key somewhere in that desk."

It was a long shot. Without hanging up, Sam began to rifle through the wooden desk. Paper clips, a letter opener, staples, stationery...but no key.

"Nothing," he said to Nina.

"Listen, pull out the drawer and run your hand on the underside of the desk top. That's where I hide keys when I have to."

Sam did as she said, and his hand felt masking tape holding something to the surface. He peeled it off carefully, and when he saw the little key, he gave a whoop.

"Nina, you're a genius!" he shouted into the phone.

"Does this buy back how dumb I was last night?"

"Twice over. I'll tell you tomorrow what else happened here tonight. I'd better get to work. Sleep well."

"Good luck," she replied.

Sam quickly inserted the key and turned it to the left. The locking mechanism popped open. He pulled out the top drawer and began to go through the files.

It wasn't until he got to the bottom drawer that he saw the old manila file with the label "NM v Trenton" on it, near where the "Trent Hurley" file had been. He carefully pulled it out and placed it on the desk. Inside was a typed letter, and just under the letter was the cover page of some sort of report. Sam's adrenalin began to pump as soon as he saw the signature and date: it was a copy of a letter written by Dr. Blair on June 20, 1979. Even before he read it, he knew he had struck gold.

The letter was addressed to Walter Fisher, Attorney at Law. It read:

Dear Mr. Fisher,

Pursuant to our many conversations, you are well aware by now that I believe the geologic formations in northwestern and western New Mexico will not support the extensive mining operations of your client FMC. I am particularly concerned about the mining complex at Church Rock, New Mexico. As I have indicated during this past year, I am convinced that the storage pond containing the uranium mill waste from the mine is particularly unsafe; there is a real and present danger that the earthen dam at the pond will break. Such a breach of the dam would have catastrophic consequences for the area immediately surrounding Church Rock—and the entire region as well if the uranium waste reached the water supply, which it certainly would. If such a breach occurred, the resulting flood would pour into the Rio Puerco, devastating the environment and the health of the local population. Let me be clear about this: If the dam fails, the effect will render the water lethal, with dire health consequences for the Navajo population in that entire geographic area.

The geologic data you requested, gathered over the last twelve months, supports the above conclusions. I am enclosing a draft of the report. Please review it at your earliest convenience and contact me if you or your client, FMC, has any questions about the facts or the conclusions presented. You are to be commended for your conscientiousness in commissioning it.

Because of the imminent threat of a dam breach and the dire consequences for the human and animal population and the physical environment of the area, I request that you provide me within fourteen days a list of proposed changes inspired by this report. I will include them when I formally submit it to the company, the EPA, the governor, and the New Mexico Corps of Engineers on August 1, 1979.

Sincerely yours,
Dr. Richard Blair
w/enc.

Sam read the letter twice, then carried it gingerly to the copy machine.

"Blair knew it was going to happen," he whispered to himself as the machine wheezed and clicked. "And Fisher duped and silenced him just as he did Mike—and then he silenced him for good."

CHAPTER 30

For the third time that week, Sam closed the door to his office, pulled out his cell phone, and punched Rio Polo's number. He had arrived at work half-expecting...he didn't know what...after his raid on Sylvia's file the night before. But she had acknowledged his arrival with her usual curt greeting and continued working. His relieved "Whew," exhaled discreetly on the stairway, showed him in hindsight just how tense he had been walking in the door.

"Rio Polo here."

"It's Sam again, Rio."

"You must have been reading my mind. I was about to call you to tell you that the DNA results are in. Hurley held that gun, not Josh Metcalf."

"Thank God!" was all Sam could say. He closed his eyes and was broadsided by a gamut of emotions: deep gratitude for justice done, high-pitched excitement, a warm feeling of satisfaction that Tua's mission had been carried out—and an overwhelming urge to tell Nina when she got back to town.

"Sam?"

"I'm here. It's just that this is such good news."

"I know. The Attorney General already knows, and a hearing for Metcalf has been scheduled for next Friday morning."

"What about Trent? I have reason to believe he's planning to leave town."

"They'll be picking him up this morning. If he leaves, he won't get far."

"Listen, I have something else to pass on. That's why I called you. In Fisher's office, I found and copied a letter from Dr. Blair to Fisher dated June 20, 1979, threatening to expose the defects in the dam. What should I do with it?"

"You're over in that part of town. Hand-deliver it to John McGarrity. I think the AG will appoint a special prosecutor, but for the moment he's the point man on the Blair case. I'll alert him that you're coming."

"Thanks, Rio. You're kind of like the traffic hub in this whole operation, making sure that people and information get to the right places."

"Happy to do it. Stay in touch."

"I will. Thanks again."

"OK," Sam said to himself after he had rung off, "that makes three things I have to do at lunchtime. My days here are numbered—no reason to punch a time clock now." He grabbed his backpack, picked up a file to give himself an official air, and headed down the stairs and out the door without so much as a glance at Sylvia.

Dr. Blair's letter was burning a hole in this backpack disguised as a letter to his mother, so Sam headed first to the Attorney General's office on Galisteo. John McGarrity greeted him cordially, took possession of the letter, and spent the next hour and a half debriefing him. It was almost noon when Sam emerged slightly spent from the building, feeling as if he'd had a tooth pulled.

His task at the Supreme Court library would take time, so he opted next for a visit to the *New Mexican*, with a quick bite at the coffee shop on Otero on the way. When he got to DeVargas Park, he sat down at a picnic table to call Nina, who was surely back from Gallup by now.

"Nina, I have news."

"The DNA?"

"It came back positive for Hurley. No trace of Metcalf."

"Oh Sam!" Then she too fell silent. Sam knew the feeling, so after a decent interval he took up the slack.

"Listen, is there any way you can meet me at the law library at about 2:00? I want to go through the Hurley and Metcalf case files, the way Mike Stone suggested."

"Sure. I'll be at the Capitol looking at the logistics for the rally with the site committee, but I'm sure I can slip away."

"OK. See you then."

The visit to the *New Mexican* took no time at all. The older man seated at a metal desk in the archives in the back of the building looked as if he rarely saw the light of day, and he grumbled when he had to put down his book. But Sam was soon scrolling through the microfilm covering 1996.

The item was on page 12 of the July 15 issue. "In the early morning hours of July 14...body of a man in a ditch on Route 76 in Española...identified as Felix Dumay...the victim of a hit and run...no leads...anyone with information...." No mention of a bicycle.

On his way to the Supreme Court building afterwards, Sam was reminded of Stone's admonition "Always be nice to clerks if you want to get anything done." The unsmiling lady he encountered at the Clerk of the Court's office did not look as if many people observed this practice.

"What file do you want to see?" she asked rather brusquely.

"Actually, I'm hoping to see two files in related cases," Sam said pleasantly. "The defendants were Joshua Metcalf and Trent Hurley. So, I guess the style of the case would be New Mexico versus Joshua Metcalf and then versus Trent Hurley."

Her sensible shoes telegraphed to Sam a working life spent on her feet. "I'm not sure I know that case. What year did you say it was filed?" She sounded friendlier; she was probably just wary of lawyers asking for favors.

"It was back in 1979. It was a murder case."

"Oh, no wonder," she said smiling, albeit wanly. "That was before my time. It must be back in storage. Wait here, and I'll get it for you."

"Thank you very much," Sam said, his smile plastered on his face. Stone was right—icicles melt.

Five minutes later, she returned carrying a cardboard box and a separate court file. She came from behind the counter. "Follow me. I'll let you look this over in the attorneys' conference room. Are you working for a law firm in town?"

"Yes," Sam said as he followed her down the hallway. "I work for the Fisher Law Firm."

"That's nice," she said as she opened the door and put the box and the file on the conference table. "Let me know when you're done."

"Thank you for your help. I should be about half an

hour." Sam took off his jacket and hung it over one of the wooden chairs.

Even though court files were matters of public record, he felt somehow privileged to be able to go through the actual documents. He shut the door and decided to start with the box labeled "NM v Joshua Metcalf." He picked up the top folder in the box and flipped through it, not really sure what he was looking for but noting the different pleadings and papers.

Slowly they brought Josh Metcalf's plight to life, making him eerily present in the room. The trial unfolded backwards, from end to beginning, since each record or set of records had been placed in the box as soon as it was produced. Near the top was the Notice of Appeal, then the final judgment order in which the judge sentenced Metcalf to life in prison. Next came the final verdict forms showing that the jury had found him guilty, followed by the judge's instructions to the jury. Read this way, they shredded any notion of logic and causality, making Josh seem doubly trapped.

It was all there: lab certificates for bullets, cartridges, alcohol and drug tests; witness and exhibit lists for the trial; pretrial motions filed by both the prosecutor and defense lawyer to let certain evidence in and keep certain evidence out, each followed by a written order by the judge making his ruling. Warrants for first degree murder, robbery, breaking and entering, and use of a firearm in the commission of a violent felony were at the bottom of the box, with the names of the attorneys involved in the case and subpoenas ordering witnesses to appear for the preliminary hearing and then at the actual trial.

Reading the records this way, like some theater of the absurd, made Sam thoughtful. "It's like rewinding a film. But in an odd way, it fits: What I want is to go back to the beginning and make the trial come out differently."

Sam shook off his disorientation and moved on to the separate file, labeled New Mexico versus Trent Hurley. It was much thinner, which made sense since Trent had not gone to trial. Sam flipped through the warrants and spotted Stone's name as Hurley's lawyer and the name of Metcalf's court-appointed lawyer.

Just then someone knocked on the door. It was Nina. He stood up, and she high-fived him. Then, very unprofessionally, she threw her arms around him.

"You did it!"

"We did it, you mean."

Then Sam pointed to the box. "That's contains all the pleadings for Josh Metcalf. I've just finished." They sat down, and he picked up the file for Trent Hurley. It was constructed of heavy-duty, smooth, gray cardboard, and each of the pleadings was attached to the file by metal fingers that went through the two holes punched at the top of the document.

"Trent's is much thinner because there was a plea bargain," Sam remarked.

"It still amazes me that a person could testify against his so-called friend and send him to prison for the rest of his life," Nina said, shaking her head.

"Well, I guess desperate people do desperate things," Sam said weakly, suddenly remembering that he too was under the shadow of a potential felony conviction. "Here are the warrants and waiver of the preliminary hearing."

"Why did he waive the preliminary hearing?" Nina asked. "I thought that's an important time where you hear the evidence to see if there is probable cause. Isn't that what you told me?"

"That's right. But he probably waived it because he knew from the beginning that he was entering a plea bargain."

"Sounds suspicious to me," she said. Sam decided not to remind her that he had waived his preliminary hearing too.

He folded the papers over the clasp to get to the next document. "Here's the plea agreement."

"What does it say?"

Sam started skimming the three-page document. "Basically it says he'll plead guilty to aiding and abetting the break and enter charge. In exchange for his truthful testimony against Josh Metcalf, the District Attorney agrees to drop all the other charges and recommend a sentence of seven years."

Nina said in a sarcastic voice, "Testify truthfully against Josh Metcalf? That's a joke."

"Supposedly all plea agreements involving a defendant who's going to testify for the government have that language. When the guy testifies, the lawyer for the other defendant will cross-examine him to show that he's testifying just to get a reduced sentence, and the prosecutor shows the jury the written plea agreement where it says that the only way the guy will get the reduced sentence is if he testifies truthfully."

"So it's all a game, to paint the witness as a great guy who would never tell a lie. How can a jury fall for that?"

"Well, that's how it is. Anyway, he apparently did a good job, because here's the final order in his case." Sam showed Nina the final sentencing order signed by the judge. "Ten years, with three years suspended. So he was left with an active sentence of seven years."

"Good for him," Nina said disgustedly.

"It's a good thing we have the gun and the letter, because I don't see anything in these files that helps prove that Metcalf is innocent."

"I'm glad you looked, though. I wouldn't want to leave any stone unturned," Nina said as she stood up from the table.

Sam pulled the box closer so that he could stack the other file on top. "OK, I'll take these back to the clerk. Maybe I can meet you later on tonight and we can do something. It's been a while since we've taken Pegasus for a spin."

After Sam closed the file, one sheet didn't line up with the others. Sam pulled it out, keeping track of its place. It had two holes punched on the top but had not been threaded into the clasp.

"What's that?" Nina asked.

"It seems to be Trent Hurley's bond papers. He was arrested and then released on bond pending the final outcome of the case."

"I don't suppose Josh Metcalf was given bond while Hurley was out getting ready to testify against him."

But Sam wasn't listening: he was staring at the paper. "Listen to the conditions," he said slowly. "Trent Metcalf is released on a secured bond of $10,000 pending the proceedings in this case. He is to be of good behavior, break no laws, stay in the state, things like that."

"OK...nothing unusual there."

Wide-eyed, he looked up at Nina. "And he is to reside at the home of his mother, Sylvia Hernandez."

Nina stared back in disbelief. "Sylvia Hernandez? Fisher's secretary?"

"Yes, it looks like Sylvia is Trent Hurley's mother." Sam reached into his shirt pocket and pulled out John McGarrity's card. "The guy I gave the letter to this morning will want to know about this," he said.

CHAPTER 31

While waiting for court to begin, Sam and Nina stood on the stone steps outside the main entrance.

"Look, here comes Smith," said Sam, pointing across the street. "I'm so glad the *New Mexican* brought him in to collaborate on its reporting of the story."

A moment later, the veteran reporter was reaching his hand out to greet them. "Good to see you two. Let's go inside. I've got something to show you."

They went inside and sat down on a wooden bench in the hallway, across from the doorway to the main courtroom. "That was some great work you two did," he said smiling. "Think of it! The DNA results from the gun you found exculpate Metcalf."

"Exculpate? You haven't forgotten your legal jargon," Sam joked.

"From "ex," "away," and "culpa," "guilt." Which, of course, is why we're here this morning."

Looking at the clock on the wall across from them, Smith lifted his briefcase to his lap and pulled out a manila folder. "We've still got a few minutes, so I wanted to show you something that my sources at the DA's office gave me."

Nina leaned over and read the title of the bound sheaf of papers that Smith took from it. "A Report of Geological Formations Affecting Uranium Mining at Church Rock, New Mexico."

"By Richard Blair, no doubt," she exclaimed. It was the same report whose cover Sam had seen in the "NM v Trenton" file in Sylvia's file cabinet.

"Blair's letter to Fisher gave the police probable cause to get a search warrant for the firm," Smith continued, "and for the secretary's house as well. Tucked way back in Fisher's office they found the report that Blair had prepared. It seems the secretary had one too. My source gave me a copy of it."

"I was out of the building when they came," Sam said, "and I left for good on Tuesday, after the shit hit the fan." It had been a pretty memorable day, actually.

"It's a beautiful day to die," Sam had said to himself as he pushed open the front door, equally tempted to turn around and walk away. He recalled how Stone had told him he often recited this phrase before his battles in the courtroom. It was apparently some Native American war chant, although Sam hadn't been able to verify it yet.

Except for the hum of the copy machine, the office was unusually quiet. When Sam stepped into the reception area Sylvia looked up from her desk, saying nothing.

In a feeble attempt to be friendly, Sam asked, "Is Mr. Fisher here?"

Sylvia's face began to turn red as she pushed the intercom button on the telephone. "Mr. Shelton is here," she said coldly into the phone and immediately placed it back into its cradle.

"A beautiful day to die." Sam felt a strange calmness as the words floated from his mind down to his gut.

The sound of Fisher's office door opening and then

closing sounded louder than usual in the surrounding silence. Wearing his trademark gray suit and smoking his Lucky Strike, he stopped six feet from Sam.

"You have broken every ethical rule of the bar and disgraced this law firm," Fisher said with a steely stare.

"Mr. Fisher, I was just doing what I thought was…"

Fisher cut him off. "You betrayed my trust," he said raising his voice.

"You're a fine one to talk about trust. Richard Blair trusted you. So did Mike Stone, for that matter."

Pushing back her desk chair as she glared at Sam, Sylvia suddenly stood up and pointed an accusing finger at him. "How could you?" she snarled. "How could you say those things?"

Sam took a deep breath and tapped into an unaccustomed reservoir of confidence. He turned to Sylvia first. "I understand your instinct to protect your son, but he's responsible for one murder and maybe another, and you let an innocent man spend thirty years in prison." Feeling his simmering anger rising, he added, "Trent deserves everything he gets."

Fisher took a step forward but stopped as Sam turned and faced him.

"Fisher, you won't be seeing me again. I could have stayed away today," he continued with controlled irony, "but I actually wanted to thank you. I got more education in the law here than I could ever have dreamed of. Maybe you'll get away with things in court, and perhaps you'll never get convicted, who knows. But I know what you did. I know what you did to Dr. Blair, I know what you did to Metcalf, and when the public finds out, I think the repeal of the mining ban will fail. I know what you did to the Navajo people by suppressing the Blair report." Glancing over at Sylvia, he added, "And I know what you did to this woman and her family."

Sylvia looked stunned at this unexpected expression of sympathy. "Mr. Fisher asked Trent to do this job behind my back," she murmured.

"I never told him to take your old gun with him," Fisher spat out.

The air reverberated with their outburst. Then Fisher took a long drag on his cigarette and stubbed it out in the ashtray on Sylvia's desk. He turned to Sam, glaring. "You're damned right I won't be seeing you again. And I will make sure you never get a job in New Mexico." He raised his hand and pointed to the door. "Now get the hell out of here!"

Sam looked the old man in the eye and shook his head. Slowly and deliberately, he turned and walked out the door. He smiled to himself as he walked toward the parking lot at the Round House, where Nina and Pegasus were waiting. It *was* a beautiful day, a beautiful day for a ride.

Now, three days later, Sam and Nina sat reading the "Summary of Findings and Conclusions" in Smith's copy of the Blair report.

The dam forms the southern wall of one of the mill's three holding ponds, which are used to evaporate tailings solution until the remaining solid waste can be buried...

Toward the bottom of the second page, Nina started to read out loud.

"Horizontal and vertical cracks have formed along the southern part of the embankment, allowing the acidic tailings solution to penetrate and weaken the embankment.

Further cracking was observed in October 1978. Despite my numerous requests, you and your client, the Flagship Mining Corporation, have failed to notify the State Engineer of the high incidence of cracking, which will contribute to the dam's likely failure, nor have you taken measures to mitigate it.

CONCLUSION: The dam is presently structurally unsound, and its imminent failure will certainly cause catastrophic human and environmental destruction."

Shaking her head, Nina handed the folder back to Smith. "They knew, they all knew, and they just didn't care. Not only that, they did whatever they could to hide the information."

Taking the folder and placing it back in his briefcase, Smith replied, "Well, from what I understand, FMC and the Fisher law firm are now under investigation. Not only that, I understand that Hurley is trying to talk his way out of this by saying that it was all Fisher's idea. I'm not sure if he can be prosecuted for Dr. Blair's murder again, but he's looking at charges for perjury and for hit-and-run homicide for what happened to Felix Dumay. It's a good thing the police moved in before he could skip town."

Sam looked up at the clock. "Time to go in," he said with an involuntary shudder. It was the very same courtroom where he would soon be a defendant himself, under the intimidating gaze of the very same judge. Josh Metcalf sat at the defendant's table with his court-appointed attorney, Michael Dickerman. He still wore his prison outfit, but Sam noticed he was not in shackles. A group of seven or eight people sat in the two front rows right behind the table. As he took a seat in the row behind them, Sam saw that most of them were holding hands. He turned around and nodded to Mike Stone and Rio Polo, who were seated in the back row. A few men and women who could have been reporters were scattered around the room.

All stood when Judge Brennan entered.

"Bailiff, call the case," the judge ordered.

"The State of New Mexico versus Joshua Metcalf."

The judge looked down at the paperwork on his desk and then at Metcalf. "Upon review of the written motions, the affidavits of witnesses, and the other evidence presented to this court, I find that you have been wrongly prosecuted and that the new evidence clearly shows that you are innocent of all charges. Therefore I grant the motion and hereby vacate your convictions and sentence." He paused and then added, "On behalf of the judicial system, I apologize for the pain and suffering you have endured during these many years, but as its spokesman, I now pronounce you a free man."

Metcalf turned to his family, his thin face transfigured. They stood up as one and cheered, surging forward to embrace him.

Sam closed his eyes, overwhelmed. Then he opened them again and put his arm around Nina's shoulder and nodded at Smith. All three of them had teared up, but they had never smiled broader smiles.

Just then the family members stood aside, and Sam

could see Metcalf looking at him. The former prisoner came out from behind the railing and walked slowly to where he stood. "Thank you," he said.

The two embraced, and Sam could feel Metcalf's body shake as he wept silently. He stood back for a second and then returned to his family and to his new freedom.

Smith put one hand on Sam's shoulder and one on Nina's. "Well done." he said, still teary. "Well done."

CHAPTER 32

The very next day—two days before the state legislature was scheduled to cast its vote on the uranium mining ban—Sam and Stone pushed their way through the crowd toward the podium set up on the north side of the Capitol. The crowd was huge, and several TV trucks were already broadcasting.

"There must be a thousand people here!" Sam shouted up to Nina, who was standing on the raised platform. Her long black hair was braided and stood out against the red shirt she was wearing. When Sam saw the bullhorn she was carrying, he was transported back to the first time he saw her.

Nina beamed back at him as she raised two fingers in a victory sign. "See you after the rally," she shouted.

Waving acknowledgment, Sam followed Stone toward the sidelines to watch. As they made their way through the crowd, Sam heard his name. "Isn't that Sam Shelton?"

More voices chimed in. "Yeah, the kid we read about in the paper." "Great job!" a man said as he passed, patting him on the shoulder. The woman beside him leaned over and added, "I'm so glad that poor man was released."

Stone looked around at the crowd from their vantage point on the fringe. "Sam, it looks like you're quite the hero."

Sam had to smile. "That headline in the paper yesterday sure helped."

Pulling the *New Mexican* from his back pocket, Stone said, "You mean this?"

Large black print ran across the top of the front page:

STUDENT INTERN FREES INNOCENT MAN AND EXPOSES CORRUPTION

"That was some article Smith wrote, wasn't it?"

"He did a great job, if you ask me. He laid it all out, the old case, the evidence of Metcalf's innocence, his release, and then all the information about how Fisher and his buddies in the state house have been manipulating the system all these years."

"Yeah. What do you think will happen to Fisher, by the way?"

"I heard from Rio that the FBI has already prepared indictments charging him with corruption and bribery, so it's safe to say that his lawyering days are over. And as you can see by the size of this crowd, the legislators are going to be hard pressed to overturn the ban on uranium mining now that you've exposed how these politician work hand in glove with outfits like FMC."

"Tom Smith mentioned that Trent was looking at a hit-and-run homicide charge in Felix's death. Did Rio mention anything about the evidence? He was going to look at the case file."

"Seems the police kept a part of the bicycle with a paint sample from the truck that hit him, and it matches the truck registered to Hurley at the time."

"That, plus his slip in the bar...is that enough to

convict him?"

"It should be." Stone looked out at the mass of people. Although standing right next to Sam, he now had to shout to be heard over the noise of the crowd. He pointed to Nina on the podium as the crowd began the series of rhythmic chants, getting louder with each refrain. "No more Church Rock! No more Church Rock! No more Church Rock!"

"The politicians and the corporations have met their match in her!" he said loudly. The two grinned at each other.

The rally concluded an hour and a half later, after impassioned speeches, eloquent speeches, and speeches that were both, punctuated by more chanting. You could have heard a pin drop when Secretary Udall reiterated his passion for the preservation of the land, reminding his listeners in passing that his work on behalf of uranium miners and Navajo who lived near nuclear test sites had begun the year *before* the Church Rock disaster. That Monday, the legislature overwhelmingly voted down the bill to lift the ban on uranium mining.

Early Monday evening, Sam, Nina, and Stone reconvened at the Pink Adobe to exhale and celebrate.

"What a great victory!" Nina declared with relief, once everyone had a glass to raise. "Cheers!"

"You all did a magnificent job," Stone said to Nina. "I've never seen such a big crowd in these parts, and they were really fired up. It was impressive."

Sam chimed in, "I agree, you did a great job! That crowd was huge and obviously made a big impression on the guys inside doing the voting."

"I hope so," she said. "It's too bad this issue hasn't been taken seriously until now. Just think of all the damage and heartbreak those corporate heads caused in the name of profit—damage to the lives and health of the Navajo people and the land." Affected by Nina's intensity, her two companions let her words hang in the air.

Stone broke the silence. "Well, if you ask me, you and Sam make a great team: you solved a horrible crime, you freed an innocent man, you brought criminals to justice, and you made major progress in protecting the environment for everyone, Navajos and Anglos alike. Not bad for a summer's work. And I might add that although you put me through the wringer, you've relieved me of a burden I didn't fully grasp."

Sam took a drink and looked over at Stone, his attorney, his mentor, and now his friend as well. "I agree that Nina and I make a great team. But at least for me, I couldn't have figured out the Blair case if it weren't for your encouragement and advice to keep pushing and digging, and let's not forget that you 'held the key' faithfully all those years. I've learned so much about the criminal justice system and about what justice really is, not least by getting mixed up with it myself. I know we still have a big hurdle ahead of us on Wednesday, but I really want to thank you for all that you've done for me. I wish I could return the favor somehow."

Stone looked across the table and nodded his head with appreciation. "Thanks for the kind words. I'm personally grateful that you were able to uncover what really happened in the Blair case, and you did it even though my hands were tied. Always remember, a really important part of being a lawyer is keeping your client's trust and confidence, no matter who he or she is or what they've done. Bottom line is, you have to protect their secrets, and I appreciate that you and Nina were able to right the wrong in this case without asking me to betray my oath as a lawyer."

"Yeah, anytime," Sam responded glibly. He looked at Nina and they smiled at each other.

"We do make a good team," she said, "and you're part of it," she added, turning to Mike. "Tua brought us together, like a good weaver, like Spider Woman herself. Think about it: the web of her existence was destroyed thirty years ago, and she took a long chance, sending Sam here with her message and her motorcycle, a chance that a new pattern could be woven linking the elements that remained. She was lucky—she succeeded despite her long delay and the obliqueness of her message. Well, it wasn't entirely luck. She had a good sense of whom to trust."

"To Tua," Mike said, raising his glass. "May she now truly rest in peace." The warmth in his voice eclipsed the sadness in his eyes.

"To Tua," his companions echoed with feeling.

CHAPTER 33

"Time to come down from our weekend high and get ready for your trial."

"Right," Sam replied glumly to Stone, as the nagging reality of his own legal troubles invaded his thoughts with a vengeance.

"As you know, your case is set for a bench trial at 9:30 a.m."

"Yeah, I have the time etched in my head. And I understand that a bench trial means the judge will hear the case instead of a jury."

"That's right. Your case rises or falls on the legal issue of the search and seizure of your wallet."

"So did you find out any thing new about that? And how do you see the trial playing out?"

"Well, normally issues like search and seizure are decided before the trial, so that the parties know whether that evidence can be considered by the jury. But in this case, the judge will decide the search issue at the same time, and if he decides for us, then the case is over."

"Tell me again how the search issue works," Sam said.

"Well, the Fourth Amendment says that the police need a search warrant before they can search you or seize your property. There are quite a few exceptions to that rule, one being that if you're arrested, the police can do an inventory search of your property without a warrant.

In your case, if it was a legitimate arrest, they get to search you. A search done by a non-police officer under those circumstances is OK as well. And finally, once you were in custody, the police needed to advise you of your Miranda rights before asking you questions."

"Hmmm. So, what's your angle?"

"Well, there's a question about the arrest in the first place. The police report says you were arrested for disorderly conduct, which would provide a reason to search you without a warrant. We know it was the paramedic who searched you and then turned your wallet over to the policeman."

Stone looked at the file in front of him and then continued, "At trial, I intend to find out exactly what happened, and in which order. I've found out that the paramedic is a rookie, and I don't trust this particular officer. I can't really probe what happened before trial because they would be alerted to what I am getting at, and they might change their stories or at least make sure they all dovetail."

"So, you're going to wait till trial. Isn't that a bit risky?" Sam's nervousness had ratcheted up.

"Everything is risky in this business," Stone answered. "But one of the few weapons that defense lawyers have is the element of surprise. In this case, and with these players, it's my judgment that we'll have to sort this out in trial, during cross-examination. If I can trip them up, then the judge will throw out the search. And if the search is out, your statement is out and you're home free, literally, I guess."

Sam gulped. "And if the search is not out, then I'm

268

found guilty of a felony?"

"Yes," Stone said matter-of-factly.

"Isn't there any other way out? I mean, I've been a good citizen this summer and I'm twenty-one now. Couldn't you, like, just talk to the prosecutor again about dropping the charges? Doesn't any of this make a difference to anyone? Do we have to go to a trial?" Sam wasn't proud of himself for pleading, so he wasn't really surprised when Stone answered rather sharply.

"Sam, that's unworthy of you. It really doesn't matter that you're a twenty-one-year-old good guy. It is all about having a fake ID. The unfortunate reality is that in this post-9/11 world, there are big consequences for being convicted of having false identification. And the prosecutor is an elected official with no incentive to give preferential treatment to well-to-do Anglos visiting for the summer, even if they do a lot of good while they're here. Quite the opposite." He picked up his pen and put it in his pocket. In a more avuncular voice, he added, "No, this case is going to be won or lost at trial. You can count on the fact that I'm your lawyer and you can always trust me. My number one job is to help you. That's the only thing that makes this whole system work."

Sam nodded his appreciation. "I do trust you, and I hope we win my case. It's just that I feel so damn vulnerable now. Following Tua's leads distracted me from my own troubles."

"I understand," Stone said, standing up. "Just remember that as your lawyer, I'm here to help you. Period." He put his arm around Sam's shoulders as he walked him to the door.

"See you in court tomorrow, young man."

To Sam's surprise, the courtroom was practically empty. The bench from which the judge presided over his court stood on a raised dais. Behind it and to the left, a bailiff stood next to the door leading to the judge's chambers. To the right, the court reporter sat next to the witness box. Sam was so nervous it could have been the scene of his execution rather than his trial.

"Is that the prosecutor?" Sam asked Stone, nodding in the direction of the wooden table across the room from their own.

"Sure is," Stone said. "His name is Matthew Casey. He's the deputy district attorney. He's been on the job for two or three years and pretty much knows his stuff."

After placing his briefcase on their table, Stone pulled a chair out for Sam. "Remember, I don't anticipate that you'll need to testify. This is all about the policeman."

Sam felt relieved in one sense, but he wondered how he could be found not guilty if he didn't testify. He suddenly felt an overwhelming sense of doom and was just about to open his mouth to see if he could reconsider the plea bargain offer for a misdemeanor conviction when the bailiff announced the judge.

"All rise. New Mexico versus Samuel Shelton, the Honorable Theodore Brennan presiding." After the judge took his seat, the bailiff announced, "Come to order. You may now be seated."

"Good morning, gentlemen," the judge said in a cordial yet businesslike voice. "I understand the defendant has already been arraigned and has pleaded not guilty. I also understand he has waived his right to a jury

trial and has elected to proceed to trial as a bench trial."
He looked over at Sam and Stone. "Is that correct?"

Stone nudged Sam to stand up with him. "Yes, Your Honor. We have requested a bench trial. In addition, as the court will note, I have filed a motion to suppress the evidence, and the prosecutor has agreed that this motion be heard as part of the trial rather than before trial, since this is the real issue for the court to decide."

The judge looked at Sam. "Is that your understanding, Mr. Shelton?"

"Yes, sir, Your Honor. Yes." All chances of making a deal had vanished, and Sam felt the sweat begin to drip under his arms.

"Very well," the judge said. He looked over at the prosecutor. "And yours, Mr. Casey?"

The prosecutor stood up. "Yes, sir."

"Since we will hear the motion first, and since it involves an allegation of a Fourth Amendment violation, the prosecution has the burden of presenting the evidence on this issue first."

"The State calls Officer Rodriguez as its first witness," Casey announced.

The police officer came in through a side door and took his seat at the witness stand. Casey began his questions after the officer had been sworn in to tell the truth, the whole truth, and nothing but the truth.

"Please state your name and occupation for the record," Casey requested.

"My name is Officer Emanuel Rodriguez. I am a deputy sheriff in the Sheriff's Office."

Casey continued, "And were you on duty in uniform

and with badge on May 16th of this year?"

"Yes, sir. I was on normal patrol working the Plaza that afternoon."

"And did there come a time when you came upon the defendant, Mr. Shelton?"

"Yes, sir."

"Please explain to the judge how it was that you came in contact with the defendant."

Rodriguez described the scene as he remembered it. "Well, there was a demonstration at the east end of the Plaza. You know, the annual protest against uranium mining by the Navajos." He smiled at the judge. When the judge did not smile back, he continued, "They were getting louder and louder."

"Go on," Casey instructed him. "What happened next?"

"Well, all of a sudden, the crowd got agitated and started spreading out. I think some girl on the stage was getting them all revved up. That's when I saw him"— Rodriguez pointed to Sam. "I moved in, along with other officers positioned around the Plaza, to arrest a number of the demonstrators for disorderly conduct." He paused for effect. "I think someone may have hit him, because when I got to him, he was down. After I sorted out the pile on top of him, I put the cuffs on him and called for a paramedic as a precaution."

Casey asked slowly, "So after you arrested him for disorderly conduct, he was taken into custody, and then you searched him."

"Yes, sir." Rodriguez leaned forward. "I had arrested him for disorderly, and then I did an inventory search.

That's when I found the fake ID in his wallet."

"And after that, he told you he had *made* the fake ID?"

"Yes, sir. After I had advised him of his Miranda rights, he told me that he was in college and had made the fake ID to buy beer before he turned 21."

Casey took the ID from the officer. "Is this the ID you took from the defendant?"

"Yes, it is."

"Judge, I move this into evidence."

The judge nodded. "Granted."

Casey glanced over at Stone with guarded triumph in his eyes. "No further questions, Your Honor."

The judge as well looked at Stone. "Your witness, counselor."

Stone stood and picked up his pad of paper. "Officer Rodriguez, how long have you been a police officer?" he asked, still standing behind the defense table.

Rodriguez was used to tricks by defense lawyers, so he hesitated before answering. "Fifteen years."

"And you were on patrol that day?"

"Yes, sir."

"Were you on foot or in your patrol car?"

Rodriguez looked over at the prosecutor, who looked away. "I was in my patrol vehicle, and then when the fight broke out, I parked and ran over."

Stone walked around the table toward the witness stand as if it took some effort.

"So, you were in your patrol car, you saw the commotion, and then you pulled over and went over to the crowd at the Plaza. Is that right?"

"Yes."

"OK. And when you got to Mr. Shelton, he was on the ground. Correct?"

"Well, I saw the commotion first, and then I saw him on the ground."

"And why did you arrest him, exactly?"

"Well, I figured he was mixed up in creating the disturbance."

"But you didn't actually see him hit anyone, did you? I mean, you run over and see everything and figure there is probable cause that he was acting in a disorderly manner, isn't that right?" Stone had stepped closer.

"Yes, I guess that you could say that."

"And, in fact, the disorderly conduct charge, the misdemeanor, has already been dismissed, right?"

"Yeah, they dropped the misdemeanor and went forward on the felony charge," Rodriguez said and then quickly added, "And I believe they offered to reduce his felony false ID charge to a misdemeanor, but you guys declined that offer."

"Objection, your honor," Stone said. "That last part was not responsive, and discussions of plea bargains are not allowed."

It was too late, however; the damage was done. The judge responded, "Overruled, counselor. This is not a jury trial, so there really is no prejudice. In any event, I'll disregard that last comment by the witness. Go on, counsel."

The knot in Sam's stomach cinched up another notch. He could see that the policeman wanted them to look unreasonable. Stone then held up what appeared to be a medical report.

"Isn't it true that when the paramedic arrived to help Mr. Shelton, you told him that he was all right and not to worry about him?"

Rodriguez hesitated. "Well, I'm not sure of that exactly. It's true that at first glance, the defendant didn't look to be badly hurt." He hesitated for a moment and then quickly added, "But the paramedic stepped in anyway."

"In what way?"

"He discovered the kid was dazed, so he looked in the kid's wallet to find out who he was. That's when he found the fake identification and showed it to me."

Stone lifted the document in front of the policeman and raised his voice. "Isn't it true, officer, that you told the paramedic to hold off for a second, that Mr. Shelton was under arrest, and that you were going to search him incident to arrest, something you didn't need a search warrant for?"

The officer stuttered a bit under the sudden verbal assault. "I... I don't remember if those were my words, but I did arrest him, and I searched him afterwards. I mean, I know I am allowed to search a person I have arrested."

"And it was after you arrested him for disorderly conduct and having the fake ID that you interrogated him and got him to say that the wallet and the fake ID were his. Isn't that right?" Stone asked.

Regaining his composure, the officer responded smugly, "That's right."

"No further questions," Stone said and sat down.

Sam leaned over. "Weren't you going to call the paramedic as a witness?" he whispered.

"Let's wait and see if the prosecutor calls him. It's easier to question him on cross," was all that Stone offered in response.

The prosecutor reviewed his notes as if deciding what to do next. Finally, he stood up. "Judge, our next witness is Peter Garcia, the paramedic."

After introductory questions about his duties at the time and place of the incident, Casey asked, "Mr. Garcia, after your preliminary exam, what efforts did you make to identify the patient?"

"I asked him his name, but he seemed a bit confused."

"So what did you do next?"

Garcia looked over at the prosecutor, and Casey gave him an encouraging nod.

"Uh, I then checked his identification in his wallet."

"And what did you find?"

"I found a driver's license from Rhode Island, with the name Samuel Shelton."

"Anything else?" Casey asked.

"I found a second driver's license, but it had a different name and was from a different state."

Casey looked over at Sam for a moment, and then turned back to Garcia. "And what did you notice about the pictures on each of the driver's licenses?"

"They were identical."

"What did you do with the wallet and the licenses?"

"I gave them to the police officer."

"And do you recognize the person in the pictures on

each of the two different driver's licenses?"

Garcia looked over at Sam and pointed. "Yes, it was him. The defendant sitting over there."

Casey cast a smug, sideways glance at Stone and then turned to the judge. "Your Honor, I move to admit the two different driver's licenses into evidence. I have no further questions."

Sam felt the blood drain from his head. He looked over at Stone, but the lawyer was already standing and had stepped to the side of the table.

"Mr. Garcia." Stone stared at the witness. "You have gone over your testimony with the prosecutor, have you not?"

"Uh, yes, yes I have."

"And isn't it true that you have talked about this case with the police officer, Mr. Rodriguez, as well?"

"Yes."

"When you were treating Mr. Shelton, you agreed with Officer Rodriguez that he was not too badly hurt, is that right?"

"Yes, that's correct."

"He hadn't passed out, had he?"

"No."

"He was able to speak, wasn't he?"

"Yes, but he was confused."

"He had no obvious signs of injury, did he?"

"No, nothing obvious."

"And Officer Rodriguez was right there with you, wasn't he?"

"Yes."

"And you are a rookie, aren't you? I mean, this was

your first or maybe your second call since you began working as a paramedic. Isn't that true?"

"It was actually my first official run."

Holding up the police report, Stone walked toward the young man. "Have you reviewed the police report in this case?"

"No. I mean we talked about it a bit, but I have never looked at that report."

Stone moved closer and held the piece of paper up, "Would it surprise you if the report said something different?"

Sensing something gone awry, Garcia looked nervously at Casey, who immediately stood up. "Objection, Your Honor!"

"Overruled," the judge responded, before Casey could state the reason he was objecting. "This is cross-examination, and I will allow Mr. Stone to ask his questions."

"Isn't it true, Mr. Garcia, that you may have made a mistake and that you saw the contents of the wallet after Officer Rodriguez had placed my client under arrest?" He moved even closer, looked at the report, and repeated, "Couldn't that be the case, Mr. Garcia?"

"Yes, I guess that could be the case." Garcia let out his breath and looked over at the judge. "It happened some time ago, and I was focused on taking care of Mr. Shelton. I guess I could have been wrong about when I looked at the wallet."

"Was this Stone's trap?" thought Sam. "And hadn't Garcia just fallen in?"

Stone stepped back and smiled, "And isn't it in fact

the case, Mr. Garcia, that it was Officer Rodriguez who gave you the wallet for you to look through in order to identify your patient? Isn't that what happened?"

Garcia nodded. "Yes, that's what happened. Things were happening pretty fast. Rodriguez told Mr. Shelton he was under arrest for disorderly conduct and then patted him down and pulled out his wallet. He checked it out, and I guess he must have seen the two driver's licenses, and then he handed the wallet over to me."

Stone looked sympathetically at the young paramedic and then turned to the judge. "No further questions, Your Honor."

Nodding his head, the judge looked first at Stone and then at Casey. "Is that it?" he asked.

Both lawyers said it was, so the judge looked at Stone. "Your motion. You argue first."

Stone began in a calm tone. "Judge, very simple. The State ended up charging my client with a felony, the fake ID charge, that was the result of an illegal search. As the court well knows, the police can arrest someone without warrant on a felony charge and then do a search, but the police cannot arrest for a misdemeanor not committed in the officer's presence. In this case, the officer did not observe the disorderly conduct that precipitated the arrest. He has said under cross-examination that he did not see my client do anything except end up at the bottom of a pile. Since he did not see the misdemeanor, it was an unlawful warrantless arrest. And once it is a question of unlawful arrest, everything that follows is suppressed."

The judge nodded. "Go on, Mr. Stone."

"In addition, Your Honor, the evidence shows that

the officer compounded his misstep. He pulled the wallet and found the two driver's licenses, but he's a veteran and knows that he isn't allowed to search under these circumstances. So what did he do? He handed the wallet over to Mr. Garcia and told Garcia to look at the wallet to identify the patient. In other words, the illegal search prompted a second search, allowing Mr. Casey to argue that the paramedic found the fake ID during the course of treatment. Such a sequence of events would have legitimized that search, of course, since the Fourth Amendment applies only to a search by a representative of government.

But the point is, Your Honor, that everything that followed that first illegal search is inadmissible. In short, the State has no evidence in this case, and the charge against my client needs to be dismissed."

The judge looked at Casey. "Argument, counselor?"

"Yes, Your Honor. I would point out that the officer made the arrest on a good-faith belief that the defendant had caused the disorderly conduct, and therefore the warrantless arrest and the subsequent search were proper, the officer's statements are legitimate, and the evidence is admissible."

The judge glanced over at Stone, who simply shook his head back and forth. The judge looked at his notes and pondered the two arguments for about a—to Sam, an agonizing—minute. He then announced, "I agree with Mr. Stone. I find that for the purpose of this motion, the officer did not have the requisite probable cause to make the warrantless arrest, and therefore the search based on the disorderly conduct charge was improper. I also find that there is a major discrepancy in the state's evidence as to who went through the wallet first. On questioning by Mr. Stone, it does appear that the police conducted the search first. The evidence stays out."

The prosecutor stood up, "But, Judge..."

"I have made my ruling, Mr. Casey. The evidence is excluded," the judge said sternly. "Any further evidence on this case?"

Casey looked down at the papers on this table. "No, sir."

"Mr. Stone?" the judge asked.

"Nothing, Judge," Stone said politely. "No evidence. We move to dismiss."

The judge nodded. "I agree. This case is dismissed."

Things were happening quickly, almost too quickly for Sam. He turned to Stone, unable to believe his ears. "That's it?"

Stone leaned over, a discrete smile playing across his face. "Yup. We just won. The case is over."

The judge stood and quickly left the courtroom, as did Mr. Casey. Sam felt an overwhelming sense of relief. Speechless, with tears welling in his eyes, he turned and embraced his lawyer.

"What do we do now? I mean what happens next?" Sam asked, stepping back with some embarrassment, disoriented by the sudden end of his nightmare.

"We go home," Stone said with a smile, as he collected his files and placed them into his briefcase.

"It's all over?" Sam asked again.

"It's all over," the lawyer confirmed. "The legal system relies on the court making a final decision and then moving on."

As they exited the courthouse, Sam, feeling jubilant, drank in the fresh air. It was still the middle of the morning, and the sun blazed against the deep blue sky.

"You're really good, Mr. Stone," he said with a big grin. "I guess that with all those distractions, I didn't fully realize how stressful this case was for me. It's a whole different story talking about criminals and trials and actually being the defendant. I mean, I felt so helpless." The relief that flooded him was about to make him tear up again, so he took a deep breath to calm himself. "I was a bit worried there for a while, but you really pulled it off. I really, really appreciate it."

"It's always more fun to win than to lose," the lawyer answered, smiling as broadly as Sam.

"Yeah, well, I realize this was not the biggest case in the world for you, but it was really important to me. How did you know to go after the paramedic like that? Was it a bluff?"

"The main thing about being a lawyer is being willing to confront people. It helps to have good evidence, of course, but most important is the willingness to be aggressive and fight for your client. In this trial, I had a hunch the officer was hiding something. It was a hunch, and so I used the medical report as a prop, assuming the paramedic would cave. In this case it worked, and he changed his story."

"Is that what it's all about? The lawyer's willingness to go for the throat?"

"I wouldn't put it quite like that...Actually, come to think of it, maybe that's not such a bad analogy. You need to want it badly enough that you're willing to take a witness down."

"Well, I sure am glad we won. Thanks again."

Stone stopped on the sidewalk and turned to his young client. "Sam, it's always good for me to be reminded that every case, large or small, is important. I appreciate your kind words."

"Well, like I said, I really appreciate your work on this, Mr. Stone. I mean compared to what happened to Metcalf in the Blair case, this is not a very big deal. I mean, I was facing a felony conviction, but at least I wasn't going to be serving a bunch of time. I am just so glad I still have a clean record."

"So am I. And you can call me Mike."

CHAPTER 34

"Let's take the High Road through Truchas and come back along the Rio Grande," Nina said. Sam had two days left before heading back east, and she was determined, after so many postponements, to show him Taos, the Rio Grande gorge, and some of the sights along the way. Sam was more than game for a ride. Besides, it would distract him. The thought of leaving Nina and Santa Fe made him feel thoroughly miserable.

They were soon on the road towards Española and Pojoaque. At Route 503 they took a right through Nambe and then past Chimayo.

"Nambe means 'People of the Round Earth,' " Nina shouted into Sam's ear against the noise of the wind. "It is part of the Nambe Pueblo."

After the High Road dipped into the green valley of Chimayo, they turned right onto Route 76 and began a climb into the Sangre de Cristo Mountains. As they passed through the tiny village of Cordova, Sam pointed to a small adobe cottage with wooden statues scattered in the front yard. Nina nodded but then alerted him to the sharp left-hand turn on the road. Soon Sam was gunning the throttle to pick up speed as Pegasus began the climb towards the small village of Truchas straddling the ridge. At the top, Sam slowed down and Nina shouted, "The settlers here dug miles of irrigation ditches to bring water into the village from a trout-filled river, and that's how it got its name."

Sam and Nina continued on Route 76 and soon passed a sign announcing the Carson National Forest. The tiny villages they passed through were all of Spanish origin and settled as part of a royal land grant. In Las Trampas, they pulled up in front of the adobe wall enclosing the Church of San Jose de Gracia. The buttress-like adobe towers on either side of the church's façade were connected by a strong horizontal roofline and an unexpected balcony.

"Classic Spanish colonial church architecture," Sam read from the sign in front of the adobe church. "It looks like it's a National Historic Landmark as well. Hmm...1776, a date even I can remember." Inside, the dark wood around the Stations of the Cross and the other vivid paintings made the freshness of the white walls stand out, but Sam's gaze drifted more vertically, to the rough-hewn floor underfoot and the painted decorations on the wooden ceiling.

Not long afterwards, they passed through Penasco, Vadito, and Talpa, finally reaching Rachos de Taos and the San Francisco de Asis Mission Church. This was the one Sam especially wanted to see. The adobe bell towers in the front curved out into impressive buttresses, but the real attraction was the back of the church. He wasn't disappointed: the massive, unbroken, primeval shapes of its rear walls and buttresses were as otherworldly and abstract as in Georgia O'Keeffe's paintings or the photographs of Ansel Adams.

"Let's keep moving," Nina said finally. "I'm getting hungry." Close to noon they rolled into the town of Taos, parked the motorcycle, and walked around the Plaza, stopping for lunch on the outdoor patio of a restaurant called the Apple Tree.

Afterwards, they headed to the Taos Pueblo, about a mile north of town. As he parked the motorcycle, Sam reiterated his frustration at the limited amount of sightseeing he had been able to do. "You know, between work and the Blair case, I haven't seen a single pueblo, not even the one at Bandelier."

"This is a good place to start," Nina replied, "though we probably don't have enough time to take the guided tour."

"How cool is this!" Sam exclaimed as they approached the compound. "It's so amazing to me what can be built with adobe." The five-story, red-brown structures were punctuated by their bright doors and the dark rectangles of door openings, and fringed with the shadows cast by the roof timbers protruding from their façades. "They look like apartment buildings, with each layer stepped back."

"I bet you don't know of any other apartment buildings that are a thousand years old!" Nina replied, picking up a brochure from a small wooden box next to the path, but she didn't need to read it. "Its official name is Rio Pueblo de Taos, but it's also just called Rio Pueblo." She pointed to a small stream running right through the middle of the compound. "That's Red Willow Creek. It originates up there"—she pointed to the towering Taos Mountain—"in the Sangre de Cristo Range. This building is called North House, and the other one is South House. Most of the pueblo is out of bounds for visitors, but we can have a look inside over there."

They bought their tickets, and Nina started scanning the brochure as they walked closer to the rough wall of the north building. "It says that these are the largest multistoried Pueblo buildings still in existence, and that the walls are often several feet thick. The primary purpose of the design was defense. Up to 1900, the only way to get to the upper floors was by ladder on the outside to the roof and then down an inside ladder. In case of attack, the ladders could easily be pulled up."

They walked around to the side of the structure and then up to the second level. A young member of the tribe was standing outside the open doorway to one of the apartments. "You can step inside and look," he said.

Nina and Sam spent a moment adjusting to the dark interior. "The homes usually had two rooms," the young man said, "one for general living and sleeping and one for cooking, eating, and storage. Each home is self-contained. There are no passageways between them."

Sam looked at the table and two chairs and the simple wooden-framed bed against the wall. "Not much furniture," he observed.

"Our people didn't have much furniture in the past, so we keep things the way they were."

Nina nodded. "They are known for being one of the most private and conservative pueblos," she said to Sam, "keeping to the old ways. You'll notice there's no electricity or running water, yet the Taos still live here."

It was a good segue for the young man. "Our pueblo is the only inhabited Native American community that is a UNESCO World Heritage site. But I should mention that there are several thousand of us, and most of us live in conventional houses outside the pueblo. We have almost a hundred thousand acres. Forty-eight thousand of these, tribal mountain lands, were returned to us by the U.S. government in 1970, after a long struggle. They include Blue Lake, the sacred lake where Red Willow Creek begins. Now that our land is whole again, we are more confident than ever that we can preserve our spiritual, cultural, and economic health."

"For at least another thousand years," Sam added warmly. "It's so remarkable that buildings made of earth baked with water and straw can last for such a long time."

"Our climate helps," the young man answered. "But we maintain the outer surfaces each year with thin coats of fresh mud and the interior ones with washes of white earth."

"Just like the colonial churches we've just seen," Nina added. "It's a major communal effort."

Their guide accompanied them outside into the bright light again. "Are you a tour guide year round?" Nina asked him.

"No, just in the summer. I've just finished my first year at Navajo Technical University in Crownpoint. I'll be getting an associates degree in environmental science. I'm really into geographic information systems, but I like returning to the old ways in the summer, and sharing important aspects of our culture with others."

"I almost went to NTU!" Nina replied. "But I decided to stay in Gallup, at UNM, and now I'm in Albuquerque. You've probably heard about the defeat of the proposal to repeal the ban on uranium mining. I worked on that this summer."

"Then I owe you our thanks. I watched those events carefully, especially since Crownpoint was directly threatened. This has been such a hard road for the Navajo, and you have never given up."

"And we never will. Good luck with your studies."

"Thanks. You too." The young man reached out his hand, and Sam and Nina both shook it as they said good-bye.

Reunited with Pegasus, they took a left on Route 64 and sped across wide-open, flat land to their final destination, bracing as gusts of wind came across the wide plateau. Nina pointed out a series of adobe houses that seemed buried in the windswept landscape. The huge Rio Grande Gorge lay ahead, but it was completely invisible on the flat terrain.

Then, about ten minutes later, the earth opened as if it had been sliced with a giant knife, and they saw, spanning the gorge, a huge steel bridge, its roadway laid across a single magnificent arch with a partial arch to each side. Sam pulled into the little parking area at its eastern side. The walls of the canyon were rocky and barren, but at the bottom flowed the Rio Grande, a robust stretch of the lazy trickle that later separated parts of Texas and Mexico.

"It looks like a little sliver of water from up here," Sam said as he kicked out the side stand with his left foot.

"Yes, it is amazing. But look down there at all the trees and brush. The river keeps things alive, even late in the summer. It's even a great place for whitewater rafting."

Nina took off her helmet, got off the bike, and started walking toward the bridge. "Come on," she said, smiling, and waved for Sam to follow.

"I hate to say it, but I'm not a huge fan of heights," Sam confessed as the wind picked up and the bridge seemed to sway. She held out her hand for moral support. "Here, I'll make sure you don't get blown off."

They walked hand in hand down a walkway to one of the small, cantilevered lookouts and peered over the railing. "It's like standing on top of a fifty-story building," Sam said unsteadily.

Nina's black hair blew towards the other wall of the canyon. She pulled it back and held it with one hand. "What we're looking at wasn't carved by a river, you know, like the Grand Canyon. It's a genuine rift in the earth's crust that eventually corralled the runoff from the higher elevations. It starts in Colorado and goes all the way to Texas. The gorge itself is only about fifty miles long, though."

"No kidding. Plate tectonics in action."

They walked to the far side of the gorge and sat down at a picnic table in a roadside rest area next to the bridge. Sam looked up at the deep blue sky and back towards the majestic Sangre de Cristo Mountains. He looked at Nina, and his heart constricted. "How can I leave here? It's hard for me to imagine being anywhere else."

She smiled. "It's going to be strange for you to be back in college. I mean, it's been a pretty wild summer for you, being the local hero and all."

"How about you? You struck a major blow for your

people and the whole state of New Mexico this summer. And you know I couldn't have gotten to the bottom of the Blair case without your help and determination. A classroom will have to feel pretty confining to you too."

"Maybe I'll have to buy a motorcycle to counteract that!"

"And maybe I'll hang up my Navajo weaving where I can look at it all the time and block out all the greenery!" They both laughed without conviction, trying to block out as well the fact that they would soon be saying good-bye.

"So what's your latest thinking about what you'll do after college? Still want to be a lawyer?"

"I think so. What I finally figured out is that in a lot of ways, being a trial lawyer is like being an athlete, and I really liked sports in high school. You know, you have two sides going at each other, each team trying their best to win."

"That's true. It's a contest, a fight. You even have the judge acting as the referee. The trouble is that you can end up representing the wrong side. That's would be my problem. I would need to be fighting for the right person or the right cause. I mean, who wants to represent people like Hurley or Fisher?"

"I see your point. But then of course, I was charged with a crime, too. In fact, the impartiality of the law is one of the things I like about it. You don't really have to think too much about guilt or innocence. You just have to use all your resources to go to bat for your client."

"How do you account for Metcalf, then?"

"Well, that's a tough one. You can't help but think

that his lawyer could have done a better job defending him."

"That's good. Blame it on the lawyer."

"Take it easy! Sure, if the law in a criminal case assumes someone is innocent until proven guilty, then it should work out that innocent people don't get convicted. It means the lawyers really have to work hard on each case. That's not easy if they're getting a lot of court-appointed cases and are not paid much."

"If I were to be a lawyer, it would be to file lawsuits against the people and companies that have been abusing my people and all the other Natives in this country. It still amazes me how much abuse has gone on."

"I agree with you. If there were more really good lawyers representing the Navajo or any other tribe, a lot of the wrongs could be fixed."

"I've thought of that, of course. I'm going to take this year to focus on college and decide what's next." She looked out over the landscape. "I can tell you that I believe more than ever in the land, the environment. My people have an expression, a saying. It goes like this:

I have been to the end of the Earth
I have been to the end of the Waters
I have been to the end of the Sky
I have been to the end of the Mountains
I have found none that are not my friends."

"And today you've brought me to a place where they all come together," Sam rejoined.

"Do you remember when we hiked to the top of the Ski Basin at the beginning of the summer? We saw that hawk, and I told you that I had often dreamed of a hawk when I was a child. Can I tell you a secret?"

"Of course."

"Ever since that day the hawk flying high above the land has reappeared in my dreams in the most vivid way."

"What do you think that means?"

"It still seems as if he's protecting the earth. I keep thinking that's what I need to do." She sighed. "It's amazing to me that people do such cruel things to the earth and to each other. And it seems like it's mostly about greed and material wealth. That damned mining company and its minions! People need to see what's really important. Like this," she said with a sweep of her arm. "The dreams also tell me that there's something about light and color that I need to explore. I have to start weaving again."

"The one you did in high school had really striking patterns and colors."

"It's a start, anyway." They looked silently out over the gorge.

"Speaking of weaving, you'll be reminded of Tua when you get back to Providence. I wish I could have met her. She must have been quite a woman when she was young, from what everyone said about her. It must have driven her crazy to keep her secret all these years. I guess a mother will do just about anything to protect her child—oh my God! Just like Sylvia!" She sat bolt upright. "It just hit me."

"With so much collateral damage in both cases," Sam said pensively. "It's strange that we have a lot of sympathy for the one and not so much for the other."

"And Stone, dear Mike Stone. Tua obviously loved him. It must have been really hard to leave."

"I know how she felt," Sam replied, and they both fell silent again until Nina roused herself.

"So what did your parents say about your trial and all?"

"I haven't told them."

"What?" She looked at him skeptically. "Are you going to?"

"I'm not sure. They'll never understand, and they'll probably just give me a hard time about doing stupid stuff."

"That sounds crazy to me. They'll understand what you did, and they'll be proud of you. You can tell them you acted like a Navajo warrior."

Sam smiled at the thought. "I guess you're right. I don't know if they'll be proud, but I need to tell them. If I can stand up to Fisher, I can take some flak from them."

"That's right."

"What's that Indian expression about a beautiful day to die? Stone told me about it, and it keeps coming into my head."

Nina laughed. "That's a saying from the Sioux leader Crazy Horse, who used to shout 'Hóka-héy!' which means 'Today is a good day to die!' It's an expression of willingness and even eagerness to give one's life for one's cause."

Sam grinned. "I'm not sure I'm quite there yet, but it pumped me up when I was going in to face Fisher."

Nina smiled back. "Another interpretation is that it expresses a belief that one should never live a moment of one's life with any regrets, or with tasks left undone. Which would make today as good a day to die as any."

"Never live a moment of one's life with any regrets or tasks left undone," he repeated slowly. "I like that."

After a short pause, Sam reached into his pocket and pulled out a small cloth bag with a pull string and handed it to Nina. "By the way, I have this for you. It's a gift to help remember the summer." Inside was a wooden weaving fork carved from juniper, about two inches wide and eight inches long.

"It's beautiful," Nina said. She turned the piece over in her hands and with a knowing touch slowly rubbed the smooth wood between her long fingers. "I will think of you whenever I use it."

"You know," said Sam, "you're going to have to work very hard to get me out of your life."

"I won't lift a finger," Nina replied, giving him a radiant smile. "And I have something to show you," she said. Pulling up her pant leg a few inches above her right ankle, she revealed a small red and gold tattoo of an oak leaf.

"That's really cool," Sam said, grinning broadly. He thought of their meetings under the oak tree at the Audubon. "It says it all."

And for Sam the dazzling day was suddenly lit from within. Elbows on the table, they interlaced fingers, shaking off their earlier dejection.

"Let's compare notes on graduate schools and make sure our choices overlap," Nina rejoined.

"And today's trip has just whetted my appetite for the great sites of the Southwest. Maybe we could ride to

Chaco Canyon or Canyon de Chelly next summer."

"If we're not too busy saving the world, that is."
They both laughed a genuine laugh this time. "And Mesa
Verde is not far over the Colorado state line."

Later, they walked arm in arm back across the
bridge. They mounted Pegasus and retraced their route to
Taos, then slowly gathered speed on Route 68, enveloped
by the steep canyon walls. The road followed the rushing
Rio Grande, and Nina held Sam tightly as they leaned
together into the twists and turns.

61631441R00166

Made in the USA
Middletown, DE
13 January 2018